A Time for Hope

A Time for Hope

ANNA JACOBS

Allison & Busby Limited
12 Fitzroy Mews
London W1T 6DW
allisonandbusby.com

First published in 2014.
This paperback edition published by Allison & Busby in 2017.

A CIP catalogue record for this book is available from
the British Library.

10 9 8 7 6 5 4 3 2 1

ISBN 978-0-7490-2149-8

Typeset in 10.5/15.5 pt Sabon by
Allison & Busby Ltd.

The paper used for this Allison & Busby publication
has been produced from trees that have been legally sourced
from well-managed and credibly certified forests.

Printed and bound by
CPI Group (UK) Ltd, Croydon, CR0 4YY

Chapter One

As Stu got out of his car, Gabi flung open the front door and hurled his suitcase at him. 'Get out of my sight, you cheating worm!'

He gaped at her in shock as the suitcase bumped to a halt at one side of him. 'What the hell's brought this on?'

'A woman phoned me this afternoon on my mobile. Radka, she said she was called. She rang all the way from the Czech Republic.' She watched him stiffen and then hide his surprise. 'Ah. I see you know her. She was very frank about knowing you and mentioned that little scar on your backside to prove it. And she also told me how pregnant she was.'

He could have been a stone statue by the time she finished speaking. 'I see.'

'Is that all you can say? Who is she?'

'You met her at the office dinner – the beautiful blonde.'

'Who danced with you twice.'

He smirked and looked round. 'Look, we need to have this conversation in private. In case you haven't noticed, our next-door neighbour is peeping through her window, and the way you're yelling, she'll hear every word you say.'

'I don't care if the Queen herself has us under surveillance. *You* aren't coming into this house again, Stu Dixon.'

He moved towards her, scowling. 'I own a third of this house, actually, so I have every right to come inside. *Every right*.' He shoved her out of the way so hard she bumped back against the wall.

But she was quick enough to push him back outside. As he raised one clenched fist, she tried not to flinch. He'd hit her a couple of times in the past year, claiming afterwards it was just rough play that had gone too far. The second time she'd waited till he was asleep and then thumped him good and hard with her rolling pin. She'd made her point. He hadn't touched her again.

'You'll have to fight your way in,' she shouted, face thrust as close to his as their six-inch height difference would allow. 'I'm not having you back, even in another bedroom. You'll not sleep soundly a single night if you try to return.'

Another silence, then he shrugged and took one step back. 'Why am I bothering? It's about time I did something about our marriage. You've been a big disappointment to me, Gabi. Radka is a much better proposition as a partner. She'll be a good support in my job, too, because she understands how businesses *really* work.'

He paused to eye her body up and down. 'You're not bad-looking for a woman of thirty-five, and you're not overweight, I'll grant you that. But your performance in bed leaves a lot to be desired. Radka, on the other hand, is superb at making love. It was a lucky day for me when my company sent me to liaise on this Czech project and I met her.'

She folded her arms, keeping back her pain at these cruel accusations.

'You should take lessons in what a man needs from a woman, or the next guy you get into a relationship with will also find you disappointing . . . and so very unadventurous.'

Gabi snatched up the pot of petunias from the porch and chucked it at him, but he dodged it easily. She'd always been terrible at throwing things, had never regretted that lack of skill more than at this moment. She'd like to have drawn blood from him.

He brushed away the earth that had showered over him. 'Look what you've done to my new suit, you bitch!' He moved forward, grabbing her shoulders and shaking her hard. 'Don't you *dare* throw anything at me again.'

Suddenly she was afraid of him. To her relief, he let go of her, but he stayed where he was, just inside the door. It was she who moved back.

'I could come right inside if I wanted, because I'm much stronger than you.' He took a step forward, moving across the threshold. 'You'd do well to remember that.'

After a pause during which she could feel her heart beating too fast, he added, 'Our break-up has happened a little sooner than I'd planned, but that's all right, Gabi my sweet. You don't think I wanted to live in a village near Swindon for much longer, surely? Bucolic life in Worton does *not* appeal to me.'

'Then why did you buy a house here?'

'I agreed to buy this house because I thought it'd increase in value in such a pretty little commuter village. I intended to sell it within a year or two. But the bottom has dropped out of the damned house market and prices have slipped.'

She glared at him. 'Too bad. I hope the house doesn't sell. I like living here.'

'Well, make the most of it, sweetie, because one way or another we're selling in the next few months. After our nice little divorce, we'll split the proceeds of the house sale and I at least will move somewhere more upmarket.'

That hurt. Oh, it hurt so much that he could toss the word 'divorce' at her casually, as if it was just a business matter, not the end of their marriage. She raised her chin and said as calmly as she could manage, 'Good. That'll suit me.'

'Oh, more than good. I'm going to take away a nice profit from our relationship, and you'd better not try to stop me.'

'Profit!' This was the last thing she'd have expected to hear. She stared at him in bewilderment. 'But house prices have slipped.'

'When we divide our goods, I shall be the winner. You brought a lot more to the marriage than I did, but you didn't document all of your contributions.' He laughed. 'In fact, you lent me quite a lot of money, some of it cash, and then I paid money out of my account as part of the deposit on this house. I have a cash trail that says I'm half-owner. Our agreement to divide it a third and two-thirds was only verbal. You are so stupidly trusting, Gabi.'

She was too shocked to reply. Had he ever cared for her?

'I came out of my last relationship smelling of roses, too,' he went on, jabbing one finger into her chest. 'Though Patricia didn't have to be bought by an outmoded institution like marriage, as you did, so breaking up with her was much easier. But it was worth marrying you, because I'll get much more out than I put in.'

He stepped back, raising one hand and wiggling his fingertips mockingly in farewell. 'I'll see you in court, pet. Keith will be acting for me, of course.'

Trust him to have a lawyer as his best friend, she thought bitterly.

Picking up the suitcase, Stu moved to his car but stopped at the end of the garden path to study the house, as if assessing its value. Then he put the suitcase into the boot of his car and brushed the last flecks of soil from his suit. The look he gave her as he did this promised retribution.

He always made a big fuss about his appearance, but, as her grandmother had said, 'Handsome is as handsome does.' He hadn't acted at all handsomely after the first few months of marriage.

Gabi let out a long shuddering sigh as she watched him drive away and rubbed the painful part of her chest where he'd poked her. She'd been afraid of him today. It was as if he'd ripped off a mask and shown her the real Stuart Dixon, someone she'd only caught brief glimpses of before.

He was much stronger than she was – six foot to her five foot six – with muscles well honed from working out at the gym. She'd take care not to be alone with him again.

Then she got angry at herself for being afraid. Profit

from their marriage, would he? She'd make damned sure he didn't get anything he wasn't entitled to.

She slammed the front door shut and leant against it, shaking. No word of regret for the end of their relationship. Not a single one.

Well, there hadn't been any affection between them for a while. At first, she'd been foolish enough to put that down to his stress at work, where his company was laying off staff in a ruthless cull and he was trying to make sure he wasn't dumped. Then he'd been away in the Czech Republic part of the time.

When he didn't want her in bed any more, she'd begun to wonder whether he was being unfaithful. But she hadn't found any real proof of it, so she'd done nothing except hope things would improve.

More fool her.

Didn't it upset him at all to break up? Had he cared about her at all?

He was right. She was a trusting fool.

Gabi went online to search for information about divorce and found government-sponsored sites, giving all the details of how to do it. It seemed such a straightforward procedure these days that she decided to save money and do it herself. After all, Stu wouldn't be contesting the divorce, and they could use a mediator to help them decide on the division of property before they got to the final stage, the decree absolute.

Stu agreed through his lawyer that the only times he and Gabi would meet from then on would be on neutral territory.

Not trusting him, she changed the locks of the house.

His secretary phoned a few days later to ask her to pack the rest of his clothes, his sports gear and his CDs.

Gabi did that, dumping the bags on the porch outside the house at the arranged time, rather than letting him come inside to collect them. She watched from an upstairs window as he picked them up, chatting to the woman in his car as he loaded his things into the boot.

When she heard the name 'Radka' and the word 'darling', she studied her successor, who was very thin, blonde and sharp-featured.

Gabi had always refused to have her hair bleached to the blonde he preferred. She liked her own colour; anyway, the dark roots showed through within twenty-four hours. What was wrong with brown hair, for heaven's sake?

And what was wrong with her? He'd really upset her saying she was disappointing in bed. She'd only slept with two or three men, ones she'd cared about, but it had been a pleasant experience.

She shouldn't let Stu get to her, but he'd always been able to press the right buttons to upset her.

She was surprised how smoothly the divorce was progressing. Well, Stu could hardly contest the reason she gave – his adultery. A couple of acquaintances had made a point of telling her that he was openly shacked up with an attractive blonde woman in Prague, where he was working on a special project.

This Radka female, no doubt. Well, she was welcome to him.

* * *

A few weeks later, Gabi came home to find her bedroom in disorder. She rushed round the house, but all the windows and doors were locked.

How had the intruder got in?

She spent a long time going through her clothes, but nothing was missing. Nothing at all! What was this? Some kind of joke?

She reported the break-in to the police, but they said she should have left things as they were and there was nothing to be gained by sending detectives round for a non-crime. They would ask the police on patrol to keep an eye on her house while she was at work.

Grimly, she arranged for the locks to be changed again and told her neighbours what had happened, asking them to keep an eye out for people loitering.

Just as she was thinking that was that, it happened again. But this time the intruder left a set of her underwear on the bed, arranged as if a person was wearing it, but with a knife stuck through the bra. That felt downright creepy.

The police did come out this time and seemed to take it seriously. So did she! But they could find no fingerprints except hers, and again there was no sign of a forced entry.

This left her so nervous she jumped at the slightest sound after dark and found it difficult to get to sleep, which was wearing, to say the least.

She began to wonder if this had a purpose.

One day, during her lunch break, she passed Stu in town. He stopped and she nearly walked past, but she decided there was nothing to be gained by antagonising him. And, anyway, it would be cowardly.

He greeted her with, 'Sleeping all right, are you? No intruders?'

Smirking, he walked on without waiting for an answer and she could only stand there and watch him in shock.

He must be the one responsible for the break-ins. But how could she report him to the police when she didn't have a shred of proof? He knew that, of course. Besides, he was part-owner of the house.

How had he got in? The locks had been changed twice.

As she watched, he stopped about fifty yards further along the mall and turned to look at her. Laughing, he blew her a kiss and carried on walking.

She hoped she hadn't betrayed her feeling of shock and betrayal, but she doubted it. She'd always found it hard to conceal what she was thinking.

Why was he doing this to her? She simply couldn't understand it. What could he hope to gain from it?

That evening, she couldn't get the encounter out of her mind. Stu was tormenting her for the hell of it, she decided in the end. He hated anyone to get the better of him, and she supposed he considered her throwing him out of the house to be just that.

The sooner she was completely rid of him, the better.

A few months after their divorce paperwork went in, the decree nisi was granted. The next step was for them to state how they would divide their property.

Stu astounded her by making a grab for everything he

could think of, even listing items she'd brought from her first marriage.

If Gabi hadn't fought back, she'd have lost a lot more, but that didn't reconcile her to having to dip into her savings to hire her own lawyer.

Stu stopped her in the centre of Swindon one day, grabbing her arm so that she couldn't get away without creating a scene. The pedestrian precinct was busy, with people streaming past, making the most of their lunch breaks, and she could have screamed for help. But that would have been embarrassing.

'You've wasted your money on that lawyer, my pet. It'd have been just as cheap to let me have what I wanted.'

'I'd rather give *him* the money and keep my things out of your greedy hands.'

'You really are stupid to antagonise me any further. Very . . . very . . . stupid.'

Her breath caught in her throat. His lips were smiling, but when the smile slipped, she saw sheer hatred. What had she done to make him hate her? It was the other way round: she had good reason to hate him. And she was beginning to.

He shook her slightly. 'I've not finished with you yet, my dear little fool. Keep watching this space.' He winked at her and moved past her, bumping into her and knocking her sideways, so that if a passer-by hadn't steadied her, she'd have fallen.

He turned quickly to say loudly, 'Oh, sorry. Are you all right?'

She thanked the passer-by and when she looked, Stu was sauntering down the street.

Once again, she felt threatened . . . and more than a little afraid of him.

She watched him till he'd disappeared from sight, wondering what he'd meant by his threat. How could he possibly get anything else out of her? She had nothing of value left and was relying on the money she'd get when they sold the house to rebuild her life.

She'd only have enough left to buy a flat or a tiny cottage, and not one in a pretty village like Worton.

She caught sight of her reflection in a shop window and was shocked to see how gaunt and strained she looked.

Why was she letting him get to her?

How could she stop him?

There was no way she could think of because she didn't know what he'd do next. She'd heard him speak vindictively of people at work who'd got the better of him – not when they were first married, but as the months passed and his facade of Mr Nice began to slip.

'I'll make them sorry one day,' he always said. Now he'd turned his spite on her. Yet it was he who'd cheated, he who was trying to take more than his fair share of their possessions.

Perhaps after their divorce she'd move away, somewhere far away.

Perhaps.

But the few friends left after Stu had offended them lived in Wiltshire, especially Tania, whom she'd known since school. If she moved away, she'd know no one.

* * *

Eventually, the two lawyers drew up a property settlement. Gabi knew she was being cheated, but her lawyer said it was the best deal he could get for her and he'd advise her to agree to it, or she'd simply be throwing her money away protesting.

He also warned her to document her financial dealings a lot more carefully in future. It would take a forensic accountant to check her financial history with Stu, and that would be extremely expensive.

On the day when they informed the court of how they'd be dividing their property, Stu waited for Gabi outside and held out his hand. 'No hard feelings.'

She made no attempt to shake it. He'd raised his voice as he spoke, presumably for the benefit of their lawyers. When she walked away without even speaking, however, he followed.

She stopped and told him in a low voice, 'I have plenty of hard feelings, you thieving rat. Leave me alone.'

Stu moved quickly to bar her path. 'Oh dear, we are in a snitty mood, aren't we? But you and I do need to discuss selling the house, Gabi my pet.'

'Don't you "pet" me!' After a moment, when he didn't move, she added reluctantly, 'I suppose you're right.'

'Come for a coffee at Parker's and I'll tell you about an idea I've had.'

'We don't need to go anywhere.' Especially not to a café they'd visited often when they were first married. 'There are some seats on the other side of the entrance. They'll do.' Without waiting for his agreement, she walked across the reception area and sat down, arms folded.

He hesitated, then came to join her, sprawling next to her on the hard upright sofa, so that she had to edge into the corner in order to avoid touching him.

'I'm sure we can agree about one thing,' Stu began. 'We both want to sell the house as fast as we can.'

'We definitely agree on that.'

'Someone at work told me about "quick house sale" agencies, so I've been doing some research.'

'What are those?'

'Just what the name says: agencies which specialise in selling houses quickly. A lot of divorcing couples use them. I've found a few online which sound OK.'

'And the snag of using these agencies is . . . ?'

He shrugged. 'Well, you don't get as much for your house as you might do if you waited. But then you don't get months of hanging around, either. After all, there's no guarantee about how much you'll sell for, even if you do wait. I have to remind you that you're getting free use of the house in the meantime. Perhaps I ought to charge you rent.'

She ignored that, focusing on the main thing. 'How much less are we likely to get if we sell this way? Do you have any figures?'

'About ten per cent on average, they say.'

She hated the thought of tossing more of her money into resolving this mess. But she hated even more the thought of being tied to Stu for one day longer than necessary. Make that one second longer. 'Email me the names of some agencies you think might be suitable and I'll look into them myself.'

She wasn't at all sure anything Stu suggested would be the right way to go. But she would like to sell quickly.

Stu gave her one of his smug smiles and pulled out some pieces of paper. 'I knew you'd be interested, so I printed some information out. The first agency looks the best to me, but I'll go with any you choose.'

She took the papers and stood up. 'Leave it with me. I'll get back to you.'

'Don't take too long.'

'Oh, I definitely won't.' But she intended to check it all out very thoroughly indeed. She was also going to check out recent house sales in the area while she was at it.

She couldn't get his earlier boast of making a profit from their marriage out of her mind. She'd hardly call his share of the goods and chattels much of a profit, not by his financial standards, anyway. He had been hungry to get really rich, and she didn't think that would have changed.

So what was he planning with this quick house sale idea? She'd have to keep a very careful eye on him.

It was all utterly depressing, and if she hadn't had her friend Tania to let off steam to occasionally, she'd have gone mad.

Chapter Two

For the rest of the day – which was one of her days off work, thank goodness – Gabi checked property sales on the internet.

First she looked at quick sale agencies. There seemed to be quite a lot of them. Strange that she hadn't heard of them before. But then she hadn't divorced anyone before and been keen to sell a house quickly.

She felt she could trust the Office of Fair Trading, so visited its website, which warned sellers of the drawbacks to using such agencies: not only lower sale prices, but tricks to push the agreed price even lower in order to sell quickly.

She read the advice carefully and decided she'd refuse to do things that way. But then she checked recent house sales and rang up a couple of local estate agencies. The news wasn't good: sales were slow, prices had fallen, and her house wasn't in a highly desired part of Worton.

The thought of hanging around for month after month, as many people seemed to do when selling their houses, upset her. She hated the idea of still being linked in any way to Stu. She wanted to get away from him, get away from the nasty tricks. She couldn't even feel peaceful in her own home any longer, because there were strange noises at night, noises she couldn't place.

Surely he couldn't be making them . . . could he?

She was short of sleep, short of peace and quiet, so she reconsidered his suggestion.

After making herself a cup of coffee, she sat by the sitting room window in the dusk, thinking it over.

Surely, in this matter, their interests really were the same? And how could he cheat her, anyway? He didn't own these agencies, had to abide by their rules as well as obeying the law about settlement of house sales.

So, in the end, she phoned him.

'I've checked things out and I'll agree to trying a quick sale agency for three months and no longer. But I'm not going below a certain price.' She named it.

There was silence. Then, 'Well, we can but try at that price. I certainly share your desire to get as much as we can for the place. I bet I can guess which agency you chose: Arcott and Wray.'

He made everything into a game, loved to gamble and often said, 'Bet I can guess'.

'Yes. I did think Arcott and Wray sounded better than the others. How did you know?'

'Simple. They sounded the best to me, too. I'll fill in their contracts and bring them round after work for you to sign.'

She was startled. 'You've been in touch with them already?'

'I downloaded their forms from the internet. I meant what I said: I want to get my money out ASAP.'

So did she, damn him.

'Gabi? Are you still there?'

'Yes.'

'Is six o'clock tomorrow OK with you? Right, then. I'll drop by after work. It'll be nice to see my little house one last time. Maybe I should bring a bottle of wine, for old times' sake?'

'No, thank you. I just want us to get the business stuff sorted out.' He had a much better head for wine than she did. He was trying to get the edge on her. He had boasted about playing such tricks – only he called them strategies – on other people.

After some thought, Gabi phoned Tania and asked her to come round straight after work to play chaperone. No way did she intend to be on her own with Stu, not after the way he'd threatened her last time.

She intended to have witnesses present every step of the way along this final stretch to freedom.

'You'd be better selling your house the normal way,' Tania said bluntly.

'Financially, yes. Emotionally, no.' Gabi couldn't stop her voice wobbling. 'I just want to get this over with.'

Her friend's voice softened. 'You've had it tough for the past few years, haven't you, what with Edward and—'

'I don't want to talk about Edward.' Especially not in the same breath as Stu. Edward had been a very special person.

'OK. Sorry. I'll come and act as your bodyguard and witness, then.'

'That's great. Thank you so much. I'm pretty sure Stu will bring Keith with him.'

'Why would he do that? He doesn't need a lawyer for something this simple. It'd cost him a fortune.'

'Keith is also his best friend. The two of them are as thick as thieves. I bet Stu won't have even had to pay him the normal rate for the divorce.'

Gabi was right. Keith did turn up with Stu. He flashed her one of his half-smiles from behind his thick glasses but didn't attempt a kissy-kissy greeting, thank goodness. She'd as soon touch a viper as either of these men.

Keith settled in a chair to one side and folded his arms, avoiding further eye contact.

Tania did no more than nod at the men as she sat down next to her friend.

The contract seemed very straightforward, but when it came to signing it, Gabi hesitated, staring down at the two pieces of paper. No, she wouldn't sign without legal advice. Not with Stu involved.

'I'll show it to my lawyer, then get back to you.' Another expense but also another safeguard.

Stu rolled his eyes at this announcement. 'There's really no need. Keith's seen it, after all. It hasn't got any concealed tricks to it.'

'Nonetheless.'

'Oh, OK! Do what you have to, but do it quickly.'

When the two men had left, Tania gave her a big hug. 'Well, at least you had enough wit not to put your head into a noose without checking how tight the rope is. Ah, don't cry, Gabi love. He's not worth it.'

'I'm crying for the house, not him. I love this place.' She fumbled for a tissue and wiped her eyes, trying in vain to stop crying.

'Of course you're crying for the house.' Tania gave her another hug.

But Gabi knew she hadn't fooled her friend. She was also crying for her marriage and for her own stupidity in letting Stu set her up for a fall.

She wondered if she was suffering from depression. If she wasn't now, she was certainly heading that way – and who wouldn't be depressed in her situation? She was sleeping badly. There were still occasional night-time disturbances and stones thrown at her bedroom window.

The police said it was youngsters and no damage had been done. She knew it was Stu. Who else could it be? He wanted her to sell quickly.

And she was even eating unwisely and had put on weight. Weren't you supposed to lose weight when you were upset?

She kept telling herself to snap out of it. Stu wasn't worth it. She should get on with making a new life for herself.

But somehow she couldn't get her act together. He seemed to have sapped her energy and willpower.

She hadn't a clue what she'd do after they sold this house, apart from leave the area. And not tell him where she was going.

When Stu got back to London, he went straight to Radka's flat. She had her feet up on the couch and was sipping a glass of red wine.

'How did it go?'

'Gabi's taking the contract to her lawyer, but I'm pretty sure she's going to bite.'

Radka smiled that lazy, sexy smile of hers that made

him want to grab her and kiss her senseless. 'Good.'

He poured himself a glass of wine and sat down on the couch. 'What's for tea?'

She shrugged. 'Whatever you care to get. I'm not hungry. Cheese and biscuits will do for me.'

He frowned and she gave him a hard look. 'I'm not a housewife, Stu, and I never will be. I don't know why you keep expecting such attentions from me. And in my own flat, too.'

'You could do your share of the shopping, though.'

'I hired a cleaning lady and I pay her. That more than covers my share of the chores. I will not live in a pigsty. I keep telling you I don't cook. And as I don't eat nearly as much as you do, why should *I* do the shopping?'

She took another delicate sip, licking a stray drop of wine from the corner of her mouth with the tip of her tongue.

Hell, she was a sexy piece! He went to get out the cheese and biscuits, his mind on other things. But there wasn't enough food in the fridge for his more robust appetite and his lust faded as his stomach growled. 'Can't you at least order in some food? You can shop online, you know.'

'Do it, then. Anyway, I've been busy this week. For your benefit.'

He turned round eagerly. 'Ah. Your friends are coming to the party? They're interested in the house?'

'Could be. We'll have to wait and see.' She went to pour herself another glass of wine.

His stomach rumbled again. 'I'll nip out for some fish and chips. Can I get you anything?'

'I'll just eat a corner of your fish. Don't drink too much tonight, Stu. It slows you down in bed.'

He drew in his breath sharply at the look on her face, tempted to forget his takeaway. But he'd be too hungry to sleep after they'd made love, so he nodded and nipped out, calling in at the mini-mart as well.

Radka was the most exciting woman he'd ever bedded. And useful to him in business. So what if she wasn't into wifely chores? A man going places couldn't find a more useful woman. And the sex was a big bonus on top of that.

His company had been negotiating with a group in Prague and he'd been able to help push that along, thanks to Radka. His senior manager had seemed pleased. As far as you could tell with that po-faced sod.

This was it, Stu knew it was: his big break into top management. Then eventually a business of his own.

He just needed more money to finance himself. Radka had said she'd come in with him and shown him how to make extra.

They'd make a fortune together. She was his ticket to real money – he knew it.

She was going back to Prague soon and wouldn't come back to London for a while. He must join her there. She had a much nicer flat.

She would see if she could pull a few strings to get him assigned to the project in a more permanent way.

The following day Gabi managed to see her lawyer for a short session. She had to ask for time off work again to do it. Her boss wasn't pleased about that.

The lawyer pulled a face at this way of selling but agreed there was nothing illegal or tricky about the contract.

'Make sure you use a good settlement agency when you do sell. Not one these people run. And not the same one as your husband.' He fumbled in his drawer and slid a piece of paper across the desk. 'These are all reliable places. We've worked with them before.'

She signed the contract in his presence and sent it to Stu by courier.

It should have made her feel better to start things moving, but it didn't. As she walked back to the car park, she couldn't put her finger on why, but she felt apprehensive. As if she was doing something dangerous.

Now where had that word come from? What could be dangerous about selling a house quickly? Especially if you used a good settlement agent and had things checked by a lawyer.

She wasn't surprised when Stu phoned her the following evening.

'I took in the contract and it's all go, my sweet.'

'Stop calling me that!'

He chuckled. 'How soon can you get the house ready for viewing?'

'I can't do anything till we get the roof repaired. You know the law about house sales and hiding defects.'

'Shit! I'd forgotten about that.'

'And don't you mean how soon can *we* get the house ready? I'm expecting you to do your share.'

'No can do. The company's sending me off to Prague to help bring in a rather lucrative deal. I'll be gone for a month or so, perhaps longer. Do you really want to wait to market the house?'

She was furious, but not surprised that he was wriggling

out of the hard work involved in sorting things out. 'I shall want your share of the money for the roof before you leave or I won't lift a finger.'

Silence. Then, 'OK.' His voice became softly persuasive. 'But you'll have the house looking nice, won't you? I doubt it'll need all that much doing. You could win gold in the Tidy Olympics. I bet the agent could bring people in to view the place right this minute.'

'Keeping the house clean is *not* the same as making it look its best. It really could do with brightening up. You never did get round to painting the living areas.'

'I don't do decorating. Anyway, I'm not spending any more money on the house, apart from that damned roof.'

'Neither am I, then. I'll just have to do my best with what we've got. Have you sent off your application for the decree absolute?'

'Of course. Keith's sorted all that out. And you?'

'Naturally. You're having an easy ride through this divorce with Keith doing everything, damn you.'

'Haven't I always told you, it's the connections you make who facilitate things, in life as well as in business? Only you were too stupid to see that.'

Too stupid to suck up to people she disliked, yes. She hated his smugness, but he had plenty to be smug about. He was doing really well in his career, and she was sure *he* wasn't going to be made redundant.

She wasn't doing nearly as well and she'd become increasingly conscious of that during their two years together. She'd never set out to become deputy manager in a big supermarket chain. She'd worked for an uncle in his shop, enjoying the interactions with customers.

Then she married quite young and moved away. That hadn't worked out as they'd planned, and the management trainee job had turned up when she needed to get another job – *any* job.

At the time, she hadn't much cared what she did to earn a living, just about the money she could earn, because she had much more important problems to deal with. More important to her in accepting the job offer had been the company's flexible attitude to hours, once she'd explained her problems.

Their training programme had been good – she'd give them that – and she'd risen to deputy manager in one of the smaller branches – not one of the giant ones. But she knew she'd get no further in the organisation, didn't even want to.

She did her job in a responsible manner, but she'd never been able to bring much enthusiasm to the act of enhancing and facilitating what they called 'the shopping experience'. Ha! She knew that most women wanted only to get their family's food supplies as quickly and cheaply as possible.

The most interesting part of the job, to her, was coaching the junior staff and mothering them a little if they needed it. Some of them were fresh from school – such babies, however grown-up they looked and tried to act.

Putting the phone down, she sighed at her own inadequacies. That's what Stu always did to her these days: made her feel stupid.

Perhaps she *was* stupid. She'd been taken in by him, after all, and had lost a lot through marrying him. Not just money but confidence. She'd *let* him dominate their marriage, take over the finances, make the important decisions about their life together. He'd done it bit by bit, and she hadn't even realised how he'd taken control.

All she'd wanted was to start a family before she grew too old and build a happy life together. But Stu had always found good reasons to postpone having children.

She could hear his words now. *Soon, sweetie. Let's get ourselves a bit better established first.*

What she should have done, if she'd had any sense, was live with him for a while and see how they got on. Tania had begged her to do that. But Stu had swept Gabi off her feet and into wedlock.

Or, in this case, into property-lock.

She had provided most of the money for the deposit on the house, but nowhere in the records did it say that. He'd switched small sums of money around various bank accounts, borrowed from her, paid it back by putting it into the house fund. And she had no way now of proving that it was mostly her money which had paid the deposit.

Oh, stop moaning, she told herself. *Get on with your life, you fool. You're still only thirty-five. The world hasn't ended.*

But her chances of having a family were slim now, and that hurt.

The trouble was, she had to figure out what to do next before she could get on with her life, and she simply couldn't decide on anything.

There was only one thing she was certain of: she wasn't getting married again.

Never, ever.

Chapter Three

Gabi got the roof repaired within a month, but by the time work on it finished, she felt exhausted, what with dealing with the builders every day before work and clearing up after them inside the house when she got home.

The men cleared most of the debris from outside, but there seemed to be dust everywhere inside, something she found hard to live with. Who wanted to eat their evening meal off a gritty table? Prepare food on a dusty surface? Not her.

There were a lot of other things to do, too, what with sorting out Stu's possessions, as well as her own. He'd taken some of his things but by no means all. He'd left a pile of boxes in the smaller of the two spare bedrooms.

The boxes showed he was a man of whims – as if she didn't know that by now. He'd gear up for some new pastime, usually involving the purchase of expensive equipment and special clothes, enjoy it for a while, then lose interest. There was kit from several interests that must have happened before they got married – weight training, fishing, a gun club even – plus the remains of the fads she'd witnessed and teased him about after their marriage, such as golf.

What fashionable pastime hadn't he tried? Even she could tell he wasn't cut out for sports requiring a lot of boring training. He was too impatient, wanting instant gratification in everything.

When she studied the living areas of the house with a buyer's eye, she knew she had to paint the walls at least, because they looked positively dingy in the bright, spring sunlight.

She was so weary by then she sat down and cried at the mere thought of all the extra work. 'Damn you, Stuart Dixon, for leaving it all to me!' she sobbed. 'I hope you get what you deserve one day.'

He wouldn't, of course: he could charm his way through any situation.

After much thought, she asked the store manager if she could take the rest of her holidays as special emergency leave. He wasn't at all pleased about that, because they had a huge healthy eating campaign about to hit all the shops in the chain.

'I don't think we can manage any leave just now, Gabi,' he said gently.

'Then I'm sorry, but I'll have to resign. I just . . . can't go on like this. I'm too tired to think straight.'

He stared in shock at this ultimatum and studied her more closely. 'You look exhausted. Two weeks, then. But see you have a good rest.'

'I'm sorry but I need a full month.' Tears escaped her control and she dabbed at her eyes. 'Sorry.'

He shook his head and gave in. 'That month is your limit, Mrs Dix—um, Ms Newman. And perhaps you should consult a doctor. You seem rather . . . depressed. It must be a very trying time for you.'

'Thank you. I will see my doctor if I don't improve; I can't seem to pull myself together. Anyway, I'm very grateful.'

He flapped one hand at her. 'Go home straight away. And take things easy.'

She only wished she could, but she had a lot to do.

It was just starting to rain and the house felt damp and cold. She didn't sort out the painting equipment, as she'd planned, but crawled into bed. As she got warmer, she let herself sink into oblivion. Just an hour or so. She'd work better after a good rest.

When she woke it was dusk. She looked at the bedside clock in astonishment. How could she possibly have slept so long?

When she went downstairs, she couldn't be bothered to cook, so made herself some toast and jam. She wasn't very hungry, anyway.

She wished Tania wasn't away on holiday in Greece, and that she hadn't lost touch with most of her other friends since her marriage. Tania wasn't the only one who hadn't taken to Stu, but the others had voted with their feet, making excuses not to get together until she stopped inviting them.

It was at times like this that Gabi most missed having close family. Her parents were dead. They had been quite old when they'd had her – a late-life surprise. They'd seen that she was reasonably well educated and had treated her with mild fondness, but they had been too set in their ways to change.

Unfortunately they'd died, one after the other, a couple of years after she finished business college. And the money she might have expected to inherit from the sale of their house turned out to have been invested in a reverse mortgage to buy an annuity, which they'd only had the benefit of for a couple of years.

Everything had been left to her, but after she'd cleared the house and paid the remaining bills from their bank account, there had been very little to inherit. She still really resented that wasted annuity – she could have found them better financial help, had they asked for it. Which they never did.

As she emptied their house, she was upset to find very little information about either side of the family – no old photos, letters or diaries. Her mother had insisted on clearing everything out after her husband died, and had refused Gabi's help.

'You won't want to go through our personal things, dear. It's a thankless task, believe me. There's nothing of interest to anyone but Henry and me. Anyway, clearing it all out will give me something to do.'

But Gabi hadn't expected her mother to destroy everything.

She knew there were still a few distant cousins and their descendants left on her father's side. They lived in the north, somewhere in Lancashire. Two of the cousins had come to her father's funeral, but not her mother's. Her mother had had a couple of cousins, too, but she hadn't stayed in touch with them, and no one but Gabi and a couple of long-time neighbours had come to her funeral.

Gabi should have paid more attention to what was being destroyed, but she'd just met Edward and fallen in love with him.

Now, she sometimes ached for a sign that she belonged to a family, however scattered. She would have liked to ask the cousins about her ancestors. Sadly, her mother had even destroyed all the old address books.

It was upsetting to know so little about your family. Maybe, when all this divorce stuff was over, she'd join one of those trace-your-ancestry organisations and look for her forebears.

The following morning, Gabi slept late, not feeling at all like painting walls. She ate some cereal, showered and dressed very casually, then gave in to temptation and went back to read in bed. *I deserve a bit of a rest*, she told herself. *I'll work better for it.*

She dozed off over her novel and woke with a start when something clunked against her bedroom window. She darted across the room, but although she caught sight of a male running away down the back lane, the figure wasn't at all clear because of the trees.

Opening the window, she stared down, wondering what had been thrown, and gasped when she saw a broken bottle containing pale pink liquid. It looked like petrol – like a petrol bomb!

Only, if so, it had failed to explode.

Why would someone do this? How could she make sure the device wasn't dangerous? Or was it booby-trapped to explode if she went near it?

She was making her way cautiously downstairs when someone knocked on the front door and she nearly jumped out of her skin.

She peered through the security peephole and saw a stranger, hand raised to knock again. It couldn't have been this man who'd thrown the bottle. He'd not have had time to get round to the front of the house. Anyway, he wasn't wearing the same sort of clothes, looked very respectable. So she opened the door.

'Gabrielle Dixon?'

She said it automatically, as she had many times in the past few months. 'I used to be. Since my divorce, I've reverted to my maiden name.'

'Sorry. Ms Newman, then.'

She was surprised. How did a complete stranger know her maiden name?

He held out a card. 'Des Monahan. I'm a private investigator, member of the British Security Industry Association if you'd like to check up on my bona fides. A lawyer called Henry Greaves has given me the task of locating you and delivering this in person.'

He held out a letter in an envelope with a company name and address neatly printed in one corner. 'Oh, and Mr Greaves would like a receipt, if you don't mind.'

She shouldn't let a stranger into the house. It was asking for trouble. And she still had to deal with the petrol bomb. 'I . . . this isn't convenient.'

What if the bomb could still explode? She began to shake.

'Are you all right?'

There was something about his face that made her trust him instinctively, so she told him what had upset her. 'Someone just threw a petrol bomb at my house. It's lying in pieces on the back patio. I can't think what to do.'

He looked past her, instantly alert. His very calmness gave her confidence.

'Did it damage anything? Did you extinguish it?'

'It didn't explode.'

'Show me.'

She took him through the house towards the back garden, opening the patio door warily. 'There it is.'

'Stay there.' He moved forward to where the pale pink liquid from the bottle had splashed across the paved area next to the house. The bottom of the bottle was still in one piece and the liquid in it was glinting in the sunlight.

He bent to dip his finger in the moisture lying in a hollow in the paving. As he held it to his nose and sniffed, he frowned, then tried another of the tiny puddles that were drying up fast. 'This isn't petrol, but it does look like it, I will admit.'

Her legs felt so wobbly, she stumbled to the little wooden bench against the wall and collapsed on it. 'So even if I call the police again, they'll just . . . say it was a prank?'

'Probably. Why do you say "call the police again"?'

She studied his face. He looked so thoroughly decent, she found herself telling him about the other incidents.

He came to sit on the bench beside her and took her hand. 'It looks as if someone's trying to frighten you.'

'And they're succeeding.'

'Have you any idea why?'

She shrugged. 'I'd guess it's my ex, but I don't understand why. Anyway, he's just gone back to Prague where he's working on a project, so this can't be his doing.'

'Let's go back inside. A cup of hot sweet tea wouldn't go amiss. You're in shock still.'

'Yes.' She stood up.

Des put an arm round her shoulders and led her into the house, locking the door behind them.

She studied him again as he did that. He was of medium height, only a little taller than her, and he wasn't remarkable in any way, except for a certain steadiness. Yes, that was a good word to describe the impression he'd made on her. He seemed decent, to use an old-fashioned word.

To her at least, he made Stu's good looks, expensive clothes and fake tan seem like overkill.

They stood still in the middle of the kitchen and Des put his arm round her again. Lightly, nothing sexual about it, just one human being comforting another. She didn't pull away because she still felt wobbly.

He didn't hurry her, just watched her gravely with grey eyes, a thoughtful expression on his face. His dark hair was neatly trimmed, with a few strands of grey at the temples. Even his clothes were about as nondescript as you could get. Not shabby, but nothing to draw the eye. She'd guess he was a couple of years older than her.

She sighed and moved away from his arm. Reluctantly.

'Are you feeling better now?' he asked gently.

'A little. I still feel shaky, though.'

'Sit down. I'll make the tea and you can direct me.'

She was glad to sit. 'Thank you. I'm sorry about the

mess in here, but I've just had the builders in and I'm about to decorate.'

'I'm feeling thirsty myself, if you don't mind.' He put the kettle on.

'You're welcome.' She stayed where she was, feeling boneless and numb. If someone had meant to frighten her, they'd succeeded big time.

'How do you like it?'

She started, not realising he'd finished making the tea. 'White, no sugar.'

He put a mug on the table in front of her. 'Could you face some sugar in it this time? It's good for shock.'

'All right. You must think I'm an utter wimp.'

'No, I don't. Anyone would be frightened by that. It was a cruel trick to play.'

She took a comforting sip of the hot liquid. And another.

When she'd swallowed the last warm mouthful, she put the mug down, feeling somewhat better. 'Thank you for helping me.'

'My pleasure. You've got some colour back now.'

'Yes. And I just realised, you said something about a letter.'

'It can wait if you need more time to pull yourself together.'

'No. I'm all right now. Anyway, it'll take my mind off . . . that.' She jerked her head in the direction of the back door.

He took her mug and put it tidily on the draining board, then pulled a letter out of his pocket and offered it to her.

She looked at the address: Rochdale. She was puzzled

that a lawyer from a town she'd never visited would want to contact her. Was that perhaps where her father's family came from? Or her mother's?

She spread out the papers and began to read. 'Oh! It's a legacy.' She gaped at her visitor. 'I can't believe this. Why should Rose King leave me anything?'

'Keep reading.'

'Yes. Sorry. I was just so . . . surprised.' She read the rest of the letter more slowly, trying to take it in. 'Ah. She was my mother's cousin. The name does sound vaguely familiar, though I don't think I've ever met her. My parents weren't big on keeping in touch with distant relatives. Rose would be my second cousin once removed, I think. Or is it twice removed?'

He smiled. 'I'm never quite sure of the exact relationships between cousins, especially those of different generations.'

'I still can't understand why she'd leave anything to me.'

'I gather Mrs King had no direct descendants, so she left her estate to a trust whose main purpose was to help any of her female relatives who were in need. She felt she'd been lucky, had a long life and good friends, so she devised her own way of helping others. Mr Greaves said the old lady could be very determined once she'd decided upon something. She planned the way the trust would do that.'

He cocked his head on one side and paused, as if to ask whether she was taking this in.

'Goodness me.' Gabi looked down at the letter again. 'It says something here about there being conditions for taking up the inheritance. Do you know what they are? I might not qualify.'

'Mr Greaves would prefer to explain the details to you himself.'

'Why did . . . I suppose I should call her Cousin Rose. Why did she think I needed help?'

'She knew very little about you when she died. She simply left instructions about keeping an eye on her female relatives and made a list of those she knew about. Mr Greaves hands over this surveillance to me, while he pursues the genealogy – which is one of his interests – and unearths the occasional distant cousin. It was he who asked me to check on you and your husband a while ago.'

She was surprised by this. 'Why would he want to do that?'

'He knew you existed, but had found it hard to contact you. Apparently, your husband had deliberately left as few traces as he could after you married. I investigated further and, quite frankly, I wasn't impressed by Stuart Dixon, so when I found out you were divorcing him, I informed Mr Greaves and he sent me to find you, in case you needed help.'

Gabi began to read the two pages of attachments. Appendix I mentioned houses Rose King had owned, which now belonged to the trust.

'One of those houses is always available for her descendants to live in,' Des said quietly. 'Not permanently, but as needed, in times of crisis. They're a bit old-fashioned, but comfortable enough. You'll be losing this house when you settle your finances, I assume.'

'But I'm not in crisis – well, except for the divorce and . . . a series of nasty tricks.' Not just nasty but frightening. Could Stu really be arranging these shocks?

'Are you all right?'

She blinked and looked at him. 'Sorry. My mind wandered for a moment. I shall have enough money left to put a decent deposit on a small house or flat, and I already have my furniture and appliances. So I don't think I shall need to use the trust house, though it's wonderful of Cousin Rose to care about her descendants like that.'

'It's entirely up to you. But have you thought that you may need somewhere to stay while you're looking for another place to live? You can't move straight into a house. These things take time. Will you stay in this area?'

'To tell you the truth, I've no idea what I'm going to do.'

'There you are, then – Rose's house might be just the thing you need till you've worked things out.'

'I suppose. But I don't know anyone in Lancashire. I'd thought of renting nearer here.'

'Whatever you prefer. There are also some boxes of documents available, which you may enjoy going through. Mrs King was very interested in family history. But we're not allowed to take them away from the houses.'

'Ah. That does interest me. I know so little about my mother's family.' Gabi looked down at the papers again. Whether she needed this help or not, it felt good to know that someone in her family had cared enough to make such provisions. It made her feel less alone in the world.

She smiled at him. 'Whatever happens, Mr Monahan, I would like to see those family documents, so I won't make a decision yet.'

She turned to the last page. 'Oh!' A further surprise was outlined in Appendix II: Mrs King had left some small legacies, one to be given to each person using a house. All the dwellings – Gabi loved the old-fashioned term – were on the outskirts of Rochdale, near a place called Littleborough. She wasn't even sure where Rochdale was, not exactly; she'd have to look it up on the internet.

'Is anyone living in a house at the moment, Mr Monahan?'

'I'm not at liberty to discuss other people's details, I'm afraid.'

'Oh. Well, can you tell me what it means by a legacy? Does that mean she's left me some money?' Gabi would need as much money as she could find after the divorce to buy a house. So although it might be mercenary, perhaps it'd be worth going up to see Cousin Rose's lawyer and find out what she had to do.

'Mr Greaves will give you all the details of the legacy when you go to see him.'

'I see. I would love to go through the family documents, I must admit. My mother threw all hers away. Only I don't have time to go up to Lancashire to see him at the moment. I have the divorce to finalise, for one thing, which means getting this house ready to sell.'

'Mr Greaves said to tell you there's no hurry, but perhaps you could go and see him within the next month or two. I'm authorised to pay your travel expenses.' Again, Des Monahan looked at her questioningly.

She pulled her wandering thoughts together and frowned at the letter. 'Unfortunately, I'll have to leave it till I've sorted everything out here.'

She couldn't believe the legacy would be anything big.

Her mother didn't come from a rich family. It was only in fairy stories that heroines inherited a fortune from a rich relative.

Des's quiet voice cut through her rambling thoughts. 'Perhaps you should plan to go and see Mr Greaves after you sell your house, then. When does it go on the market? How are property sales going round here?'

A tired sigh escaped her. 'Sales are very slow. And I can't put it on the market till I've painted the ground-floor rooms.'

He looked surprised. 'You're not hiring someone else to do it?'

'I can't afford to. I've taken a month's leave from work to deal with the house and . . . and because I feel a bit run down. There's such a lot to do and I've only got one pair of hands, so it'll take time.'

'I can't help being nosey – blame it on my profession – and I shan't be upset if you don't want to answer, but surely your ex should be helping with that?'

'Stu? He doesn't do decorating. Or anything practical in the house.' She couldn't keep the bitterness from her voice. 'Besides, he's in Prague for a few weeks.'

'I see.' Des looked round. 'The place does need a bit of a touch-up, I agree. It looks shabby.'

'We never got round to decorating it, as we'd planned. No, as *I'd* planned.'

He went across to run his fingers across one wall and squint sideways along it. 'The plaster's not in too bad a state. It'll only need one coat of paint if you keep it to some similar pale colour. Look, I know this sounds crazy, but how about I help you with the decorating? I'm a dab hand with a paintbrush.'

She was rather taken aback by this offer from a complete stranger and couldn't believe he meant it.

He gave her a wry smile. 'My horoscope this morning said I'd be helping a friend and would greatly benefit from doing so.'

This was weirder and weirder. 'Do you believe in horoscopes?' she asked.

His smile broadened. 'Not at all, but I thoroughly enjoy reading them all the same. And I actually like painting and decorating. Just occasionally, you know. It gives you such an instant reward, don't you think?'

She still didn't know how to respond to his offer.

His voice was gentle. 'Sometimes it's good to do something for another person. And if you don't mind me saying so, you look as if you've reached the limit of your endurance, physically and mentally.'

She couldn't hold back tears, could feel them rolling down her cheeks. This sympathy and understanding from a complete stranger was more than she could cope with.

Des pushed the box of tissues across the table to her. 'Here. If you want me to mind my own business, just say so and I'll leave you to it.'

She blew her nose firmly, but the tears still kept coming. To her surprise, she didn't want him to leave, didn't want to be on her own again. 'I can't understand why you'd offer.'

'A few years ago, when I was going through a hard time, someone was kind to me. It wasn't anything big, but it made all the difference to my life. He didn't want anything from me in return except the promise to help other people now and then. So I do. Hence my offer of help.'

He smiled reminiscently. 'I've never failed to benefit from doing that – not necessarily financially, but in some roundabout ways. One old lady gave me a bowl because she couldn't afford to pay me. I didn't need payment, but it made her feel better to give me something.'

Gabi nodded. She could understand that.

'The bowl turned out to be quite valuable as well as beautiful – early Moorcroft, a rare piece. I didn't sell it. I have it on display in my house and look at it every day when I'm at home. I've had such pleasure from that bowl.'

'What a lovely story! I like Moorcroft, too.'

Des stared into space, still lost in reminiscences. 'Another old man died happily because I'd been able to help him find his grandson. I went to a bit more trouble than he could afford to pay for, but I didn't tell him. I found the young man in time, and that, too, gave me great satisfaction. Some people scorn private investigators, but I really enjoy what I do.'

She wished she enjoyed her job.

He looked at her. 'Well? Am I hired?'

She was definitely tempted to accept his offer. 'Do you have time to help me? What about your business?'

'I'm in the fortunate position of being able to pick and choose my cases. I can take time off whenever I want.' He saw her expression and laughed at her puzzlement. 'I'm not rich. It's just that I'm an only son and I inherited the family house from parents who'd been careful with their money, a trait I've inherited. I'm not extravagant. I don't need a lot of money to live comfortably.'

She wished her parents had had more sense about money. And her ex. 'Well, then . . . if you're sure you don't mind helping.'

'I wouldn't have offered otherwise.'

'I'd be very grateful for any help you can give me, Mr Monahan. You're right. I'm finding it hard to get through all this on my own. I'm a bit run down, I think.'

'That's settled, then. And do call me Des. You're Gabrielle, I gather.'

'People usually call me Gabi.'

'Seems a pity. Gabrielle is a beautiful name. But hey, if you want me to call you Gabi, I will.'

She looked at him thoughtfully. 'I prefer Gabrielle, actually, but Stu said it was old-fashioned and changed it to Gabi. My parents always used my full name, though. Yes, please do call me that. In fact, I think I'll ask everyone to call me Gabrielle from now on.'

'Signalling a new start.' He gave an understanding smile.

'Exactly.'

'I'll go and see if I can get a room in that nice-looking bed and breakfast I saw at the lower end of this street. Then I'll come back and we'll plan how to tackle this job.' He stood up. 'Do you have some paint already or do we have to buy some?'

'I haven't got anything, not even the painting equipment. I thought . . . white. People say you should go for a neutral look if you're selling.'

'Off-white would be better, or it'll look too stark.' He glanced at his watch. 'I'll go and book a room. If I come straight back, we can go out and buy the paint today, then get an early start in the morning.'

He stopped at the door to say, 'Leave the broken glass. I'll clear it up later.'

When he'd left, she stood in the doorway, watching him drive down the street and stop outside the B and B.

This had been the strangest encounter she'd ever had. She couldn't believe what she'd done – first invited a complete stranger into her house and then accepted his offer to help her paint it. And what about the legacy? And the offer of a house?

It all felt unreal. But nice. The nicest thing that had happened to her for a while.

She frowned. Was Des Monahan really passing on a kindness? Or did he have an ulterior motive for helping her?

She knew what Stu would have said: nobody does anything for free. They're always looking for a kickback of some sort.

But she wanted quite desperately to believe that there were good people in the world, people who really did help their neighbours. Not everyone was like Stu.

The legacy couldn't be much, anyway – probably just a token amount. It was the family documents that interested her most. And the more she thought about it, the more she liked the idea of getting away to think about her future.

For the present, she was going to work really hard on getting the house ready to sell, so that she could get completely free of Stu. And she wouldn't have to do it on her own. That was such a load off her back. How kind of Des!

Afterwards, she would try to make some new friends. Perhaps contact some of her old ones. She would just go with the flow, as Tania would say, till she saw her way clear.

She couldn't imagine this house selling as quickly as the agency had said, so she'd need to go back to work after her month's leave was up.

She was dreading that.

But she did like the idea of her new start, including a return to her full name. It was a small thing, but a first step towards . . . something different. A better life, she hoped.

Des came back an hour later, casually dressed, carrying a shopping bag with a brand-new set of overalls in it.

'You must let me pay for those,' Gabrielle said at once.

'No need. I'll be using them for years, probably. My old overalls are ragged and stained now, full of holes. Shall we go?'

'Go?'

'Shopping for paint.'

'Oh, yes. We can go to one of the shops in the chain I work for. I'll get a staff discount there.'

'Sounds good. And I rang up my friend to ask the exact name of the paint he used in his house. It looks great – a very subtle colour, neither cream nor white. Shall we go in my car? It's bigger than yours, in case we have to carry things. Do you have a ladder?'

Gabrielle felt as if she'd been swept away by a gentle whirlwind, and she didn't mind at all. She felt safe with

Des. Maybe whoever was threatening her would stop if she wasn't alone.

However hard she racked her brains, there was no one she could think of who might be trying to upset her, except the man who'd once said he loved her. Stu was extremely eager to get his money from the house; he'd soon lose interest in tormenting her once he got that.

Till then, she'd be careful not to be alone with him again.

Oh, she was full of foolish ideas today. She needed to pull herself together. This was starting to sound like a bad B movie, full of gangsters and threats.

Wouldn't it be amusing if it also involved a creepy old house on the edge of the moors? Shades of *Wuthering Heights*. She'd never liked that book. It was so miserable a tale.

Henry Greaves picked up the phone that evening.

'Des here, reporting in. Is this a convenient time, not too late?'

'Very convenient. My wife's out at her book club meeting. And you know very well that I'm a night owl. I don't consider nine o'clock late. So, how's it going?'

'I've found your Gabrielle. She's almost finalised her divorce, and she's using her maiden name again: Ms Newman. We chatted for quite a while. That husband of hers seems to have made sure she cut off all ties with her past life. I told you I didn't like him. It's strange, though, how thorough he was about that. I had trouble finding his trail. Most amateurs don't hide their whereabouts nearly as well.'

'What's he like?'

'I haven't met him – only seen him in the distance. Good-looking, I suppose, if you like the showy type. She's almost free of him now, so I probably won't have anything to do with him. She's just waiting for the decree absolute and to sell the house.'

'How is she coping?'

'At the moment, she's run down and, I think, a bit depressed. She'd be pretty if she wasn't so pale and didn't have such dark circles under her eyes. I think she's had a rough time. She was trying to prepare the house for sale on her own. Her ex is apparently too busy to help get it ready.'

'Do you think she'll want to collect the legacy?'

'Depends how much money she gets from the house and what she plans to do with her life. She doesn't know much about the north of England, or her family, and she has a southern accent.'

'Rose would be pleased you've found her. I still miss the old lady. She could hold a truly intelligent conversation that always caught your interest. She was a lateral thinker, too – had some unusual ideas. Ah, well. That's life. We all have to die one day.'

'The later the better, as far as I'm concerned.'

'When will you finish there, Des? Have you thought any more about moving up here and accepting my offer of the job as manager of the trust? Those investments of Rose's have paid off big time and there's a lot more to dealing with them than I'd expected.'

'I'd very much like to accept the job. It's interesting and worthwhile work.'

'Good.'

'I'll move to Rochdale when I get a few weeks clear. About time I found a different house – something more modern, perhaps.'

'Are you working on another job now?'

'I have one that I need to finish off. I've promised to help my client with that. In the meantime, I'm helping Gabrielle decorate her house.'

'You're what?'

'You heard me perfectly well, Henry.'

'That's above and beyond the call of duty, isn't it? We don't need to know what she has for breakfast – just whether she needs help or not.'

'It's got nothing to do with duty. As far as I'm concerned, I've more or less finished the job you gave me with her. This is just . . . I couldn't bear to see her struggling and I quite like decorating, so I offered to help.'

'You're a kind man. I've seen you help people before.'

'Painting a few rooms isn't much.'

Henry smiled. Des hated his little philanthropic gestures to be made public or considered anything but normal. Nice fellow, Des. 'Rather you than me. I loathe the smell of paint. We had to decorate a house ourselves when we were first married. Devil of a job getting the paint out of your fingernails. We were both delighted when we had enough money to pay someone else to do it the next time.'

'I'll get back to you when Gabrielle is ready to see you about her inheritance.'

'Don't tell her the details.'

'No. Of course I won't.'

'Mrs King didn't have much else to enjoy towards the end. She was riddled with arthritis, poor thing. The planning of the trust cheered her up enormously.'

Des put the phone away and went to lie on the bed with his new novel. But he didn't get much reading done. He kept thinking about Gabrielle. She was in for a few surprises after the divorce – nice ones, he hoped.

He was looking forward to spending a few days in her company. There was something about her that attracted him. It had been quite a while since he'd felt this interested in a woman.

She wasn't the only one to have been burnt by a previous relationship, so he wasn't rushing into anything and he was pretty sure she wouldn't want to, either.

No, they had plenty of time, and if she settled in Rochdale for a while, it would be perfect. They could become friends, take things slowly.

Chapter Four

Gabrielle was grateful to Des for helping her with the painting. He was thorough but quick, and they got through the work sooner than she'd have believed possible.

She enjoyed his company greatly. He made no attempt to flirt with her, which would have made her wary, but they talked, really talked, and she soon began to feel she'd made a new friend.

She so needed friends now.

It was two days before she found out Des had been married and, like her, was divorced – had been for several years. The end of his marriage had been easy compared to hers, because his wife had a good job and wanted only her fair share of their joint possessions.

'She needed a man with more pizzazz,' he said ruefully. 'We didn't quarrel or anything like that, but I was too quiet for her.'

Gabrielle liked Des's quietness, the way he didn't speak unless he had something worthwhile to say, the way he smiled at her occasionally, for no other reason than that it was his nature to be friendly.

One thing was worrying her, though. 'Shouldn't you be

at work? I don't want to stop you earning a living.'

'I inherited my parents' house a couple of years after my divorce. They died in a car accident in France. I miss them, but not having a mortgage makes life a lot easier for me financially. I can please myself what jobs I take on – or have a few days off, if I fancy it.' He patted her hand. 'Don't worry. I'm enjoying the change, and enjoying your company, too.'

That made her feel good.

When he'd finished painting the final wall, he came to stand next to her and they studied the living/dining area together. 'There. That looks very nice, don't you agree? I can't think of anywhere else on the ground floor that needs painting and, as you say, the upstairs will do. How about we go out for a pub meal to celebrate?'

'I'd like that, Des – as long as you let me pay my own way.'

'If you prefer.'

'I do. We're just . . . friends.'

'For the moment.'

She looked at him in shock, but he changed the subject and she didn't dare pursue it in case she was mistaken. But she couldn't help wondering exactly what he'd meant.

If it was what she thought, she wasn't ready to start dating anyone. Not till she received the decree absolute and knew her marriage was completely over, anyway. But she did like Des.

Although she was feeling a little better now after a few peaceful days, she still couldn't face going back to work. That was weighing on her mind.

When Des drove her home after their meal, he said

abruptly, 'I have a job starting soon in London. It'll last a week or two, I should think. Would you like to keep in touch?'

'Yes.' Two glasses of wine made her brave enough to add, 'Very much.'

He smiled at her and pressed a business card into her hand. 'Good. I'd like to keep in touch, too. You have my mobile number and I have yours, but this answering service will get a message to me if I'm out of range, or if my mobile dies.'

He leant forward to kiss her cheek very gently. 'I like you, Gabrielle. I'm looking forward to getting to know you better.'

'Are you sure you want to? You're not just saying it to let me down gently?'

He stared at her in surprise. 'Of course I'm sure. Why would you doubt it?' He took her hand. 'You're an attractive, intelligent woman.'

She could feel tears welling in her eyes.

Des pulled her into a gentle hug, murmuring, 'That ex of yours did a real job of putting you down, didn't he? Don't sell yourself short, Gabrielle. He sounds like a chancer to me, a fly-by-night, to quote one of my mother's favourite insults – which suits him perfectly, from what you've told me. Does he ever settle to anything?'

'Stu certainly has a short attention span.' It hadn't really sunk in before, she realised, that her ex's push, push, push attitude might result from fault and weakness, not from vitality and strength of character.

Des stepped back. 'All right now? Good. I wish you luck

with selling the house. Keep me in touch with what happens.'

She wondered if he really would phone, if he was telling the truth about wanting to get to know her better. Maybe he'd grow tired of her and the phone calls would tail off.

It was better not to count on him, even though she did allow herself to consider it fairly likely they would stay friends. She couldn't help hoping she was right, but she didn't dare put all her faith in anything or anyone at the moment.

The next day, Gabrielle nerved herself to phone Stu. She didn't give him time to ask questions, just said, 'The house is ready. It'd look better if you took those boxes of rubbish away, though.'

'I'm still in Prague. How the hell do you expect me to do that? Wave a magic wand?'

'You could find a firm online and arrange to have the boxes put into storage.'

'Why pay for storage when there's a whole garage standing empty?'

He must be short of money. Had he been spending lavishly again? Stu did that from time to time. Living in high style was like an addiction for him. She'd never been into fine dining where waiters fussed over you and charged you a fortune for a few artistically arranged leaves topped by a minuscule portion of something exotic.

'Let's focus on selling the house now, Gabi. Leave informing the agent to me. I got on well with Peter.'

'Please yourself.'

To her surprise, the agent phoned her early the

following day, wanting to bring a couple of people to view the house. She sat outside in her car and watched them. Both were men, hard-eyed, unsmiling, in and out quickly.

She didn't expect either of them to make an offer, but one did. Only it was for a ridiculous amount, way below what she and Stu had agreed was their lowest limit.

When Peter rang that evening to tell her, he suggested she make a counter offer.

She was feeling tired, wondering if she was coming down with a cold, and said sharply, 'I'm not playing games about this, Peter. That offer is way below our bottom line, as you well know. If this man cares to make a serious offer, we'll certainly consider it. Otherwise, we're not interested.'

Stu rang later that same night from Prague, waking her up. She snatched up the phone, wondering what the bad news was. It took her a moment or two to realise it was Stu.

'You sound puddled. Are you drunk?' he demanded.

'No, of course not. You woke me up.'

'You always did go to bed ridiculously early. Anyway, you were right not to accept that offer, but you ought to have made them a counter offer.'

'No way. That guy was just fishing for a knock-down bargain. I doubt he'd have come anywhere near our bottom line, whatever I countered with.'

'Actually, you can never tell. People do try to get things cheaply, I agree. You can't blame them for trying. I'd do the same. But sometimes they really do want to buy a particular property and then they gradually increase their offer to something more reasonable.'

'He'd have had to up his offer a long way to reach our level.'

'Nonetheless, next time damned well make a counter offer.'

'If you were here, Stu, *you* could do all the bargaining. You've always boasted how good you are at selling, so I'd expect you to get far more for the place than I ever could.'

He didn't sense her irony; he never had. 'Well, I'm coming back to England next week, so you and I can meet to discuss tactics then. I want to get that house sold ASAP.'

'Don't forget to bring your magic wand. Sales are not good in this area at the moment.'

'Bye, Mrs Grumpy. Go back to your snoring.' He put the phone down.

She couldn't get back to sleep for ages, didn't want to see Stu, was dreading his return.

Every time she spoke to him, she felt less sure of herself. Why did she let him get to her like this? No matter how many times she gave herself a talking-to, she never stood up to him as she would have liked.

It wouldn't be possible to stop him coming to see the house. He was still part-owner, after all. Half-owner, according to the settlement. She hoped a miracle would occur and they'd sell quickly! Oh, please let it happen!

She'd just fallen asleep when something hit her bedroom window. It didn't break the glass but it startled her and made her sit up in bed.

She listened carefully. The thump couldn't have been a bird in the middle of the night.

She didn't hear footsteps, but something else thumped

against the window pane and a man's voice called, 'Get out of here, you stupid bitch!'

When she looked sideways, there were no lights in her neighbours' houses, but then Mrs Starkey was rather deaf and the people on the other side were only weekenders.

What the hell was all this about? Why would someone threaten her?

If they decided to break in, they'd have little trouble, because there were a lot of windows. And however loudly she called for help, no one would hear her.

She pulled a chest of drawers across the doorway. There were no more noises, but she couldn't get to sleep again. She only managed to doze uneasily. The night seemed to go on for ever.

The next morning, Gabrielle nearly didn't answer her mobile. Then she looked at the caller ID and saw it was Des. At the sound of his voice, tears came into her eyes. He really did want to stay in touch.

'How are things going, Gabrielle?'

She tried to stay calm but couldn't and gulped back tears.

'Tell me.'

'I had another disturbance during the night. Someone throwing things at my window.'

'I'd like to set vandals to breaking up stones till they swore never to damage things again.'

'Why would a vandal shout, "Get out of here, you stupid bitch"?'

Silence, then: 'He wouldn't. He must have been paid to shout that. Were you scared?'

'Yes, I was.'

'What did the neighbours say about it?'

'Mrs Starkey wouldn't hear it if an elephant landed on her roof, and the people on the other side are weekenders.'

'Maybe I could get up to see you for a day or two.'

'No. You've got a job to do. I'll inform the police and see if they can help.'

'This particular job is at a crucial stage, but if the harassment continues, let me know and I will come. I don't like to think of you on your own.'

'Thank you.'

'Is the house in the agent's hands now?'

'Yes. And he brought two people to look round. One of them made an insultingly low offer.'

'Tell the agent not to bother you with offers that low.'

'Stu would go mad if I did that. He told me I should have made a counter offer. He's coming back next week, so I'll let him take charge of that side of things.'

'Don't give him a completely free rein. Keep a careful check on what he's doing.'

'Why do you say that? Do you know something about him that I don't?'

There was silence. Then, 'I'm not sure. I thought it worthwhile looking into things a bit. You're too trusting. Did you know he's dealing with two companies in Prague? One for his own firm, the other presumably a job on the side – only . . . well, that one's with a rather shady group. What's he doing mixed up with people like that?'

'Oh. He doesn't tell me anything.'

'I'll see if I can find out anything more definite. Just . . .

keep an eye on him and don't sign anything without checking it with your lawyer.'

She needed to spell it out. 'Do you think he'll try to cheat me?'

'I don't know. But I think you're an honest person and you don't necessarily see the dishonesty in others. Even when we listened to the radio together while we were painting, you always gave people who called in the benefit of the doubt.'

'Stu says I'm a trusting fool.'

'No. You're not a fool at all. You're a genuinely nice person.'

His compliments made her feel warm inside.

They chatted for quite a while, and when Des said goodbye, she was smiling.

The phone rang almost immediately and the desire to smile vanished when she looked at who was calling.

'You've been on the phone for ages. Who were you speaking to?'

'None of your business, Stu.'

'Well, don't hold long phone conversations from now on, even if you have got yourself a fancy man.' He sniggered as if this was an utter impossibility. 'The agent was trying to get in touch with you and had to call me instead. Peter is an on-the-ball kind of guy. He wants to bring someone else round this afternoon at two. Give him a call and confirm that it's OK.'

Stu put the phone down without waiting for her reply. She felt tempted to phone him back and tell him she didn't appreciate him ordering her around, but she didn't do it.

Of course she didn't. He'd find some way of turning on her if she tried.

Once the money side of things was settled, she'd never willingly speak to him again, would block his calls. She would move away from the district and leave no forwarding address.

And she even had somewhere to go, thanks to Cousin Rose. She was definitely going to take up the offer of a house. Her spirits lightened at the thought of getting away, of living somewhere peaceful.

She had been right to agree to a quick sale agent, she decided. The quicker they sold, the better. And if they got a little less for the house, well, it'd be worth it to get rid of Stu.

Her ex turned up two days later, using his key to try to get into the house and banging hard on the door when he found it no longer fitted the lock.

He was looking vibrant and full of energy, but sporting a silly new, gravity-defying haircut more suited to a younger man than a thirty-eight-year-old, in Gabrielle's opinion.

'Well, aren't you going to let me in, Gabi?'

'No. I'm about to go out. You should have rung, Stu.'

'That's all right. I can look round the house on my own.'

'Come back later.'

When she didn't move out of the way, he shoved her aside much harder than he had last time, so that she bounced back several metres, jarring her elbow on the hall stand.

Stu shut the front door and walked into the living

room before she had recovered from the shock of this rough treatment.

'Why did you do that?' she demanded.

'What?'

'Bump me against the wall. You could have hurt me.'

He turned to stare at her coldly as if she was something strange he'd picked up. 'Yes, I could, couldn't I? You might care to remember that and stop being so bloody awkward about selling the house.'

'Awkward! I painted it.'

'Wasn't necessary. Anyway, I'm warning you to be more cooperative with Peter and the buyers he brings from now on, or I'll make sure you regret it.'

'I'll report you for assault if you dare touch me again.'

He backed her against the wall with an abruptness that took her by surprise and held her there by the weight of his body. He pushed her chin up so that she couldn't get away from him without a struggle, smiling as she tried and failed to get away. 'You'd need proof of an assault, my pet, and I'm not stupid enough to give it you. Where are your bruises? Where's my history of assault?'

He gave one of his scornful rasps of laughter. 'No one would take any complaint *you* might make at all seriously. I can see it now. You'd break down and weep all over the police, and they'd realise you're a hysterical fool who's making things up.'

He shoved her away as forcibly as before and walked on into the kitchen without waiting for her to regain her balance. 'It does look better, but, as I told you, I won't pay for the paint.'

'I didn't ask you to. I made it more attractive because I was eager to sell the house and get away from you. You need to take away that stuff in the garage now and—'

'Stop harping on about that. Not going to happen. Oh, and by the way, you've changed the lock. I need a key to the house.'

'No, you don't. You're not living here any more.'

'The place is half mine. You had no right to change the locks without my permission.'

'I had intruders. The police suggested I do it. It made me feel safer. I'd never know who you'd give a key to.'

'Well, pay attention: if you don't give me a new key, I'll break the front door down. Keith says I have a right to do that. And I may choose to do it at night. That'd really put the wind up you. I might even creep into your bedroom, for old times' sake.'

She couldn't hold back a shudder at the thought of him coming near her in bed. He'd looked positively gleeful as he made this threat, she thought. Like a naughty boy enjoying tormenting a creature smaller than him. 'I'll get you a key cut.'

'You'll have been given a spare. I want it now.'

She hated the thought of him being able to get into the house and decided to put a bolt on the inside of the front and back doors, so that she'd feel safe from him at night, at least.

'Well?'

'Wait there.' She started to go upstairs. As he tried to follow, she stopped and folded her arms. 'I won't get it out if you spy on me.'

He rolled his eyes and backed down the stairs. 'Well, hurry up then.'

She pulled the chest of drawers behind the bedroom door before she opened her hiding place. There was a loose bit of skirting board, but it didn't show unless you knew exactly where to push it. She'd found it by sheer accident when she was cleaning the room.

She'd refused to give the agent a key but she'd bet Stu would give him one now.

Stu had never been this bad before. She was shocked by the way he was bullying her openly. He'd carry out his threat to break down the door of the house if she didn't give him this key, she was sure.

She stole a glance at him when she took the key downstairs and handed it over. He had a restless, glittery air to him today, as if he was on drugs. Was he?

What had she ever seen in him? Whatever it was, it'd gone completely now.

A couple of days later, Gabi picked up the post from behind the front door as she came home from the shops. There was an envelope from the divorce court. She ripped it open before she even moved a step. Yes, there it was in black and white: the decree absolute, the official statement that her marriage to Stu was completely and irrevocably over.

She'd vowed never to shed another tear over the end of her marriage, but, before she knew it, she was sobbing, unable to hold back loud, raw sounds of grief and pain. She had expected so much from this relationship and it had lasted less than two years.

Her only other serious relationship had been so wonderful that she'd been shocked rigid when this one began going wrong. She still didn't understand why Stu had changed so radically.

Annoyed with herself for giving way like that, she blew her nose and dried her eyes, then looked quickly through the rest of the post: an electricity bill and an offer to sell her house. Ha! Hadn't they noticed the 'For Sale' sign already outside?

When she was coming home from the shops the next day, Gabrielle took a minor road which had wonderful views of the countryside. It was one of her favourite drives and she often stopped at a lookout to soak up the peace.

Was any country in the world as beautiful as rural England?

It had been raining overnight and there had been another light shower a few minutes previously. Drops of water were sparkling on the branches, catching the sunlight and showering down as branches were blown about.

But before she reached the lookout, another car drove up behind her, accelerating till it bumped into her.

She yelled, 'Get back, you idiot!' As if the driver could hear her!

The man at the wheel sounded his horn and bumped into her car again. She couldn't see his face, or his passenger's, because they were wearing knitted hats pulled down and scarves round their mouths.

He was doing it on purpose, she realised in horror as

he bumped her car again. That was why he was hiding his face. What was he trying to do? Kill her? Why?

She memorised the number of the other car and tried to accelerate just as it was about to bump her again, but it accelerated too, blasting its horn in a long blare of sound. The thump from the much bigger vehicle made her skid on the wet road and she lost control for a few seconds.

She braked hard and was coming to a halt by the side of the road, thinking to lock up the car and stay there until he'd moved on. But the other car braked hard, too, and then accelerated towards her so that it nudged her right into the ditch before she had come to a halt.

Then it sped off, sounding its horn triumphantly.

She screamed as she was jolted about badly. An airbag exploded in front of her, sending white dust all over the interior.

When the car stopped, she heard her breath rasping and couldn't hold back a moan. It was a few moments before she thought to switch off her engine, afraid of something catching fire.

The silence that followed was just as overwhelming as the noise of the crash had been. She didn't move – couldn't, just sat there for a few moments, covering her face with her hands, as if that would hold in the panic. Her heart was thudding so hard that it felt as if it'd jump out of her chest.

She couldn't think straight, let alone move, but as she calmed a little, she realised she ought to get out of her car and phone the police.

Someone spoke to her, but it was a moment or two

before she looked up in the direction of the voice.

A young woman was standing beside her car. 'Are you all right?' she repeated.

'I . . . think so.'

'Can you open the door?'

Gabrielle tried, but the door refused to budge. Panic made her whimper in her throat.

The young woman ran round to the other side and opened the passenger door. 'Here you are. You can get out this way. But check that no bones are broken before you move.'

Gabrielle wiggled her feet obediently, then her hands and arms. 'I'm all right. Just bruised and battered.'

'Can you get out now? I don't think you ought to stay inside. I can smell petrol leaking.'

'I think I can manage.' Gabrielle edged slowly across the middle of the car, catching her skirt on the handbrake.

The stranger leant in to help her out. 'I'm Sarah, by the way. I've called the police. They'll be here in a minute or two.'

'Right. Thank you.'

'Are you sure you're all right?'

'Yes. A bit shocked.'

'Did you skid?'

'No. Another car deliberately bumped into me and pushed me off the road.'

The other woman's face was a series of O shapes – eyes and mouth wide open in shock.

They turned to look at Gabrielle's car and, sure enough, there were dents and scratches of red paint on the rear bumper.

'The driver must have been drunk,' Sarah said.

'I suppose so.' Or had someone paid him to frighten her? She was suddenly sure it hadn't been an accident that the driver had chosen to harass *her*, not after the other things that had happened.

A police car drew up and a young female officer got out, followed by her male companion.

Their questions seemed to go on for ever, and they even breathalysed Gabrielle. Of course, that only proved she hadn't been drinking at all.

'Are you sure you couldn't tell what they looked like? No details at all?' the female officer asked again.

'I've told you. I think they were men, but they had hats pulled down and scarves round their faces. It's hard to see inside a car at night.'

'Well, if you do think of anything else, get back to us.'

'You won't be able to drive this car home,' the male officer said. 'We'll have to get it towed away and the paint of the other car checked before you can have it repaired. It doesn't look like a write-off, but I'd get it checked out by a good mechanic. You seem to have had a lucky escape.'

Sarah gave her particulars and drove off, but the police officers stayed with Gabrielle till the tow truck arrived, and then took her and her shopping home.

When they'd gone, she sat slumped at the kitchen table, not knowing what to do next.

The phone rang and it took her a minute or two to pick it up.

'What took you so long to answer?' Stu demanded.

'I've been in a car accident. Someone deliberately drove me off the road.'

'Don't be stupid. Why would anyone do that? You always were a timid driver. You probably swerved to avoid him and skidded.'

No word of sympathy. No belief in what she'd told him. She put the phone down and didn't answer when it rang again.

It took her a while to realise what she needed and then she phoned Des.

In jerky half-sentences she explained what had happened.

'But you're all right?' he asked.

'I'm in one piece, yes. Couple of bruises but that's nothing. I'm upset, though, as you can imagine. I can't seem to think clearly.'

'Don't try to do anything till you feel better. I'll be there in a couple of hours.'

'But your job!'

'I can spend tonight with you and drive back early tomorrow morning. I'd stay longer but I'm at a crucial point in an investigation. It'll take me two hours to get to you, Gabrielle. Can you hang on till then?'

'Yes.'

'If you're worried about being in the house on your own, call your friend Tania.'

'No. I'll be all right. Really.'

But as it grew darker, she wasn't so sure. She jumped at every noise and started to listen for Des's car long before he could have got there.

Chapter Five

Des set off immediately and drove as fast as he felt was safe. He didn't like the way problems were escalating in Worton. Someone had moved from trying to frighten Gabrielle to what could have been a life-threatening attack on her.

He couldn't bear the thought of losing her now, when he was just starting to feel . . . With a wry smile, he admitted to himself that the word he was reluctant to use was 'involved'. A car accident could end in more than a few bruises, as he knew only too well, but this time, thank goodness, Gabrielle had escaped without injury.

He'd do his best to ensure there wasn't another incident, but he couldn't quit this job in the middle.

Seriously worried about her safety, he didn't bother to stop and book in at the B and B, even though it was getting late and the 'Vacancies' sign was switched off. He drove straight up the street to her house, which was brightly lit, with all the downstairs lights on and the curtains open, as well as the porch light shining along the front path.

She must have been watching for him, because by the time he'd parked his car and run to the front door, she was there to fling the door open. When he reached out to pull her into his arms, she came willingly, huddling against him with a long sigh of relief.

'Are you all right, Gabrielle?'

'I am now that you're here, Des.'

He turned to aim the remote and lock his car, then walked with her into the house. 'Let's draw the curtains, shall we? You should have done that before you lit up.'

'I wasn't sitting downstairs. I was upstairs, moving to and fro, looking out of the windows. I wanted to be able to see if anyone approached. I suppose that was silly, but it made me feel better.'

'Then it was worth doing.' He studied her face. 'You look pale. Are you sure you're not hurt?'

'I'm all right. A bit bruised is all. I was lucky.'

'Well, now that I'm here, we need to keep inquisitive eyes away.'

'Who is there to be inquisitive?' she asked bitterly. 'There aren't any close neighbours who'd wonder about me, as I told you before.'

'Someone attacked you. They might still be watching out for another opportunity.'

She shivered and went with him round the house drawing the curtains, till they were enclosed in a brighter, cosier world. 'Are you hungry?'

Des shook his head. 'Not yet. Look, I want you to tell me exactly what happened today. Would you mind if I recorded it?'

'Why do that?'

'You never know when a piece of evidence will come

in useful. It'll still be fresh in your mind if we do it now.'

She shrugged. 'Whatever.'

He went through it with her, switched off the tiny recording device, then switched it on again. 'It's my bet they'll have stolen the car and burnt it after they'd attacked you. Do you think this is down to your husband?'

'I've been wondering that, but I didn't think even Stu would try to kill me.'

'He isn't . . . mentally ill, is he?'

'Why do you say that?'

'I don't know. From what you've told me about him, it doesn't sound like the sort of thing he'd do. But you never know. People continue to amaze me.'

'Who else is there but Stu? I've no family to care whether I'm alive or not. I think he's been trying to upset me so that I'll sell the house for a lower price.'

'And will all this stuff do that?'

'I don't know. I'm longing to be rid of him once and for all.'

'I can't understand the urgency. One modest house in a residential street doesn't attract developers and cause cut-throat land grab wars, or give the buyers huge profits.'

'But selling this house will give Stu some money and he sounds desperate for it.'

There was a knock on the door and Gabrielle sprang to her feet, looking at Des in alarm.

'I'll answer it,' he said.

'There's a peephole.'

A quick glance outside made him fling the door open

and call over his shoulder, 'It's the police, Gabrielle. All right if I bring them in?'

'Yes, of course.'

The same two officers who'd attended the accident, looking weary now, stood in the doorway of the living room.

'We won't stay long,' the woman said. 'We just wanted to inform you that a red car, which is probably the one that attacked you, has been found burnt out fifty miles away. Luckily, a passing motorist put the fire out before it destroyed the vehicle completely and it was identified as one which had been reported stolen.'

'Probably joyriders,' the male officer added. 'But burning it will have destroyed any fingerprints or other biological evidence.'

'I don't think they were joyriders,' Gabrielle said. 'I think they were sent to hurt me.' She hadn't made that clear at the scene of the incident; she had been too upset to think clearly.

They looked surprised. 'Why would they do that? Is there something you haven't told us?'

'Not that I can prove, but there have been other incidents.' She listed them.

The man had been scribbling notes. 'We'll bear in mind what you've said, Ms Newman. Please take every precaution from now on when you move about the village and stick to the main roads when you're out driving.'

She nodded.

'If you sell your house and move away, please let us know where to contact you.'

While Des showed them out, she sat down, feeling drained. When he came back, she asked, 'They think I'm imagining things, don't they?'

'They're not sure. Trouble is, they're so busy they can't deal with everything that gets piled on them. But I'm quite sure you're not imagining this.'

'Are you?'

'Oh, yes. Now, it's getting late and I think you won't want to be left alone.'

'You're right. I'd not sleep a wink.'

'I'm happy to stay with you. Can I beg the loan of your couch for the night?'

'I can do better than that. I have a spare bedroom. It won't take me a minute to put the sheets on the bed.'

'Let's do it together.'

'OK. Afterwards I'll find us something to eat. I didn't have any tea and I'm starting to feel hungry. Thank you for coming, Des.'

He pulled her close and dropped a quick kiss on her cheek. 'I was worried about you. We'll get up early tomorrow and have a quick look at security here. If I make a phone call, I don't have to get back till the afternoon, so, if necessary, I can nip out and buy a few bolts. Old-fashioned but cheap and still good at deterring casual break-ins. I hope you can sell the house quickly and then drop off your ex's radar.'

'That's what I plan to do.'

They sat chatting over a scratch meal of tinned soup and sandwiches. Then she yawned and he followed suit, laughing at the way yawns always seemed infectious.

He covered her hand with his. 'Let's go to bed. I don't think anyone will attack you tonight.'

Radka was waiting for Stu when he came back from a meeting.

'You went too far, you idiot!'

He gaped at her. 'What the hell are you talking about?'

'Did you intend those youths to kill your ex-wife? Do you *want* to face a charge of murder?'

'I don't know what—'

'Your tame vandals sideswiped her car deliberately, made her crash and gave the police something to bite on.'

'How did you know about them?'

'I have friends in the UK.'

'I only told the lads to annoy her a bit if she went out for a drive.'

'Even that was stupid. Next time, you will take more care who you employ. Contact them only by phone – no names, no faces that way. And tell them exactly how far to go. Because if you show your hand so clearly again, you're on your own and I will find someone else to work with. *And* sleep with. You're good in bed, but you're not the only man in the world.'

'All right. But I still don't see why you're making such a fuss.'

'The whole point of bringing you into our operation was that you have no police record and have good business connections in the UK.'

He considered that and nodded. Then something occurred to him. 'Is Gabi badly hurt?'

'They didn't take her to hospital, so I doubt it.'

'Damn! I wasn't trying to have her killed, Radka. I wouldn't. She's a fool, but I wouldn't *kill* her, or anyone else for that matter.' He went and poured himself a whisky with hands that shook.

'Get one for me, too.' She studied him through narrowed eyes. 'Anyone would think you still cared for her.'

'Me? Care for *her*? It's you I care for. You know it is. And I thought you cared for me, yet you talk of getting rid of me so casually.'

'I am very careful. Always remember it.'

That night was the first time he failed to satisfy Radka in bed. He couldn't get the image of Gabi being pushed into a crash out of his mind.

'I'll ring her in the morning, see how she is,' he muttered as he turned over to try to sleep.

Radka's sharp voice stabbed at him through the darkness. 'You will do no such thing. Might as well tell the world you arranged the attack. You will wait for us to find out what's going on and tell you.'

He didn't answer, pretended to be asleep.

She really did fall asleep soon after that. He knew her patterns of breathing by now.

It took him a while to follow her example. He was still feeling guilty. No, not that. He didn't do guilty, had nothing to be *guilty* about, but he was annoyed at himself for not being more careful, not choosing his helpers more carefully. He'd been trying to nudge Gabi into doing the sensible thing, not kill her.

He looked at the woman sleeping so peacefully beside

him, frowning as he studied the fine-boned face, the slender arm curved across her pillow. Radka was gorgeous, but she had been more than a bit scary tonight. As if she was in charge and he was there to do her bidding. He'd never associated with a powerful woman, and there were aspects of it that worried him.

She seemed to find things out amazingly quickly, and to know everything about him. In fact, she knew far more than he'd ever told her. How?

What had he got himself into? A way out, that's what. He'd had no choice but to find some method of paying his debts. Lady Luck hadn't been with him lately. She'd come back, though; he was sure of that. And, in the meantime, he had Radka.

But who exactly was he working for here? That thought had started to really worry him. Big-time business was one thing. Big-time crime was quite another.

Who exactly was *she* working for? Oh, she'd given him a company name and said they did behind-the-scenes stuff, but that told him very little.

By the time Gabrielle waved goodbye to Des, she felt a lot more secure in the house. Strange what a difference a few little bolts had made.

She also felt more secure about her developing relationship with him. She'd never moved so slowly before, taken such care of where she was giving her affections. That suited her mood at present. She was afraid of making another huge mistake.

But she was almost free of Stu now. There was just the

house to sell. What a relief that would be! She might even go down a little more in the price she would accept, if only to expedite matters. What was money compared to peace of mind?

Soon after Des had left, the post arrived. She picked up the envelopes and opened the electricity bill there and then. She always had to find out how much a bill was for as soon as she got it. She knew it was a silly quirk, but what harm did it do anyone if she opened her bills in the hall? There was no one to sneer at her about it now.

As she turned to go back into the kitchen, another flyer was pushed through the front door. This one was from the new beauty salon she'd seen on the way to town. She'd driven past *Pampered* a few times and thought how attractive the place looked. She wished she could afford to book a session there because she loved relaxing in a bubbling spa or treating herself to a soothing massage.

It seemed such a long time since anyone had pampered her.

She was about to throw the flyer away when a piece of card fell out. As she retrieved it, she saw the words 'Free Gift' and couldn't help noticing what it was offering: the chance of a full day's pampering session totally free. This would begin with a massage and spa, go on to a facial treatment, hair wash and blow dry, then finish with a professional make-up artist giving her some advice and then doing her make-up. They were only giving this prize to three lucky people.

'Scratch the silver bar of soap to see if you've won,' it said in big print.

'Ha! As if.' She threw the card into the rubbish bin without trying to scratch it. There would be a catch to winning. There always was. She didn't have time for messing around, had to finish packing up her life. It was part of the agreement with the agency that she would get out of this house as soon as it sold and settled, so she had to be ready to leave.

Only she still hadn't worked out where to go. Should she really take the offer of a house in Rochdale, or find a place where she could make a home? Buy a small place, even? Not round here, of course. She'd not have enough money for that.

The quick sale agency had guaranteed settlement within five working days, which amazed her. She'd never heard of that happening so quickly.

They were certainly trying hard to sell the house, she'd give them that. Nearly every day that week, she'd had to get out to let another potential customer look through it. But none of them had made an offer that was even halfway decent, and though Stu had suggested lowering the price, she'd refused to do that. So far, anyway.

There were more disturbances during the next two nights. She called at all the nearby houses, but none of her neighbours had experienced any problems. It was just her, it seemed. No damage had been done to her house, though the garden plants at the rear had been pulled up one night.

The broken sleep was very wearing, and she didn't know what to do about it. She was getting too tired to think straight. Des said to hang in and, if she felt in danger, to book into a hotel. If she could last just a few more days, he was working longer hours to finish his job earlier.

She contacted the police, who said the same as last time. There were vandals everywhere, but because of her history of troubles, patrols of the area would be increased. Big deal! How could you increase nothing? She hadn't seen any patrols round here before and she hadn't seen any since they'd said that the first time. And she'd been up a few times in the night just looking outside and checking her garden for intruders.

She went back to packing and throwing things away, yawning. When she opened the kitchen rubbish bin and saw the voucher lying on top of some papers, she pulled the brightly coloured piece of card out, drawn again by the words 'Free Gift'.

Oh, why not scratch the silver image? If she found out for sure that she'd won nothing, then maybe she'd stop longing for the impossible.

It couldn't do any harm to give herself a few minutes to dream of luxury and pampering, so she waited until she'd finished a leisurely cup of strong coffee, designed to keep her awake and alert. Only then did she get out a ten-pence coin and scratch the card.

She stared at it, then cried out loud, 'No! I don't believe it. I *never* win anything.'

But however carefully she studied the card, the word 'winner' still sat there in big black letters, with CONGRATULATIONS! in bright red slanted at an angle beneath it.

There must be some catch. She studied the conditions,

reading them several times. The winner had to agree to have her name used in promotions. Fair enough. And the day's pampering had to be taken on a Tuesday or Wednesday. Also reasonable – obviously these would be their quiet days.

She walked to and fro, still unable to believe this had happened to her. She'd never won anything except two pounds from a scratchcard in her whole life. Should she claim the prize?

That was a no-brainer. Of course she was going to claim it. And she was going to enjoy every minute of being pampered.

When should she go? She didn't have to go back to work for another week and intended to ask for more time off anyway. The mere thought of going back to that horrible, windowless building made her feel ill, and she didn't know how she'd ever paste a smile on her face, let alone keep it there all day.

But it was easy to smile today in anticipation of such a treat. She picked up the phone to book the pampering session. 'Um, I've won your free gift of a day's pampering.'

A soft, cooing voice said, 'Congratulations, madam. I'm sure you'll enjoy your special day. When would you like to claim it?'

'Would a week on Wednesday be all right?'

'That would be fine. We'll look forward to seeing you at 9 a.m. Could I have your name, please? Thank you, Ms Newman. And your phone number? Right. Got it. Don't forget to bring your winning card with you. Um, just one thing. You do realise it's a condition of the free gift that we can use your name for publicity? And we'll give you some free beauty products if you let us take your photo as well.'

'Yes, I understand about the publicity. As for the photo . . .' What the hell? she thought recklessly. 'Yes, all right, you can take a photo. As long as you make me look good for it.'

'Oh, we'll do that, don't worry. We have a brilliant make-up artist and hair stylist.'

Gabrielle smiled as she put down the phone. She didn't care about the photo or them using her name, because she'd made another decision. She was going to move right away from the district.

In fact, she was going to Rochdale. Not only because there was a house available rent-free and information about her family, but because she'd checked on the internet several times and hadn't seen anywhere suitable near here – well, not in her price range for buying. And not even in her rental range. She needed to save money, not spend it on high rents.

Tania said she could stay with her for a week or two if a sale really did happen quickly, but Gabi would only do that if she was desperate. She'd hate to impose on her friend, who only had a small, two-bedroom flat. Besides, Tania was kind, but loud and slapdash. They might be good friends, but they weren't the sort of people who should ever share accommodation, not if they wanted to remain friends.

No, she'd have to find something else for herself and the lawyer was offering her a house.

* * *

Spirits lifted by the prospect of the pampering and the fact that no one had been to look round the house that morning, Gabi picked up the phone the next day without checking who was calling. 'Yes?'

'Stu here. I'm coming round. Be there.'

Her heart started thumping at the harsh tone in his voice. What did he want now? Every time she saw him or heard from him, he nagged her about lowering the house price so that they could sell quickly.

She might lower it a few thousand, but she didn't intend to give her hard-earned money away to the extent he was demanding. She'd rather wait and sell for a fair price – well, as fair as you could get in a quick sale.

When she heard his car, she waited for him to knock, but he used his key and marched straight in. She stayed where she was at the kitchen table, hands clasped round a mug of tea, glad of its comforting warmth.

He took a chair, twisted it round and sat astride it, scowling across the table at her. 'I'm here to talk some sense into you.'

'Oh, really?'

'That last offer for the house was nearly good enough. You have to face facts about house prices, Gabi. Peter thinks we can push the guy up a bit, but not much more.'

'That would still be fifty thousand pounds under our lowest price.' She was about to offer to go down a few thousand when he interrupted.

'So what? The money's doing us no good locked in this damned pile of bricks. And house sales aren't improving, either in this area or in the country as a whole.

If you're intending to buy another house, you can simply screw someone else into accepting a much lower price. Swings and roundabouts. Surely even your tiny mind can understand that?'

When she didn't respond, he thumped his clenched fist suddenly on the table, sending tea from her mug spurting in every direction.

She had to make a stand. 'Stu, I can't afford to lower the price that much. Fifty thousand pounds is more than I earn in a year!'

'Twenty-five thousand pounds. We're splitting the house sale money down the middle, remember.'

'I still can't agree to throwing my share of the money away. You shouldn't be getting half of the house money, anyway. You cheated me on that and I don't intend to lose any more of what is—'

Before she realised what was happening, he was up and out of his chair. Moving round the table, he grabbed her by the front of her T-shirt and dragged her to her feet. This sent her mug flying and she heard it smash against the cooker.

'Stu, don't!'

'*Don't!*' he mimicked, then shook her like a rag doll. 'If you don't change your mind, *Gabi my pet*, I'm going to do a lot more than give you a shaking up. I'm going to get rather nasty about this.'

She tried to push him away, but he only laughed and shook her again, after which he grabbed her hair with one hand and twisted it round so hard she cried out with the pain. Then he lifted her up by it.

'We are going to push this guy up a little, then accept the offer. *Is that clear?*'

He thumped her down in the chair again, but kept hold of her hair.

She didn't know how to get away from him, couldn't think clearly because of the pain in her head.

He laughed, a low, feral sound. 'Now. Are you going to listen to sense or do I have to get seriously nasty?' He let go of her hair and sat down on the chair beside her this time, not the one opposite, his eyes watchful.

She knew she hadn't a chance of standing up, let alone running out of the house, before he caught her, but she tried to speak assertively, only to hear her voice wobble. 'If you touch me again, I'll complain to the police.'

'What precisely will you complain about?'

'You. Hurting me.'

'I haven't even begun to hurt you. *Yet*. It's quite possible to do that without leaving an external mark, believe me. I've heard of several ways. How brave are you feeling today, Gabi? How much pain can you take?'

She swallowed hard. Suddenly, the days of anxiety and the harassment all piled up and it was too much to bear. Even the money didn't matter. What mattered was getting right away from this madman.

Yes, madman. She stared at him and he stared coldly back. He didn't say anything, and the way he was studying her seemed just as frightening as when he'd hurt her. No sign of emotion, no trace of caring about her as he'd once sworn to do for ever.

The silence went on and on as she tried to think what to do.

His expression was so different today, so full of suppressed violence, that she was terrified of him hurting her permanently.

'You're such a fool – too stupid to know how to play against major league characters like me.' Stu grabbed her hair again before she could move away. As he used it to lift her from her seat again, she screamed loudly.

He laughed. 'You can end this whenever you like. Just agree to lower the price.' He shoved her backwards and banged her against the wall a couple of times.

She snapped. 'All right. I'll sell. Stop it, Stu! I'll sell.'

But she hadn't given in because he was hurting her. Not exactly. She'd given in because she wanted to get as far away from him as she could and never, ever see him again. And because she'd suddenly realised he must be mentally ill.

Marrying him had been the worst mistake she'd ever made in her whole life. The money didn't matter nearly as much as escaping from him permanently.

He thumped her down hard in the chair. 'Very sensible. But let's make sure you don't change your mind. We'll ring Peter straight away and you'll tell him yourself that you want to sell. Right?'

She could only nod.

When he held out the phone, she identified herself, listened to Peter's soothing platitudes about the state of the market and then waited till he stopped. 'Yes. I agree to sell at a lower price.'

Stu grabbed the phone from her. 'There you are. Settled. How soon can you find out if he'll accept our counter offer, Peter? I know he's representing a company. How long will it take him to get permission from them to offer more?'

He listened intently, then raised one thumb in a sign of triumph. 'Good. I'll stay here at the house till you phone me back.'

He put the phone down. 'We'll know within the hour, but Peter thinks the company has given their buyer carte blanche up to a certain limit.'

Turning his back on Gabrielle, he went to fumble in the pantry and pulled out from the back the bottle of whisky he'd left there. It still had two inches in the bottom. He got a glass from the cupboard and emptied the rest of the whisky into it, admiring the colour for a moment against the light.

Taking his place at the table again, he took a sip. 'Aaah! Good whisky, that.'

As she continued to sit there like a broken automaton, he picked up the newspaper and began to flick through it.

She couldn't bear to go on watching him for a minute longer, so found the strength to stand up, intending to go into another room.

He pointed his forefinger. 'Stay there.'

She didn't argue, sat down again on the chair. He'd gone mad. She had no doubt about it now and was genuinely afraid he'd murder her if she didn't do as he said.

How could this be happening to her? It was like a horror movie.

He still had a gleeful, demonic expression on his face, and it frightened her more than the violence had. He raised his glass to her in another silent toast and took a sip.

If she survived this, she was not only going to move to Lancashire, she told herself: she was going to change her name.

She just had to hold it together till he'd got what he wanted. Surely he'd leave her alone then?

The minutes seemed to tick past with extraordinary slowness.

Chapter Six

An hour later, Peter phoned and Stu put the phone on speaker so that Gabrielle could hear what they were saying.

'The offer's gone up by another ten thousand, but he won't go any higher.'

'Take it, then. Who is the buyer?'

'Ah. Well, he's doing this on behalf of a company, so that's fairly irrelevant. You won't recognise his name. He's only their agent in this. You probably won't recognise the company, either. They're a behind-the-scenes sort of outfit. Big. Fingers in a lot of pies.'

'Is this a cash offer?' Stu asked.

'Of course it is. Didn't I just say they were big? This will be peanuts to them. I'd not have advised you to accept the offer otherwise.'

When Stu put down the phone, Gabrielle gathered her courage together and asked, 'Are you sure you don't want to wait a little longer? We're losing a lot of money.'

'I thought we had discussed this. I'm losing chances to *use* my money by waiting. I don't give a damn what *you're* losing. *I* have a deal pending – a private deal that's going to make me a lot of money. I didn't waste my time in Prague and I need to go straight back there once we've signed the contract.'

He drained the last of the whisky and stood up. 'I think it'd be better if I drive you to the agency and we sign the papers there.'

'I'll drive myself. My car is OK now.'

'No, you won't. I'm not letting you out of my sight, or out of range of my hands till you've signed on the dotted line. Go and change into something smarter. I don't want to be seen out with a fat, badly dressed frump.'

'I'll put my best coat on over this.'

'You'll change into something decent.' He gave a nasty grin. 'I'll strip those things off you myself if you don't.'

She couldn't help shuddering at the thought of him touching her again.

He roared with laughter. 'You're frightened I'll want you. Dream on. I'm with a real woman now, who is *verrry* satisfying in bed. You're useless to a real man.'

'Then why did you marry me?'

'I was in an optimistic mood – thought I could improve you, bring you out of your shell. And you had the money for the deposit on a house. Dear Edward did me a favour there. People said we were in for a property boom. The financial side of things counted most of all to me. People were wrong, though. I'd just missed the boat. But I don't intend to do that again.'

He yanked her to her feet and pointed her towards the stairs, pushing her hard with the flat of his hand, so that she stumbled forward. 'Go and change, damn you. And be quick about it.'

But as she was coming down, the phone rang again. Stu ended the call and turned to her. 'Peter thinks it'll be more efficient if he gets us to sign the contracts here and then takes them to our buyer for his signature.'

'But—'

He poked her hard with his forefinger. 'You aren't going to make any trouble, are you?'

'No.'

'You'd better not.'

When Peter arrived, he hardly looked at her.

Stu read the contract from beginning to end, amended two minor points and made her initial his changes too.

She gathered her courage together. 'I need to read it as well. I won't sign it till I've done that.'

Peter looked at Stu, who stared down at the pieces of paper, then shoved them across the table to her. 'Read it quickly, then.'

She read it through carefully, amending the way the money was to be paid to her.

Stu sucked his cheeks thoughtfully, then shrugged. 'No skin off my nose.'

She waited, aching to get this over and done with.

'I will need my own copy,' she said, as Peter gathered up the papers. 'There's a photocopier in the corner shop at the end of the street.'

'Good idea,' Stu said. 'I'll get a copy, too. Then you can take the original to the buyer and get his signature, Peter, so that we can set things in motion. You can send another copy to us to initial if the buyer wants any more amendments.'

'He won't. I've worked with him before. This is his standard contract.'

Stu insisted on taking Gabrielle to the corner shop in his car. 'Don't want you running away,' he said cheerfully as he drove her there.

After they'd made the copies, she said, 'I'd like to walk back, if you don't mind, Stu. I need some fresh air.'

'Suits me. Things to do. Faces to meet.'

She no longer cared what he did. It was going to cost her financially, but she was almost free of him.

She stood in the street watching him drive away. She felt numb with misery – and shame. She'd been a coward, given in to him too easily.

But she'd been terrified, not so much of the pain itself as of the pleasure he was taking in inflicting it on her. That had been the most terrifying thing about it.

And she was so weary of fighting him.

She had a sudden thought and went back inside the shop to ask if they had any empty boxes. She needed to start packing the last of her things now.

'We've lots of boxes, dear. Save us taking them to the tip.'

'I'll come back in my car to collect them. I got it back from being repaired yesterday.'

The shopkeeper smiled. 'No need. My son can take you home in the van. We can fit as many boxes as you need into that. And it'll save me disposing of them. I really like it when people move house. Are you staying on in the village?'

'I'm afraid not.'

'We'll miss you.'

She looked round as she was driven back. The village had lost its charm. She was glad she had to get out of the house quickly.

The next time Des phoned her, she told him the house had been sold and pretended it was for a bearable price.

There was silence for a moment, then he said, 'Don't tell me the price if you don't want to, but please don't lie to me, Gabrielle.'

She gasped. 'How did you know?'

'The tone of your voice changed and you stumbled over some of the words. You find it hard to lie, don't you?'

'Yes. Sorry. And . . . it was a really low price. Stu insisted.' She didn't elaborate.

'I see. What are you going to do now?'

'Get ready to move out. I'll have to ask for more time off work to get out by the agreed date. There are all sorts of details to attend to.'

'Stu isn't helping at all, is he?'

'No.' She was even going to have to pack his remaining possessions. She was relieved when Des didn't comment, just left silence to bind them for a few moments.

'When's the agreed removal date?'

'A week on Thursday.'

'Damn! I wish I could help you prepare for it, Gabrielle, but something else has come up and I can't get away yet.'

'I'll be fine, Des. And you did help me enormously by doing some of the painting.'

'That was my pleasure.'

'Besides, there'll be no reason for anyone to harass

me now I've signed the contract to sell, will there?'

'If even one thing happens, promise me you'll call, and I *will* drop everything to come to you.'

'I promise.' She heard the sound of voices in the background and waited to see what was happening.

'I'm afraid I have to go now. I'll phone you in a couple of days. And don't forget that number. They'll contact me straight away in an emergency. Bye.'

She listened to the dial tone purring away to itself. She wished Des was still at the other end. Even their shared silences were comforting.

With a sigh, she phoned her boss. Best to get this over with. To her relief, he was available to speak to her straight away.

'I'm afraid I need to ask for more time off, Mr Buckley. We've sold the house and I have to get out in less than two weeks.'

He made an angry noise. 'Gabi, I told you we can't extend your leave. I've got other people going on holiday and I need you here. We'll give you the moving day off – of course we will – but other people get ready to move house in their own time and so must you.'

'Well, I can't do it.' She closed her eyes, admitting to herself it was more than that. She hated the thought of going back to the noise of the supermarket: people, trolleys, trucks unloading and the eternal muzak playing in the background, even in the offices. Dammit, she wasn't going to do it. She'd reached her sticking point for things she didn't want to do. 'I think I'd better resign. I'm still not feeling well. And I'll probably be moving away from here.'

'Ah. Well, all right. I'll – um, be sorry to lose you.'

He hadn't tried to persuade her to stay on, though, had he? That said a lot.

'You'll need to come in to do the paperwork and collect your things. Any day after today will be fine. We'll have everything ready for you.'

'I'll do that tomorrow.'

She put the phone down with a shuddery sigh. She was out of work now, would soon be homeless, and she hadn't got nearly as much money in reserve as she'd had when she met Stu Dixon, damn him.

It couldn't get much worse.

Yes, it could, she told herself firmly. She could be killed or badly injured in an accident, or get cancer. There were plenty of worse situations. But this was definitely the second lowest point of her whole life. She didn't let herself think about the worst thing that had ever happened to her. She always pushed that to the back of her mind.

Had she made the right decision about going to Lancashire? She'd soon find out, wouldn't she?

If she didn't feel she could settle in Lancashire, she'd have a look at other parts of the country. She could go where she wanted, do what she wanted . . . until her money ran out.

Then she remembered that Cousin Rose had left her some furniture and a small legacy. She had to go to Rochdale to see the lawyer and find out exactly what she'd been left.

For the first time in days, her spirits lifted slightly because she had some sort of a plan.

* * *

By the time the pampering day arrived, Gabi was exhausted, not only from packing and clearing out but also from going through all the checks now in place for selling houses.

She'd managed to keep this day free, because it would be bliss to let someone else look after her, pamper her. Surely that treat would energise her for the move?

Things were definitely looking up. Des had phoned to say he would be able to finish his job in time to help her move. He would set off early from London and be with her by nine or ten o'clock. She was looking forward to seeing him again.

It'd be good to have someone else around, just in case she needed help. You might think you'd covered everything, but she knew from experience that there would be glitches, queries, things needing her presence.

Stu, naturally, was going to be away at a conference on removal day and wouldn't be able to help.

'You ought to be here,' she'd insisted when he phoned.

'Why? It's mostly your stuff. Anyway, this conference is important.'

'And the boxes of your things aren't important? Shall I just throw them away? Or give them to a charity shop? Yes, that's what I'll do.'

'Oh, how you harp on about those stupid boxes! Look, the reason I phoned was to tell you I'm sending someone to pick them up the day before you move out, all right? Satisfied now?'

'I'll be out for most of the day. Can't you do it a day earlier?'

'No, I can't. You change your appointment.'

'I can't. I've won a day's pampering at a local spa. I'm not giving that up for anything.'

'They're backing a loser trying to improve your looks. You'll have to find some way of letting my carrier in.'

'I'll leave the side door of the garage open. There are only your boxes in it.'

'Yes, Madam Nag.'

'We have to get the house clear, Stu.'

He laughed suddenly.

'What's so funny about that?'

'I just thought of something else. Sorry. We will get the house clear, don't worry. I want my money.' He began laughing again as he cut the connection.

She didn't like the sound of that laughter. It had a nasty, mocking edge to it. He couldn't be plotting something else, could he? No, of course not. He was probably delighted at the thought of being rid of her.

On pampering day, Gabrielle told her neighbour, a nice old lady, not to worry if people started taking things away from the house, then drove off for her day of relaxation, confident that she'd done everything she could to make things go well for the removal tomorrow. She only had to get through one more day and then she really would be free of Stu.

She felt ashamed that she'd caved in to his bullying, but it was done now, and the main reason was just as valid: selling the house would rid her of him for ever. She would make a better life for herself and be extra careful about future relationships, if any. Men could start off seeming great, but people only revealed their true selves when you lived with them for a while.

What was Des's true self? She smiled involuntarily. She liked him, trusted him – well, she thought she could trust him. Only time would tell for sure. At least he was different from Stu – not showy, but quiet and steady. That spoke in his favour.

She found a parking place in a quiet side street and strolled along to the beauty salon, giving herself up to the bliss of a whole day's pampering. Never mind that the weather was overcast and a bit chilly. It was warm and cosy inside the salon.

The staff of *Pampered* were wonderful, overwhelming her with offers of tea, coffee, herbal concoctions. They provided a healthy lunch, which she enjoyed greatly. At the end of the session, they photographed her and she didn't mind that, because she was definitely looking her best. She wished Des could see her now.

By the time she left the salon, after a final glance in the mirror at her new and more flattering hairstyle, she felt as if her whole body was glowing, ready to act. She smiled up to see the sun shining through the patchy clouds, as if welcoming the new Gabrielle back into the world.

That happy mood ended abruptly when she reached her car. It looked wrong as she approached it, but she couldn't work out why until she got nearer. The tyres had been slashed – not just one or two, but all four of them.

As she let out a cry of despair, a woman turned to look at her in surprise, then hurried away round the corner, clearly not wanting to get involved in someone else's trouble.

Gabrielle looked round frantically for help, but there was no one in sight. She'd let her membership of the RAC lapse to save money, because she didn't travel very far these days and her car had never let her down. Tania was away on holiday and there was no one else she could ask for help.

With only an old-fashioned mobile phone that she hardly ever used, Gabrielle knew of no way to access a phone directory. She couldn't think who to call for help. Her mind was a blank. She couldn't remember the name of a garage, only of her petrol station. Stu had always organised car servicing and she'd not had anything done to hers since they parted.

She couldn't help it: she burst into tears right there in the street, sobbing loudly, leaning against the car.

An elderly man stopped to ask her what was wrong and she pointed to her tyres, too upset to string words together.

He walked right round the car. 'The rotten devils! Fancy slashing all four tyres! Whatever will this generation do next? You poor thing.'

'I don't know what to do, who to call.'

'Better call the police, love. This is a crime.'

'I can't dial nine-nine-nine for slashed tyres.'

'Hmm. I suppose not.' He fumbled in his pocket and pulled out a larger than normal mobile phone, probably even older than hers. 'My daughter programmed some numbers into this for me.' He clicked and muttered for a moment or two, then said, 'Aha!' loudly and held it out to her with an expression of triumph. 'There you are, love.

That's the number to dial if you need police help but there isn't a life-threatening emergency.'

She did this with her fingers shaking and was put through to a woman with a kindly voice, who said the police would be with her within the hour.

'I'll leave you to it, then,' the man said. 'I'm meeting someone or I'd stay with you. Cheer up, love. This isn't the end of the world.'

No, but it was the final straw in a trying period of her life. The tears were still flowing, but she managed to say, 'I'll be all right now. Thanks for your help.'

She could do nothing but walk up and down. The sky clouded over completely and the very air around her seemed grey and cheerless. Then a light drizzle began to fall and she remembered that she'd left her umbrella at home. She could have sat in the car, but she wasn't sure whether that would damage the wheels; anyway, she felt too angry to sit still.

Her thoughts were dark and unhappy. She couldn't help wondering if it was Stu who'd arranged for this to happen, but she couldn't figure out why he would bother. She had done what he wanted now, hadn't she?

Who else but him would target her, though?

No, this must be blind chance. Hooligans.

No passer-by stopped to ask if she was all right, let alone offer to help her, even though several people slowed down to gape at her slashed tyres.

By the time the police arrived, she was wet through and cold, which was stupid of her, but there you were. She *was* stupid: Stu had told her so enough times. But the most stupid thing she'd done had been marrying him.

The police officers examined her tyres, then one said, 'There's not much we can do to catch the perps, love. They won't have left any clues. We'll report the incident, of course, and we can get you help, at least.'

They phoned for a tow truck and it came within five minutes. When she explained that she was moving house the next day, the man promised to replace the tyres by the following morning.

'You can pick it up at ten o'clock,' he told her as he got back into his vehicle.

She watched her poor little car being driven away and thrust her cold hands into her pockets as she waited for the taxi the police had called for her. They had to move on to their next case and left her to wait on her own.

'Will you be all right?' the older police officer asked. 'You look very upset and you're soaked through.'

She patted her hair involuntarily. It was dripping down her neck and all the styling had gone out of it. 'I'll be OK. Thanks for your help.'

'You should join a motoring association.'

'I will.'

When the taxi arrived ten minutes later, she gave the driver her address and leant back in the seat, eyes closed.

She'd thought things couldn't get worse! How wrong she'd been. This might only be a minor setback, but it couldn't have happened at a more inconvenient time.

And it'd spoilt her lovely day.

Chapter Seven

As the taxi pulled away from the house and she began to walk up the path, Gabrielle saw that the front door was slightly ajar. Had the people picking up Stu's boxes gone into her house? He must have given them his key. Why would he do that?

She walked more quickly. The door lock had been forced. She peered inside, listening, but could hear no one, so went in.

As she looked to the right, she cried out in shock. The front room was empty. Not a single piece of furniture was left. She closed her eyes and opened them again. It hadn't been an illusion. Someone had taken all her furniture.

She walked round one empty room after another, too numb with distress to cry or make any sound beyond the occasional whimper.

Some of her food had been left in the pantry cupboard, cheap perishables like potatoes and onions, and a few open packets, but the rest had been taken. The few remaining items of frozen food, one of which was supposed to be a meal for tonight, must have gone with the freezer.

Upstairs was in a similar state. There was no furniture

left. Not a single piece. All that was left of her clothes was her worn underwear and a torn, frayed pair of jeans. They had been left in a small heap on the floor in a corner.

Worst of all, they'd taken her computer. It wasn't a new one, but she had all sorts of information stored on it. Well, she'd find out now if storing things in the cloud worked. That was the least of her present worries, though.

She was too numb with distress to look in her hiding place, but then it occurred to her abruptly that the thieves would have searched for anything of value that had been hidden. She ran back upstairs, hoping they hadn't found the cache. Did people usually hide their valuables in the bedroom? Or had Stu told the thieves she had something of value hidden there?

She stopped dead for a moment on that thought. Yes, Stu. She was quite sure he was involved in this.

They hadn't found the hiding place. She groaned in relief. She still had her mother's wedding ring and the pretty gold and seed pearl brooch that had belonged to her grandmother, one or two other treasured items as well.

But she'd lost nearly everything else that she owned.

It took her a while to realise she should be phoning the police.

It took them forty minutes to answer her call for help. They sounded astonished that someone should clear a house out so thoroughly.

'Didn't your neighbours notice what was happening?'

'They knew I was going to move and I told Mrs Starkey that someone was coming to collect things today, but I didn't say what. It should just have been a few boxes, stuff belonging to my ex.'

'Has that gone as well?'

'I haven't looked. It was in the garage.'

She led the way there and, sure enough, Stu's things were gone as well.

'Who was supposed to be coming today?'

'I don't know exactly who. My ex had arranged to have the rest of his stuff picked up. We've just got divorced and sold the house, you see.'

'We'll have to contact him. Do you still have his number?'

'Yes.' She gave it them.

'Was your furniture valuable, Ms Newman?'

'No. Some of the electrical equipment was fairly new. I bought the fridge and freezer after we split up, and the washing machine was only a couple of years old.' She gulped back tears. 'I don't understand why someone would do this.'

'It isn't common unless you've a house full of valuables, I must admit. Could your husband have taken the furniture? People do strange things out of spite after divorces.'

She shrugged. What could she say? She couldn't accuse Stu on a mere feeling. 'He was going to a conference all day, so it'll be easy to check on him.'

'Do you have somewhere to go tonight?' the woman officer asked. 'Obviously you can't sleep here. There isn't even a blanket left.'

'My friend's away on holiday.' Anyway, there was only one person she wanted. 'There's a guy I'm seeing. I'll call him. I haven't known him for long, but I'm pretty sure he'll help me. He was coming here tomorrow anyway to help with the move.'

And if Des didn't want to help her, it was best to find out now.

'Don't touch anything, Ms Newman. We'll get the crime scene people in to examine the place. Why don't you call your guy? We'll stay with you for a while.'

So she phoned Des.

When he answered on the second ring, she burst into tears and couldn't speak.

The male officer took the phone from her while the woman put an arm around her and made soothing noises.

Gabrielle fought to control her emotions and after a few moments was able to take the phone back. 'Des?'

'The officer told me what's happened. I'm sorry, so very sorry, Gabrielle. I'll be on my way to you within a few minutes. Why don't you book rooms for us at the B and B where I stayed last time? I'll meet you there in a couple of hours.'

She smeared away more tears and managed a choked 'Thank you. I'll do that.'

'I wish I could get there more quickly. You must be dreadfully upset.'

'Mmm.' The first shock was passing. She had gone into a sort of numbness.

She left the officers to keep an eye on the house and walked down the road to the B and B.

Even here, her luck wasn't in. They had only one room left, though at least it had twin beds.

'I'll take it.' She had no choice. She couldn't go

anywhere else easily till she got her car back. Des could go to another hotel . . . or he could take the other bed. She stood very still as she realised she'd welcome his company, hoped he'd stay with her.

She walked slowly back up the hill to the house and found the detectives examining the crime scene.

'Strangest crime I've had for a while,' one of them was saying to the other.

'Excuse me. I'm the owner. Is there anything I can help you with?'

They asked her a few questions and then one said thoughtfully. 'They seem to have been very careful about leaving no traces. Must have been watching those crime scene shows on TV.

The other nodded. 'I doubt we'll find anything here. We'll continue looking and be in touch when we've checked everything. Did you have your mobile phone on you or did they get that as well?'

'I still have it but it's an old one. I don't use it much.'

'Give me the number and I'll call you tomorrow. We'll shut the house up and string crime tape tonight. Can't do much more in the dark.'

'I'm supposed to clear the house for handover tomorrow.'

'You'll probably be able to do that by the afternoon. It's not a major enough crime to throw a taskforce at it, I'm afraid.'

'No. Look, can I get some things for overnight?'

There were only a few garments left, mostly ready for the ragbag, and as the thieves had taken all her suitcases, she had to put her clothes into a plastic dustbin liner. The intruders had missed a roll of those because it was right at the back of a drawer, but they hadn't missed much else.

What sort of thieves took every single item?

What were they going to do with them? Set up home?

That was the only half-sensible reason she could think of. But what if she was right? What if Stu had arranged this? Perhaps he was setting up a home in Prague.

Would he keep on harassing her? Or was this his parting shot?

The owner of the B and B looked at the plastic bag disapprovingly, so Gabrielle had to explain what had happened, by which time she was in tears again.

As she slowly climbed the stairs to her room, she heard the woman mutter to her husband, 'I thought I'd seen and heard everything, but this takes the prize for nastiness. Poor woman. Tyres slashed and everything she owns stolen in one day.'

'More than a coincidence, if you ask me,' he said gloomily. 'Mark my words, someone's got it in for her. It'll be someone she knows. Always is.'

As Gabrielle went into her room, the owners' words echoed in her brain, making her more certain than ever that this was connected with Stu.

She didn't even start to unpack her clothes, was too wrung out with emotion to do more than dump the rubbish bag, then collapse on the bed and lie there, curled up, waiting for Des.

Surely he would come to her as he'd said?

What would she do if he didn't?

She didn't even try to work that out tonight. She was too numb and weary. It'd been a very long day.

Des told people he was leaving early to deal with a family emergency, then hurried back to his hotel room. He'd done what was needed on this job, anyway, and Leon understood the fact that people had personal crises.

He did jobs for Leon's small government agency every now and then. They paid promptly, the jobs were fairly interesting, and the people at the agency seemed to appreciate his efforts.

They had offered him another job, but Gabrielle desperately needed help and she was much more important than any job.

He stood still in shock as he realised that. For all his talk of taking things slowly in their possible relationship, she'd rapidly become important to him. He shook his head at his own weakness, then smiled at the thought of her as he slung his things into his suitcase.

The sound of Gabrielle's muffled weeping on the phone kept replaying in his memory as he drove. It had hurt him to hear how upset she was. Why the hell would someone do that to her, steal all her possessions?

Her furniture wasn't particularly valuable, so this was a crime which didn't seem worth the trouble. That was what puzzled him. However, a removal van would surely be easy to trace, even if it had been stolen. They weren't exactly ten a penny on the roads.

Who could have done it? How would they dispose of

her possessions without anyone noticing something from a police list?

He drove to Worton with his usual care and attention to traffic and weather conditions. Having lost a cousin to a pile-up on the motorway when he was twenty, he never let his emotions take precedence over safe driving. Human life was too precious to risk.

It was dark when he arrived in the village, and he could see from the end of the street that there were no lights on in Gabrielle's house, so he went straight to the B and B.

'Is Gabrielle Newman staying here?'

'And you are?'

'Des Monahan.'

'Ah yes. She's expecting you. Room six. Up the stairs and to the right, end of the corridor. Here's your key.'

'Thank you.' He mounted the steps two at a time, eager to see her.

When he knocked on the door of number six, there was no answer. He knocked again, more loudly, and waited. Still no answer. Where was Gabrielle?

He tried the handle and found the door unlocked, which made him frown as he went in. She should have locked it. Anyone could have got to her.

A bedside lamp was switched on and Gabrielle was curled up on one of the two single beds, asleep but looking troubled. Even as he watched, she moved restlessly and muttered in her sleep.

He went closer. Her hair was a tangle and her make-up smudged. She didn't usually wear make-up – well, not that he'd seen. Then he remembered that today had been the pampering day. He knew how much she'd been looking forward to it, and even that small treat had been spoilt for her.

Had the thieves fallen lucky, finding an empty house? Or had they known she'd be out? He felt they were more likely to have known, because they'd come with a removal truck, prepared to take everything away quickly.

But the crime still didn't make sense.

He cleared his throat loudly, but she didn't stir, so he switched on the overhead light and nudged the bed with one knee.

She turned a little, half opened her eyes and threw one arm across them to shield herself from the bright light overhead.

'It's me, Gabrielle. Des.'

This time she opened her eyes fully. 'You did come.'

He sat down on the edge of the bed, which brought him close enough to see her puffy, reddened eyes. 'Did you think I wouldn't?'

'I wasn't sure. I don't feel sure of anything lately.'

'You can always be sure that I'll do what I promise.' As tears filled her eyes, he pulled her into his arms and held her close. She felt so right there.

She didn't speak, only nestled against him. But a warm tear rolled on to the back of his hand, then another.

'You've had a dreadful day,' he told her softly, stroking her hair. 'Maybe we can start to turn that around from now on.'

'I can't understand why he would do it to me.'

'He? Do you know who did it?'

'It had to be Stu.' She raised her head to look him in the eyes. 'Who else could it have been? They came prepared with a big truck, so they must have known I'd be away.'

'That's what I was thinking. But how would your ex know you'd be out?'

'Stu wanted to have his boxes picked up today and I said I wouldn't be in. I even told him about the day's pampering I'd won. How stupid was that?'

Des couldn't resist dropping a kiss on her damp forehead. 'Well, let's go out and get some food before everything closes. Which is my room? I need to drop off my luggage and wash my hands.'

She flushed bright red. 'Um. There was only this room free.'

'Ah.'

'It's got twin beds. We could share it, if you like. It'd save you a lot of trouble and . . . I'd feel safer. I feel as if someone might attack me at any minute.'

'People usually do feel violated and threatened when their home has been broken into. It's normal.' He surprised himself by adding, 'I won't let anyone hurt you like that again, Gabrielle.'

After a short silence to let that sink in, he added in a more upbeat tone, 'So, which bed do you want?'

Her voice was flat. 'It doesn't matter. This one will do.'

'Let's get something to eat, then. I have a very healthy appetite, I'm afraid, no matter what happens. The unpacking can wait. Where do you suggest we go?'

'They do decent meals at the local pub, or we could get a curry. We're probably still in time for either.'

'Which do you prefer?'

'I don't feel hungry.'

'If you were hungry, which would you choose?'

'Indian.'

'Good. So would I.' He pulled her to her feet. 'You'd better wash your face. Your make-up's run. Sorry about your day of pampering being spoilt.' He gave her another quick hug. There were no words capable of taking away the sting of this spiteful crime.

Her lips trembled but she pressed them closely together, laid her hand on his cheek for a moment, then went into the tiny en-suite bathroom. She came out with her skin looking fresh and clean, which he thought suited her much better than make-up, anyway. Who wanted to kiss a cheek covered in gunk?

It surprised him all over again how much he wanted to kiss her – and keep kissing her.

The restaurant was brightly lit and full of people laughing and talking. A waiter showed them to a corner table, which had just been vacated, and handed them menus.

'The food smells wonderful,' Des said. 'Glass of wine? Beer?'

'Beer with a curry, don't you think?'

'It's what I prefer. What do you fancy to eat?'

'Order whatever you like. I can eat anything, but I don't feel very hungry. I'll probably just pick at things.'

When the food came, he bullied her into eating poppadums and onion bhajis, then some chicken tikka. He was relieved to see a little colour come back into her cheeks.

She patted her hair self-consciously as she leant back afterwards. 'I must look a mess.'

Her hair had dried in a tangle of curls, which he thought looked gorgeous. 'I like your hair that way.'

'You do? Really?'

Why did she look so surprised at this compliment? 'Yes. I wouldn't say it otherwise. I guess you must usually straighten it. Why?'

'My hair is *too* curly. It doesn't look professional. They said that on the first management training programme and Stu said it too. He hated it to look messy.'

'*Messy!* It looks gorgeous, makes me want to run my fingers through it. Anyway, you said you'd resigned from your job and you've certainly resigned from your marriage. Why not wear your hair the way *you* want? I really do like the way it curls round your face.' He reached out and twisted a curl round his finger for a moment, then let go.

She looked at him doubtfully. 'I don't own the straightening equipment any more. The thieves even took that. So I have no choice about how I wear my hair.'

He was annoyed with himself for not considering the ramifications of her losing just about everything she owned. 'Your insurance will pay for replacements if you need them.'

She flushed and stared down at her clasped hands. 'I let the house insurance lapse. It only ran out last week and . . . well, it didn't seem worth it when I was moving in a few days and wouldn't have another house to insure for a while.'

'Oh, Gabrielle! You poor thing! No, don't cry. We'll work something out.'

She bowed her head, but tears were trickling down her face again. And she had every reason to be upset.

'Look, I'll go and pay for the meal, then we'll go back to the B and B.'

He put his arm round her without thinking as they strolled back, but she went stiff, so he let go again.

Once inside the B and B, she said, 'I think I'll go straight to bed, if you don't mind, Des. I'm exhausted.'

'Fine by me. You use the facilities first.'

She picked up her rubbish bin liner full of clothes and vanished into the bathroom. When she came out, she was wearing some faded pyjamas. She blushed as she saw him looking at her.

'I don't have a dressing gown now. I suppose I'm lucky even to have these pyjamas. I was going to use them for cleaning rags.' Her voice caught as she said that.

'This isn't a fashion show. They cover you up – that's the main thing you need from them at the moment. And I care more about what sort of person you are than whether you look glamorous.' He grinned. 'After all, I'm not exactly the most handsome man on the planet, am I?' He went to complete his own ablutions without giving her a chance to reply to that.

When he came out, she was standing in front of the dressing table, on which were a few neat piles of clothes. Her expression was bleak as she said, 'Just checking what I've got left.'

He waited, but she didn't say anything else. 'Do you want to read in bed for a while, Gabrielle?'

'I just realised: they took my books. *All* my books, even the tattered ones I've loved since I was a child.'

He could have kicked himself for not thinking of that. She must have lost a lot of small possessions she cared about. Unable to leave her to bear her pain alone, he moved slowly over to where she was standing. 'I'm not trying to have my wicked way with you, Gabrielle, but I think you need another hug.' He held open his arms, leaving the choice up to her.

With a sound of sheer anguish, she walked into them, and he held her for a while.

Then he pulled back a little. 'How about we get into bed? We need to talk, but sometimes it's easier to talk freely in the dark, don't you think?'

She immediately stiffened.

'Get into our separate beds,' he corrected. 'I phrased that badly.'

'No, you didn't. Sorry. I'm too suspicious.' She got into her bed and lay down, looking suddenly boneless and white with fatigue.

He switched off the overhead light and got into his own bed, yawning. It had been a long day.

Her voice came softly through the darkness. 'I do appreciate you coming to help me, Des. I can't thank you enough.'

'That's all right.'

'Why did you come so quickly?'

He didn't hesitate. 'Because I'm attracted to you, starting to care about you. Can't you tell?'

Silence, then, 'I suppose.'

'I'm the sort of man who takes things slowly, though,'

he said as the silence continued. 'And I can take no for an answer, if you're not attracted to me.'

'Oh. Well, actually I *am* attracted to you, Des, but at the moment so many horrible things are going on that I can't face another relationship.'

He decided to lighten things up a little. 'We haven't got a relationship yet, so there's nothing to face.'

She gave a slight huff of laughter. 'Then what are we doing sharing a bedroom?'

He was glad to hear the laughter, brief as it was. 'Apart from fate leaving only one room free here, we're sharing for the usual reason: we both needed somewhere to sleep. And I don't think you wanted to be alone tonight, so I was happy to stay with you.'

There was silence, then she said unexpectedly, 'You're right. I didn't want to be alone. And . . . I do like you, Des Monahan. A lot. But that's as far as I'm prepared to go at the moment.'

He felt as if he'd won a major victory and snuggled down, smiling. 'Good. I like you, too.' A yawn overtook him. 'Don't take it wrongly if I fall asleep on you in the middle of a sentence. I'm exhausted.'

There was no reply, only a soft whiffle of breath. She'd beaten him to it, falling asleep between one word and the next.

He was happy to follow her example. It had been an arduous day for them both. Tomorrow they'd decide what to do next. Tomorrow . . .

Chapter Eight

Des woke at his usual six o'clock. He didn't want to disturb Gabrielle, so lay in bed, thinking over what had happened.

'Are you awake?' Her voice was hesitant and not much above a whisper.

He hadn't moved, but she must already have been awake, too, listening to his breathing. 'Yes. I'm an inveterate early riser.'

'Oh, good. So am I. I'll just use the bathroom.' She got out of bed and went into the tiny en suite.

When he came back from the same errand, she was standing by the window, staring along the street towards her former home.

Her voice sounded steadier this morning. 'There are crime scene tapes at the house. The tape shows very clearly, but it wouldn't stop anyone who wanted to get inside, would it?'

'Not for a second.'

'Thieves would be disappointed if they broke in.'

'Very.'

'I suppose they took Stu's boxes of things, too. They're gone from the garage, anyway.'

Another pause, then, 'Des, I've been awake for a while, thinking what to do. First I have to stop the real removal people from coming today. Then I have to get all the remaining bits and pieces of rubbish out of the house and throw them away.'

He went to stand beside her. 'And after that? Do you have somewhere to go for a few days, or are you going straight up to Rochdale?'

'I thought I might as well see that lawyer in Rochdale about my inheritance. No use hanging about here. Mr Greaves – isn't that his name?' She let out a mirthless laugh. 'They even stole his letter in amongst my papers, so you'll have to give me his address again.'

'I can do that. I think it's a good idea for you to get away from here. Why don't we travel to Rochdale together? I have business there, too. I'm thinking of moving up there and taking on a job offered by Mr Greaves.' He was even more eager to do that now.

'Go in a two-car convoy, you mean? I'm supposed to get mine back today.'

'That's not very sociable. I can come in yours or you in mine – whichever you prefer.'

She turned to give him another of those long, searching looks.

He held his breath, surprised all over again by how much he wanted her to say they could travel together.

She gave a little nod, as if he'd passed some sort of test. 'We'll go in your car, then. I can put the remaining bits and pieces in mine and leave it behind Tania's place. Besides, Stu might be able to trace me through my car. He won't know anything about you or yours.'

'I'll leave my car here at the back of the B and B when I come to help you clear your house, so that your neighbours won't be able to link you to it if anyone comes round asking.'

She laughed suddenly. It was the first time he'd seen her laugh properly and it lit up her whole face.

'What's so amusing?'

'It's just struck me. This is like a mystery novel – no murders, but a few brushes with cops and robbers.'

'They call such stories "cosy mysteries" these days.'

'Cosy. I like that name. I'd love to feel cosy again. And it is a mystery what's going on with me, isn't it? I don't understand it at all.'

'The police may get to the bottom of it eventually. Or else I might have a go, out of sheer curiosity. I don't like to leave ends dangling.' Especially when it concerned someone he cared about, but he didn't say that.

They tried the removal firm's number, but got only the answerphone. They left Des's mobile number and asked them to call back urgently.

'Breakfast isn't served till eight o'clock at the soonest,' Gabrielle said.

'Too late for me.' He picked up the packet of two biscuits left beside the tea-making equipment in the corner and offered her one.

She shook her head.

'Mind if I eat them both? I have a fast metabolism.'

'Go ahead.'

He began munching and said between bites, 'Shall we

stroll up to your house and check that it's all right? By the time we come back, breakfast will be served.'

'Fine by me.'

'You still need to contact the removal people.' Des checked his watch as they wandered back to the B and B half an hour later. 'There may be someone there now.'

To her relief, a woman picked up the phone.

After Gabrielle had explained what had happened and cancelled the job, Des grinned at her. 'Let's go and eat our "full English breakfast" now. I'm ravenous.'

'You must have hollow legs.'

He chuckled. 'My grandma always used to say that.'

'So did mine. Granddad was the same, always ready for something to eat and never putting on weight.'

Gabrielle was as hungry as Des and they ate cereal and fruit, followed by bacon, eggs, sausages, tomatoes and baked beans. Des ended up with toast and honey as well.

After paying their bills, they went back up to their room.

'Good thing I had my credit card with me,' Gabrielle said, patting her stomach ruefully. 'I don't usually eat such big breakfasts. I shan't feel hungry again for a week, I'm sure.'

'I enjoyed every mouthful. How soon will your car be ready?'

'About ten, they said.'

'Let's go and chivvy them to do it faster. How soon can you pack your things?'

'In two minutes flat.' She sighed. 'I'll need to buy a few more clothes today or tomorrow. They even took my everyday clothes, leaving only the ragged, worn-out things. I'm ashamed to leave the house looking like this.'

'Do you have enough credit on your card to buy what you need?'

'I'll be all right as long as the money for the house goes into my bank account at noon, as it's supposed to do. Oh! I don't have a computer any more. I won't be able to check that online. I'll have to go into a branch of my bank. Thank goodness I've still got ID in my handbag.'

'You can check your account on my smart phone.'

'Thank you.' She put one hand on his shoulder and leant across to kiss him on the cheek. 'You've been wonderful to me, Des. I don't know what I'd have done without you.'

'My pleasure. And isn't that what friends are for?'

'Yes, but somehow you always make me feel good about myself. That's such a bonus.'

He was sorry when she stepped back, ending the physical contact quickly. But at least she had initiated this brief touch. 'I only speak the truth as I see it, Gabrielle. Do you have the number of the tyre place? I'll give them a quick ring and ask them to hurry up.'

Fortunately, the car was almost ready, but after they'd picked it up, they had to go back to the house to deal with the handover.

The detectives were there, taking a last look at the scene of the crime.

'We got some tyre prints,' one of them said. 'Lucky it rained yesterday. We think we've found the deeper indentations of the removal truck.'

When the police had left, Gabrielle filled the dustbin

with rubbish, but couldn't sweep the house. She packed the few remaining bits and pieces into her car, then stared down into the boot. 'Not much to show for thirty-five years, is it?'

Des was horrified by how little there was left, but tried not to show it. Even the food from the cupboards had gone. 'No, it doesn't seem much. But you'll gradually acquire other things. This is a consumer age, after all.'

'Other things won't be the same. They even took my photos, Des. What use would those be to anyone?'

He gave her another quick hug and felt her take a couple of deep breaths, as if pulling herself together.

'No use crying over spilt milk. I'll leave my car at my friend Tania's when we head north. She has a spare parking space. She's on holiday but I'll leave her a note and phone when she gets back.'

The estate agent arrived at eleven-thirty, ignoring Des as he looked round disapprovingly. 'Couldn't you at least have vacuumed the place?'

Gabrielle controlled her anger at his rudeness and explained what had happened.

He gaped at her. 'You're joking.'

'I wish I were. I've lost everything I own.'

He looked at Des. 'Who are you?'

'Detective Sergeant Barlow,' Des answered promptly. 'Just finishing up here.' He flashed a card at the agent, but gave him no time to study it and find out he was lying. 'And you are?'

It was Gabrielle who answered, managing to keep

a straight face as she introduced the estate agent, then added, 'If you want anything doing about cleaning this house, contact my ex, I'm sure he'll have more resources than me at present. I don't even have anywhere to live.'

He didn't seem to know what to say to her. 'Well, yes. Sorry about your problem. I'll – um, see to it. You just . . . get on. You must have a lot to do.'

Des came across to murmur in her ear and she nodded, turning back to the agent. 'I'll need to check my bank account to make sure the money's gone through, before I hand over the keys. But as I've had my computer stolen, the DI has kindly agreed to lend me his smart phone. Unless you want to lend me yours?'

'No, no. I'll wait for you to check. There won't be any problem, though. Our accounts department is very efficient.'

To her relief, the money had been paid into her bank account. She turned to Des. 'I'm ready to go now.'

They left the agent speaking urgently on his phone.

She didn't turn back to look at the house as she got into her car.

'You all right?' Des asked.

'I'm managing OK. Thanks for asking.'

She looked at her rubbish bin liner half-full of clothes, sitting limply on the back seat. 'Do you think I'll set a new fashion in designer luggage?'

'Bound to. Shiny black, soft, pack in style, very cheap. Who could resist such a bargain?'

That brought a genuine smile.

They left Gabrielle's car at Tania's building, pushing a note to her friend and the remaining car key through the letter box of the flat. By now, the thieves would probably have thrown away the spare that had been hanging in her hall.

Des's phone rang just as they were about to set off. 'It's the police,' he mouthed at her, then listened intently.

'He was just letting us know that no one has reported a removal truck stolen, but they found a witness who'd seen it leaving. The lad said it was plain grey, shabby, nothing remarkable about it, no company name on it.'

'So that's that. They've got away with it.'

Des looked at his watch. 'We're not going to get to Lancashire before everything closes. How about we stop for the night on the way up and make an early start in the morning?'

'Whatever you like. Perhaps we can stop somewhere with shops. I won't take long, I promise you. I'll just buy a few necessities. I need clean underwear and I prefer not to wear items saved for cleaning the floor.'

'Of course we can find some shops. And you can take as long as you need.'

Des watched her buy swiftly and frugally in a big chain store, comparing jeans and tops by price and quality. But she fell for one pretty skirt and a top with a glittery band round the neckline. She looked good in it, had a better colour in her cheeks this afternoon. And he noticed her buying two simple cotton nightdresses and a matching dressing gown.

He bought a couple of books while she was trying another pair of jeans on. He chose cosy mysteries, of course, was addicted to them.

Then they went to find accommodation.

'Separate rooms?' Des asked.

She swallowed hard. 'Would you mind twin beds again?'

'Of course not.'

But there were only rooms with double beds left.

Again he let her make the decision. 'One room or two?'

'One will be fine. If it's all right with you. I'm still feeling a bit nervous and don't fancy being on my own in a strange place, even though I know Stu has no way of tracing me. It's not logical, is it?'

He lowered his voice, for her ears only. 'No, but it's normal for people in your position. I value your trust in me very highly, and I promise I won't abuse it.'

She nodded, but she didn't even know whether she wanted him to make a pass at her or not. He had been so restrained, without making a fuss about it. Perhaps he didn't fancy her.

She was torn both ways, valuing his restraint and yet wanting him to hold her close, touch her . . . and perhaps more.

It had been a long time and she was only human. Other women had casual relationships from time to time. She never had. Tania thought her mad.

She'd decided she was picky.

And then she'd gone and fallen for Stu. Picky *and* a fool.

But Des was different. He was a steady sort of man – wasn't he?

* * *

The hotel room was cramped but clean with adequate facilities.

Des dumped his suitcase on the small stand and took out his phone. 'I'll just call Mr Greaves and find out when he'll be free to see us. He doesn't finish till six most nights.'

He waited till someone picked up. 'Henry! It's Des here. Look, I'm bringing Gabrielle to see you. She has nowhere to live and will need one of the houses, I think. We'll tell you all about it when we arrive tomorrow. Do you have a free slot? OK. We'll be there.'

He turned to Gabrielle. 'Henry can see you tomorrow afternoon at two-thirty. Unless there are huge hold-ups, we should be able to make it easily.

Then he looked at the bed. Not even a king size. 'Are you sure you're all right with this?'

'Yes.'

'Let's go and find some food, then.'

She smiled. That man did seem to love his food, and yet he was trim and looked muscular. 'Do you work out to use up all those calories?'

'I run sometimes, try to get in a few walks, even in cities. I like walking.'

'So do I.'

'Good. We'll go walking on the moors together, if you like.'

There he went again, making plans for their future. She wasn't certain what she wanted, but she did enjoy his company . . . and his touch.

They ate in the café attached to the hotel. It was adequate but she couldn't finish her meal.

When they went back to the bedroom, Gabrielle waited to see if she felt nervous about sharing the bed. But she didn't. The more time she spent with Des, the more at ease with him she felt.

'Shall I use the bathroom first?'

He waved one hand. 'Be my guest.'

She came out wearing the new dressing gown. 'Do you have any scissors or maybe a penknife? I can't get the label off the back.'

'I have my trusty Boy Scout knife. Turn around.' He fiddled with the label and snipped off the plastic strip which had defied her fingers. 'There.'

'Perhaps we could do the same to the other new clothes while we're at it?'

'You hold them out, I'll use my masculine muscles.'

By the time they'd fiddled with several different types of label, they were laughing together over the vagaries of clothing sellers.

When he put away his knife, the laughter faded and something else replaced it in his eyes. But he still held back, so Gabrielle took the initiative, grateful that he was allowing her this choice. She moved closer. 'I'd very much like you to kiss me, Des.'

'I'd very much like to oblige.'

The kiss was slow and gentle, yet it made her want him even more and she pressed against him, realising from his physical state that he too wanted more.

'No need to stop there,' she said.

He studied her face. 'Sure?'

'Very.'

'Good.'

In the darkness he gathered her to him, and though she felt nervous at first, that soon vanished, because he was a wonderful, caring lover . . .

When they lay together afterwards, she decided that whatever she'd done to deserve this man, she hoped it continued.

'That was wonderful,' he murmured in her ear.

'Yes. You've got hidden talents, Mr Monahan.'

He chuckled. 'So have you.'

It was, she thought dreamily, just as wonderful to be able to laugh together afterwards and not make a competitive performance of the act of love.

It had been, she realised as she was drifting into sleep, a true act of love.

Still nestled in his arms, she contemplated the realisation that she had fallen in love with Des. She hadn't intended to. She still wasn't quite sure how he felt about her.

But she trusted him to treat her with kindness, whatever came of their budding relationship, and kindness had been in short supply in her life for a while now. It would be enough to start with.

She sighed and nestled closer to the sleeping man, slipping her hand in his.

Des's happy smile and quick kiss were enough to dispel any embarrassment Gabrielle might have felt on waking beside him the following morning. But they didn't linger over the breakfast they'd ordered, which had been left on trays outside their room.

They were ready to set off by eight o'clock, as they'd intended.

'Lay on, Macduff!' Gabrielle said, picking up her various packages and the rubbish bin liner of old clothes.

Des grinned at her. 'You even got that quotation right. Most people don't and it irritates me. It shouldn't, but there you are – I'm a stickler for detail. I might irritate you a bit with it, only you have to focus on details in my profession.' He began to recite the whole sentence from Shakespeare's play and she joined in.

'*Lay on, Macduff, and damned be to him who first cries, Hold! Enough!*'

'That should be our motto for this puzzling situation of yours,' he said.

'All right. Lay on, Mr Monahan! We won't give in, whatever happens.'

He noticed that she smiled for a while after that, and he did too. It was a strange thing to link them, quoting Shakespeare, but he was happy to find anything that made her feel more comfortable with him. She had a lot of reasons for mistrusting men, thanks to Mr Stuart Bloody Dixon.

Once he'd seen her through to the other side of the mess . . . if the attraction continued to grow, as he rather thought it might . . . well, it might change his whole life.

He cut those thoughts off short. He mustn't lose his focus. Not till things were settled and explained, anyway. Something about this situation worried him, though he couldn't work out what exactly was making him feel uneasy.

He wished now that he'd met her ex, or at least had a surreptitious look at the guy. You could usually tell a lot from someone's appearance.

Perhaps it was the money thing. In Des's experience, some swindlers never let go until they'd milked a victim dry, and Gabrielle still had quite a bit of money – enough to put a deposit on a modest house, from what she'd said. Would this Stu fellow come after that next?

They seemed to be getting away from him too easily.

Maybe he was worrying for nothing and they'd never see Dixon again.

Or maybe he'd come after the rest of her money.

There were a lot of maybes hanging over them at the moment.

He fell back on his old mantra: one day at a time, one step at a time.

Chapter Nine

The first sight of Rochdale was a big disappointment to Gabrielle. The streets and buildings looked rather tired and shabby as they drove into the centre.

'It's because they've had hard times here in recent years, a lot of unemployment,' Des murmured.

'How did you know what I was thinking? Are you a mind reader?'

'No, a face reader. And you have a very expressive face. Wait till you see the Town Hall. There – look!'

He stopped the car in a parking bay in the big open space in front of the Town Hall, and she got out to stare at the huge stone building, with its tower at one end. 'Wow! It's beautiful. Victorian Gothic, like the Houses of Parliament.'

'Not the same architect, though. This was done by William Crossland – one of his earlier works. We'll do a tour of it one day, if you like. It's even more impressive inside. The people here are rightly proud of it – and, of course, it's Grade One listed.'

They stood for a moment, admiring the beautiful, ornate building. 'I love old buildings,' Des said. 'Modern ones, like those towers on the horizon over there, look like piles of egg boxes to me. Any child could design the outside of one by piling up toy bricks.'

He glanced at his watch. 'Unfortunately, we'd better get moving. We're cutting things rather fine, thanks to those traffic jams on the M6. Henry appreciates punctuality.'

The lawyer worked from the ground floor of a restored Edwardian house, whose garden had been turned into a car park. Other businesses occupied the first and second floors, according to a signboard in the entry.

Henry was well-dressed, the sort of man who might have been called a 'gentleman' a hundred years ago, Gabrielle decided. He was quietly spoken and exquisitely dressed, which made her feel even more shabby in her cheap and practical new clothes.

Stu would have been scornful about the lawyer. He always claimed that the world had moved on, and the only people who counted were those who had moved with it. But not as many things had changed as he claimed, and some people ignored passing trends until they had proved themselves. He had always leapt from one fad to another, like a frog crossing a pond by jumping on lily pads.

She realised the lawyer was speaking to her. 'Oh, sorry. What did you say?'

'Des told me about the robbery. Shocking thing to happen. Would you like a cup of tea, my dear?'

'I'd love one.'

'I'll ask Mrs Hockton to get us some. She makes a perfect pot of tea. Excuse me a moment.'

Gabrielle stared round. Beautiful antique furniture,

glass-fronted bookcases, and a fire so realistic that it took her a minute to realise it wasn't a coal fire but a gas imitation, which looked just right in the old-fashioned fireplace.

Des sat slightly to one side, as if keeping out of the conversation.

When Mr Greaves came back, he took the armchair opposite hers and studied their faces. 'You both look tired.'

She could feel herself blushing, but Des stepped in quickly. 'Neither of us slept well last night. Not the most comfortable of hotels and Ms Newman is still upset about the robbery.'

Gabrielle bent her head to hide her smile at this explanation of their weariness.

'Yes, of course. I hope they catch the thieves. However, we have some rather more pleasant business to deal with today. What did Des tell you about your inheritance, Ms Newman?'

'Not much. I know only what you said in your letter. He told me you'd explain the details.'

'Yes. Quite right. Well, for a start, Rose King has left provision for any female relative in need to be given twenty thousand pounds.'

'That's . . . a very helpful sum.'

'There is a condition to it, I'm afraid. You have to live in the area for six months in order to claim it, but while you're here, you'll be given a living allowance, and, if you wish, you can stay in one of the trust's houses rent-free, with electricity and all services paid for you. She felt that would give people time to get on their feet again, mentally and financially. You can stay longer if you wish.'

'It'd be wonderful to have somewhere to live! And my ex won't be able to trace me as easily if I'm living in someone else's house.'

He looked at her shrewdly. 'You think he might come after you?'

'Only if he feels he can get more money out of me. Which I won't let him do.' She quoted the old saying, 'Fool me once, shame on you; fool me twice, shame on me.'

'Very true.'

'However, I'd rather avoid trouble. Perhaps I'm worrying for nothing. I may never see or hear from him again.' She hoped. 'I'll have to buy some furniture for the house, because they took all mine, but I'm sure I can find what I need in the second-hand shops.'

He smiled gently. 'Mrs King's houses are all furnished – some more sparsely than others, I will admit. They're rather old-fashioned, but everything is in working order and they have all the basic appliances, so there's everything you need except for food and your own clothes, of course.'

Mrs Hockton came back just then with a large tray full of pretty china.

Des stood up. 'Shall I fetch the teapot for you, Mrs H?'

'Yes, please, Mr Monahan.'

When they were all supplied with tea and biscuits, Mr Greaves continued his explanation. 'Mrs King lived in one of the cottages in Top o' the Hill until she died. That's a village near Todmorden. She didn't hanker after a large house, even though she'd made quite a lot of money on the stock market.'

He smiled fondly, 'She seemed to have a knack of

buying shares which would shoot up in value, and she was usually just as good at knowing when to sell. She called it her little hobby. Few people have such lucrative hobbies, but she didn't care about the money she made nor did she spend much on herself. What she enjoyed was using it to help people.'

He studied Gabrielle thoughtfully. 'There are two cottages available in the village she lived in and there are a couple of other houses in slightly more isolated surroundings – in the same area, though. As the name suggests, the village is right at the top of a hill, or rather at the edge of the uplands – the moors, that is.'

He looked sideways at their companion. 'I'd suggest Mr Monahan shows you the houses tomorrow so that you can choose which one you'd like to live in.'

'I can choose?'

'Of course. Subject to the trustees' approval. I'm hoping to persuade Des here to become manager of the trust, especially the financial side of things.' He shuddered eloquently. 'I really have no head for dealing with stocks and shares, let alone the requirement to keep an eye on Mrs King's relatives.'

He looked at Des. 'Unless you have strong views about which house Ms Newman should live in?'

'Whichever takes her fancy. I'm not going to prejudice her for or against any of them. I'll enjoy taking her round them all tomorrow.' He glanced towards the window. 'I think we ought to find somewhere to stay before it grows dark.'

Mr Greaves nodded and held out four envelopes. 'Here

are the front door keys. The addresses are written on the envelopes. I'll see you tomorrow afternoon at about the same time to hear your decision, if you think you'll have gone round them by then.'

He smiled at Des's nod, then turned back to Gabrielle. 'There will be other things to discuss once you've made your choice.'

She walked out with Des, feeling a lot better than when she'd gone in. Outside, the words burst out of her. 'I shall have somewhere to live! Oh, you don't know what a relief that is!'

'I can imagine. I'm really glad for you. Come on. Let's get a room and then—'

She finished it for him. 'Then we'll find somewhere to eat. You're hungry again.'

'Can't help it. It's part of my charm.' He looked at her quizzically. 'We're sharing a room again, aren't we? I'd hate to think you were just using me for a one-night stand.'

She chuckled. 'We'll share if you're a good boy.'

He pulled her to him for a quick kiss. 'I'm a very good boy.'

It took her breath away, that kiss did, for all its gentleness. He was easy to like and relax with, but when he kissed her, fireworks seemed to explode around them, as if they sparked something in each other.

Stu leant back in the big comfortable armchair and smiled at Radka, enjoying being back in her beautiful luxury flat. 'Told you it'd work. Gaby was so easy to dupe and the beauty salon didn't mind that way of me giving her a day's treat.'

'Yes, you were right. I was pleased with the way things went. And you even had the sense to phone the beauty salon this time, not turn up in person. Clever boy. You're learning.'

'Hardly a boy.'

'You seem like one to me sometimes.' She frowned at him. 'Now, can you please stop talking about your ex. You mention her at least once an hour. She's the past – done with. Say *Bye, bye, Gabi! Hello, Radka.*'

'Hello, Radka,' he repeated, smiling.

But she didn't smile back at him. 'I'm your future now and don't you forget it. I don't share my men with anyone.'

'Men?'

'One at a time, but, obviously, you're not the first.'

He frowned. 'I don't talk about Gabi that often, surely?'

'Oh, but you do.'

He shrugged. 'Well, she was so profitable. Good housekeeper, too. I miss being looked after. Pity I can't think of a way to get the rest of her money. She still has a tidy sum left. Maybe she—'

Radka gave an elaborate yawn.

'Sorry. Do you want to go out and get something to eat?'

'Again? You ate only three hours ago.'

'Are you never hungry?'

'I don't allow myself to get hungry. I have no wish to become fat.' She walked across to stare at herself in the mirror, turning from side to side, preening a little.

'You're on the scrawny side of slender, if anything,' he said without thinking.

A cup sailed through the air and hit him on the side

of the head, before crashing to the floor and breaking into several shards.

'Hey! Stop that.' He rubbed his head and used his handkerchief to wipe off the splashes of coffee.

'I warned you. I will throw things if you criticise my appearance. Or make you sorry in other ways. I'm happy with how I look. If you aren't happy with me, find yourself another woman and I will find another man.'

'Don't be silly. You're beautiful and I love being with you.'

Another glance at the mirror. 'No, I'm not beautiful. But I am attractive and sexy. That is just as useful.'

She turned to smile lazily at him, in that certain way she had when she wanted him, and he could feel desire rising. 'Extremely sexy,' he said in a voice gone suddenly husky. 'In fact, why don't we—'

She held up one hand to keep him at a distance and her voice became sharper. 'Not now, but definitely later. I have to go out to see someone about selling the incidental goods we acquired from your ex. I will also tell my main partner this may be a good way to bring the special items through customs in future. If he likes the idea, he will make it happen and then we will give you a share.'

'Make sure you tell him it was my idea in the first place.'

Her voice was utterly flat and cold, very much a foreigner speaking English at this moment. 'No. I am one of the partners and I employ you. I will tell the others only what they need to know about you. You must stay in the background, continue working for your company, or you will lose your usefulness.'

'But—'

'When I get back, I will tell you only what *you* need to know about the situation, too. Better, if anything goes wrong, that no one knows any details about the others.'

'Except you know about me.'

She inclined her head. 'Yes. Except me. But I found you. And you will benefit from those precautions.'

He looked at her with sudden anxiety. 'Why should it go wrong?'

'Darling, what we're doing *is* against the law in both countries.'

He tried not to think about that side of things. 'Well, if it does go wrong, I shall insist that I knew nothing about what you were doing. After all, my reason for being in this country is an entirely different project for the British company which employs me.'

'Yes, of course. That is a very useful excuse for you being here. But it is a very small project compared with the ones in which I'm involved.' She moved towards the door, stopping to say provocatively, 'Later on, if you are a *verrry* good boy, we will go to bed and test your staying power.'

Another of those smiles and she'd gone. Stu began to pace up and down. The details she gave him about what she did for a living kept changing. He had assumed she was a manager of some sort, or maybe the owner of a small company. Now, she was saying his job was small beer and that she was a partner in a major company of some sort. He scowled. He wasn't used to being with a woman who was more successful than he was.

Moreover, he still hadn't worked out how to manipulate Radka, which worried him. He was usually good at dealing with women, but she was unlike anyone he'd ever known before. And he had to admit that she managed him more than he managed her. He didn't like that.

Only she was rich. Judging by this flat, *very* rich.

The nature of her business interests was beginning to seriously worry him. He didn't want to get in trouble with the law, but he needed the money his involvement with Radka brought in quite desperately, to pay off some rather larger debts than usual. If he didn't pay them, he'd be in trouble with people who didn't mind what they did to wring their money out of you.

He was never going to gamble in the big league again. He hadn't been at all lucky in the past year. Once he was clear of all this, he'd find himself another hobby instead.

And whatever Radka said, it might be useful to get the rest of that money from Gabi, especially if he could do it without being caught out. Gabi would only spend it on a deposit for another stupid little house. He had a much greater need for it.

He walked across the room to smile at his reflection in the mirror. He'd still got his youthful good looks, give or take slightly fewer strands of hair. He bowed to the image in the mirror. Nature had been kind to him.

Feeling at a loose end, he went to stare out of the window of the flat, wondering if he should go out for a stroll. No. He couldn't be bothered.

His thoughts turned inevitably to his ex and her money. It might be fun to let Gabi get settled in, then take away for a second time the stupid bourgeois bits and pieces she'd probably already started accumulating. He'd enjoy organising that, especially if he could hang around this time and watch her reaction.

How to do it without being caught was what he hadn't quite figured out yet. He had a copy of her signature, could write it perfectly, and knew which bank she used, what her account and credit card numbers were. He'd kept her laptop from the goods that had been stolen, and had found all the details of her account passwords on it. What a fool she was, keeping such information in a file with such a simple protection system.

He'd have to find a way to keep a watch on what she was doing.

He wondered where she'd buy a house next. No, it'd be a flat. She'd not be able to get a big mortgage on her pitiful salary. She'd probably buy nearer town, so that she could get to work easily. Till she got somewhere, she'd be staying with that ditzy friend of hers – what was her name? Tania. Yes, that was it. She lived in a ghastly little block of flats near the centre of the village.

He paced to and fro in the flat. Dammit, for all Radka's charms, he really missed England. He hadn't expected that.

Since he had nothing better to do, he opened the laptop his employer had given him. Better check the afternoon's emails. Oh, bugger! There was one from his boss.

Need to see you about something important. Thursday at ten a.m. My office. Charge your flight to the company as usual. Patrick

Maybe this wasn't going to be as long an exile as Stu had feared. Well, he hoped it wasn't. He'd had enough of Prague. Life was a lot pleasanter when you spoke the local language and weren't dependent on an uppity female for so much of your leisure-time activity. And Radka seemed to go to London regularly. It wasn't as if he'd not see her again.

He frowned as he reread the email. He didn't appreciate the way he'd been treated by his company lately. He'd been very neatly sidelined to Prague and he knew who to thank for that. Maybe Patrick had thought better of this posting. Stu felt he was wasted here, absolutely wasted. Yes, that'd be it. They wanted him back.

He knew who to blame for his exile and one day he'd pay Patrick's damned personal assistant back for sending him here. In fact, he'd take great pleasure in doing it.

After sending off a reply, he began pacing to and fro again, got himself a whisky but only sipped at it. He wasn't into heavy boozing, didn't like the feeling of getting drunk and losing control. Drinking couldn't hold a candle to trying to coax a win from Lady Luck.

He couldn't think of anything he wanted to do tonight. Walking round Wenceslas Square with the tourists was all right once or twice, to say you'd been there, but what did he care about cathedrals? And as for that weird-looking Dancing House, you could keep it. He didn't even know what 'deconstructivist' meant, let alone have a taste for modern architecture and buildings which looked as if they were going to fall over any minute.

What a pity he'd never had a really big win. Without

that he still had to climb corporate ladders, and that meant kowtowing to old fools with no hair and big bellies. Or putting up with Radka's moods. She could be a real bitch at times, however good she was in bed.

He sighed. Just one big win at the casino would have done it, set him up for life. Then he could have lived in style.

He might go back a day early and have a sniff round Worton, see what Gabi was doing with herself. The thought of a few days in England cheered him up.

Des took Gabrielle to a hotel in Rochdale where he'd stayed before.

'We'll take the main suite. It's worth the extra money for the space.'

She must have looked worried, because he added, 'The trust will pay your share.'

'Are you sure?'

'Yes. Half the price of the suite is no more than a modest room.' He winked. 'There are some advantages to being a pair.'

'A lot of advantages,' she said demurely.

He drew a deep breath and approached the reception counter. 'Hello, Jenny. This is my partner, Gabrielle. We'd like the main suite.'

The middle-aged woman behind the counter gave them a sentimental smile. 'Certainly, Mr Monahan.' She validated a pair of electronic card keys and held them out. 'Early breakfast as usual?'

'Yes, please.'

She nodded to Gabrielle. 'I'm glad he's found himself a partner. He's a kind, loving man.'

Des blushed and hurried Gabrielle away to the lift. 'She will try to mother me.'

'I liked her compliment.' She gave him a little nudge. 'And I loved the way you blushed.'

The lift came just then and she didn't comment on the way he blushed all over again. But it was cute!

Their room was a lovely, comfortable space with a super-king bed.

'A six-foot bed!' Gabrielle gloated, bouncing on it. 'Lovely.'

'Unless you want me to take advantage of you this minute,' Des said, 'we'd better go out for some food. I'm assuming that you don't want fine dining or room service here?'

'I'd rather go out somewhere casual, given my lack of smart clothes,' she said with a sigh. 'I noticed that you didn't give the receptionist my surname.'

'I thought it might stop you worrying about your ex finding you. I wondered if you were going to give a false surname.'

'Reading my mind again?'

'No, your face. I love reading your face. Now, I desperately need feeding. Come on.' Laughing, he tugged her out of the room and took her to a pub he knew from his previous visits. It had an excellent bar menu.

The pub was full of people, even though it was only midweek. Good hearty food was on offer. She chose a 'jacket' with chilli con carne, grated cheese and salad.

The potato was huge and she couldn't finish it.

'You'll fade away,' he commented, seeing her push the remains of the potato to one side and lay down her knife and fork tidily to signal that she'd finished.

'I ate plenty.'

'Call that eating?' He finished his meal, then picked up the menu. 'What do you want for dessert?'

'Nothing, thank you. I've had an elegant sufficiency. I would like a decaf cappuccino, though.'

But he tempted her into a couple of mouthfuls of his chocolate mousse, and as she took the food from the spoon he was holding out to her, she suddenly felt warm with desire for him. Again.

'*Tom Jones*,' he said. 'The scene where they were eating.' He offered another half spoonful of mousse and she sucked it slowly from the spoon, this time exaggerating the sensuality.

It was his turn to go rigid for a moment or two.

She smiled cheekily at him. 'Cat got your tongue?'

'No, but you've taken my breath away, Gabrielle.' He took hold of her hand and kept hold of it till they'd finished their coffees.

She didn't pull hers away. It felt right to be touching him.

'What time do you want to leave tomorrow on our tour of the houses?' he asked as they strolled back to the hotel.

'Immediately after breakfast. I don't want to be escorted round the houses by a hungry tiger.'

He chuckled. 'I've been here a few times before. They'll do us a breakfast at six or seven o'clock, whichever you prefer, if you ask ahead. All we have to do is pay the morning cook for an hour's extra work, which I always do. She's used to me now.'

'I usually eat at about six o'clock,' she admitted.

'Good. So do I. We fit together surprisingly well in the details, don't we? Unless you like cricket.'

'Cricket? I can't be bothered with it. I find it boring.' She held her breath, hoping she hadn't annoyed him, because some people loved the sport.

He laughed. 'It's all right. You won't upset me. I can talk about it a little, so that I don't stick out like a sore thumb with other guys, but I never watch it by choice.'

'So we're a pair of early birds,' she agreed with a smile, 'who like to quote Shakespeare accurately and don't enjoy watching cricket. We clearly have a lot in common.'

He gave her a smouldering look. 'Oh, I think we have more in common than that.'

Which caused her to blush.

When they went back to the hotel, she unpacked her new clothes, laying them in piles on the bed. Four small piles and a fifth pile that she decided was finally really for the ragbag.

'You'll soon find other clothes you like.'

'Yes. Of course I will.' She pasted a smile to her face, but knew she hadn't fooled him about her feelings. Well, seeing how few clothes she now owned would upset any woman. You didn't have to be a fashionista for that.

Des held out a book. 'Here you are. I bought you a present when we were shopping. Bedtime reading. You said you liked cosies. I must be a terrible sleuth, because

I didn't guess who committed the dreadful deed in this woman's last book.'

She cuddled the book to her chest. She hated not having a book on the go. This small thing made her feel better, more normal, and showed yet again how perceptive and caring he was about details. 'Thank you.'

He held out a tissue. 'Nothing to cry about.'

'Only happy tears.' She mopped her face.

When she yawned, he said quietly, 'Come on. Let's get you back to bed, Cinderella. You'll sleep much better tonight, I'm sure.'

'I am rather tired.' She yawned again.

They both took showers. As she lay in bed, she listened to his going on for rather a long time and she wondered if it was a cold shower. That thought made her giggle and feel good.

She opened the book and tried to read, waking briefly when it fell out of her hands and landed on the floor with a thump. She saw him smiling down at her as he picked it up off his side and laid it on the bedside table.

'Sorry. I'm so tired.'

'Don't worry. You've a lot of poor sleep to catch up on.'

That was the last thing she remembered till morning.

Chapter Ten

The first thing Gabrielle saw when she woke was Des's face, his fine hair ruffled, greying a little at the temples, thinner on top. She had grown to love that face.

He opened his eyes and reached out to touch her curls. 'Hey there, curly!'

'Hey yourself.'

'A quick cuddle, then we'll go down for breakfast.'

But they didn't get up as quickly as they'd intended.

Gabrielle was eager to look at the houses on offer. She wasn't surprised to find they were the only ones eating in the hotel dining room at seven o'clock in the morning.

'You're a pair of real early birds,' the woman who served them said cheerfully.

She soon came back with their order. 'Good thing I like to earn the extra money by coming in early. Breakfasts are easy to prepare. Most of our guests like to stay in bed as long as they can.'

'I'd just lie there awake, fretting to get up,' Des told her.

'We're all different, aren't we? Me, I enjoy lying in bed. Only time I get a bit of peace with my kids racing round the house from dawn till dusk.'

By eight o'clock Des and Gabrielle had been supplied with plenty of good food and cheerful chat about the town, and were on the road for Top o' the Hill. The roads into Rochdale were full of cars now, so it felt good to drive out towards the countryside.

The village was reached by a winding road which followed what seemed to be a natural fissure that zigzagged down a steep slope at the edge of the moors proper. The cleft must have been gouged out over the centuries by a rushing stream, which was still there to one side of a road so narrow that it had to have passing places.

Des drove slowly up it and through the tiny village, which consisted of little more than a main street, fringed by three hundred yards or so of houses, and containing, in the centre, one general store, a kindergarten and a pub. A couple of short lanes led to houses planted in small groups behind the upper side of the street.

They followed the road out of the village and up the hill, turning left just before a small church. Des stopped the car and gestured towards the building. 'I'll show you inside that church another day. There's a plaque to the King family members lost in the two wars. We might have time for a quick look at the graveyard today, at least.'

He smiled at her and added ruefully, 'Here I am promising future visits again, but we will go to these places once we're both settled in the district.'

'Does that mean you're definitely taking the job as manager of Cousin Rose's trust fund?'

'Yes.' He hesitated. 'Well, unless it'd upset *you* to live here?'

She stared at him in shock, not sure if this meant what she thought.

As usual, he seemed to understand without her needing to explain. 'We won't go into any other details about the future yet, but that one's rather urgent if I'm to accept the job.'

'It wouldn't upset me at all to live here,' she said, choosing her words carefully. 'The people seem friendly, and I like the way the towns and villages seem to nestle against the edge of the moors, or in hollows below them. But I can't commit myself to anything else yet, Des, I simply can't.'

'Of course you can't. This job was more or less a done deal before I met you, but your positive attitude to the area does make it easier for me to accept, whatever we decide finally about our – um, future. It's exactly the sort of job I like: part-time, so I can do what I want with the rest of the week – take on other jobs pro bono or whatever. And the trust job involves helping people.'

'People like me.'

'Yes.' His smile was as intimate as a caress. 'Just so you know where I stand, I've already had an offer on my house in the south.'

'It must be great.' She had been worrying about getting a mortgage, even if she got a job, because she'd only have been in that job for a short time. 'Won't you miss your old home, though?'

'No. The house is old-fashioned with no charm whatsoever. I think my parents chose it because Dad loved gardening, whereas I find the big garden rather a burden. The house was built in the 1930s and is at the stage where it needs a lot of work doing to bring it up to scratch. It's not worth it. I've sold it to a builder who's paying an excellent price, considering. He's going to knock the house down and build two or three others in its place. The local council planners are more liberal about allowing that sort of infill development these days.'

'And have you found a house you like here in the north, or are you going to rent?'

'I'm not certain yet what I'm going to do. Maybe when things have settled down, we could go house hunting together. It'd be good to have a woman's viewpoint.'

'I'd enjoy that.'

'Good. We'll add that to our list of things to do.' He pulled up in the parking area in front of a terrace of four dwellings, three storeys high, and turned her attention to them with a wave of his hand. 'These are the cottages Rose left. They have handloom weavers' rooms on the top floor.'

'How can you tell?'

'By that row of mullioned windows, each separated from the others only by a narrow stone column. They did that to give maximum light for weaving before the days of gas or electric lighting. It was the equivalent in the eighteenth century of a picture window. Working folks' houses didn't usually have big windows in those days.'

He led the way towards the house on the left. 'This is the one that's available. The next one to it also belongs to the trust, but it needs attention before it can be used again.'

Inside, the house felt dark and still, as if no one had been in it for a good while – as if the very air had sat quietly waiting for someone to come in and breathe life into it.

But the house hadn't been waiting for *her*, Gabrielle

decided almost immediately as she followed Des round. The only room she liked was the big one on the top floor. The rest was too dark, with a shadow cast by the moors behind it. The kitchen at the rear would probably be in shadow for most of the day.

Des didn't comment till they came back down to the kitchen. 'Not to your taste, eh?'

'That sounds ungrateful. If it was the only house available, I'd take it happily, but as there are others, I'd rather see them before making a choice.'

'It *is* rather gloomy. Come on, then. No use wasting any more time here. But I will show you the graveyard before we leave.'

This seemed a strange focus, but she didn't quibble. He must have some reason for doing it.

He drove up the hill for about two hundred yards, stopping the car in a parking area in front of a small, plain, stone church. When they got out, he walked past the church, whose door was padlocked, and led her up the final part of the slope, stopping at a wall and opening a tall wrought-iron gate to let her in.

Gabrielle caught her breath as she stopped inside the graveyard. It was like a scene from *Wuthering Heights*: a windswept oblong of ground, about as big as a football pitch, sloping slightly down from the crest of the hill, where they were standing, towards the moors behind it. It was surrounded by drystone walls, with grave markers leaning this way and that, some lying flat, half covered by long strands of unkempt grass.

Beyond the graveyard stretched the moors, and her

eyes were immediately drawn to the hilltop land, which spread out in gentle undulations towards the horizon. They called to her, those moors did, made her want to stride off across their wide spaces. A wind was blowing steadily towards them from the 'tops', as Des said locals called them, sending Gabrielle's hair flying and making her pull her thin jacket more closely round her body.

He didn't speak, letting her gaze her fill and breathe in the clean upland air. She liked the way he didn't push her to do things instantly.

'These northern moors are more beautiful in real life than when you see them on the television, aren't they?' she said at last. 'Are there walks across them?'

'Yes. Some of the most used walks are well signposted, with indications of how long and difficult each walk is. I'll take you one day.' He laughed. 'Another place to put on our to-visit list.'

'I'd like that. It's a wild, lonely place, isn't it? I bet it's bleak in winter. Is this where Cousin Rose is buried?'

'Yes.' He pointed. 'She's lying in that far corner. Come and see. She had to get special dispensation, because the graveyard is officially full and closed to new occupants. But her ancestors are here and there was still room among them, so she got her final wish. She'll be the last King buried here, though.'

They had to wind round lines of graves and clamber over a few headstones to get to the corner. These graves were better tended, standing in a neat little group. To one side was a modest, new-looking headstone with *Eleanor Rose Josephine King* and the date of her death. Underneath it said simply *With her family now, but missed by her many friends.*

'I'm glad she got her wish to lie here,' Gabrielle said. 'She sounds to have been a lovely person.'

'I never met her, but I get the same impression. Mr Greaves always speaks very warmly of her. And look at how she's left her money to help others. I even liked the way her own house felt when I visited another member of your extended family who was living there for a while. I meant to tell you when we were there. Libby's only just moved out. She and Joss are renting till they buy a house together.'

'I'm not the only one the trust has helped, then?'

'No. That's another thing I'll do soon – introduce you to your umpteenth Cousin Libby by adoption.' He laughed. 'I can work out the exact degree of cousinship if I look at your family tree, but I haven't connected the two of you in my mind yet.'

'What's she like?'

'Nice woman, about your age. She has a young son from her first marriage, a lively little lad, and she's hooked up with a friend of mine, Joss, an ex-policeman. They're planning to marry soon.' He glanced at his watch. 'I'll tell you more about them later. We have three more houses to inspect before two o'clock.'

'I'd like to come back another day and put flowers on Cousin Rose's grave,' Gabrielle said as they walked back to the car. 'I'm very grateful to her.'

'Good idea. I'm grateful to her, too.'

She glanced quickly at him.

He winked, then tugged her towards the car, making her run, so that they arrived slightly breathless.

Had he been giving her another hint, or was she reading too much into what he was saying? She hoped she wasn't. Suddenly, her life seemed to have hope creeping back into it again. She'd felt very downhearted for a while. Not clinically depressed – at least she didn't think so – but definitely on the blue side.

It was time she had something to hope for.

The second of Cousin Rose's houses was in the village itself, slightly smaller than the first one, with only two storeys because it didn't have the weavers' upper room. It had two bedrooms and was more than adequate for one person. The furnishings were in good order and the windows of the ground floor seemed to let in more light than those on the ground floor of the first house.

Still, nothing about it made Gabrielle want to live there.

She shouldn't be so picky, she thought guiltily. She was lucky to have the chance of any free accommodation. But Mr Greaves had said she could choose which house she lived in, so she didn't need to make a decision till she'd seen them all.

Des read her mind again. 'Not this one?'

'No. Well, not if there's a better choice.'

'Which of these two do you prefer?'

'The first one.'

'I thought you might. I'll be interested to see how you react to the next place, which is different again.'

'In what way?'

'Aha! Wait and see.'

He drove down to the main road, turning on to a side road which ran along the floor of a small valley, then turning left along a narrow lane barely one car wide. The gravel at the edges was patterned by the marks of car wheels, and there were a couple of wider places near each of the three houses they saw, with a car parked outside one house.

About a hundred yards up the hill from the other houses, the road stopped at a dead end with a small turning circle. To the right lay a single detached dwelling.

'This is it,' Des said.

As she got out of the car, Gabrielle stopped to study the house, which was much larger than the first two they'd looked at and appeared quite old. It was bordered along the front garden by a narrow stream, and they had to cross this on a little bridge made of two huge blocks of stone. There were no walls to the bridge, which felt like a continuation of the footpath.

'How lovely!' She stopped to peer down into the water. 'Are there any fish in the stream?'

'Shouldn't think so. It trickles out from the edge of the moors and probably rushes down the hill in rainy weather in a torrent. See how deeply it's cut into the ground below us. That must have taken decades.'

From the bridge they moved along a crazy-paving path to the front door, and Des opened the envelope to get the key, which was large and old-fashioned, made of wrought iron.

But Gabrielle's eyes were still on the house and she took a couple of steps back to study it again, glad that he was waiting to open the door. It was like a child's drawing, with a central door framed by a small, glassed-in porch with an inverted V of a roof in dark slate to match the house roof. There was a window on either side of the front door, and identical windows above these on the upper floor, with a smaller window between them, presumably to illuminate the stairs.

'Will you let me open the door?' She took the key Des held out and inserted it, listening in delight to the loud clunking sound as the tumblers moved in the lock. When she turned the handle and pushed open the door, bright morning sunlight flooded inside with her, revealing an old-fashioned, stone-flagged hall. It seemed lit up in a cheerful greeting.

There was a door on the left; beside it, well-worn wooden stairs led upwards. They must have been carpeted once, because the screw marks of carpet holders were still there in the bare wood.

There were two living areas at the front, one to each side. The one to the left was stiffly formal, filled with dark, old-fashioned furniture. Somehow, she didn't think many people had ever used it. The room to the right wasn't untidy, but it gave the impression that it had been well used and might become untidy at any minute.

She had the fanciful thought that if she turned quickly, she might even see the smiling, ghostly faces of people who'd been happy here in the past.

Des didn't break the silence as they went back out into the hall, and for that she was grateful. She wanted to listen to the house, its faint creaks, the sound of the wind against the panes.

At the rear was a large, old-fashioned kitchen, and to the left a door led into a dining room. Beyond the kitchen, to the right, was a narrow scullery and washhouse, rather like those her grandmother had had. A relatively modern washing machine was installed in the washhouse next to the ancient copper boiler, which needed a good polish. The sink was still what her grandmother had called a slopstone, low and square, made of stone, and there was a dusty enamel washing-up bowl standing in it beneath the rather newer taps.

'I remember Henry once telling me that Mrs King had intended to live here herself,' Des said. 'It was the last house she bought and she knew it from her girlhood, had always loved it. But she fell ill soon afterwards and didn't have time to renovate it as she'd planned. The place is very old-fashioned, but . . .' He looked sideways at her.

'But rather charming,' she finished. She went back into each room on the ground floor, then returned to the kitchen, which had a coal-burning range with stove and hotplate, as well as a gas cooker. The big wooden table was dusty but had been scrubbed white over the years – and would be again, she vowed.

'I can imagine cooking meals here, sitting at that table to eat them, with my book propped up against a bowl of fruit,' she said.

'I like to read with my meals, too. When you live alone, it keeps you company. There's a bookcase with some old books in it in the best room, did you notice?'

'No. How lovely! I'm going to need something to read.'

Upstairs were four decent-sized bedrooms, complete with old-fashioned beds. Des tried one and grimaced. 'You'll need a new mattress at the very least, if you come to live here.

She sat down beside him. 'Wow, it's like lumpy concrete.'

'Probably a flock mattress. Goodness knows how old it'll be, but out it goes. Give me springs and comfort any time. Let's look at the bathroom.'

It was large, with a claw-footed tub on a low platform at one side.

She went to look at the various fittings more closely. 'These look like original Edwardian pieces. Look at the patterns on them. They'd be worth a lot of money in an antique shop because they don't seem to be chipped or cracked, apart from a little crazing, which is only to be expected.'

'I doubt you'll want to use such big pieces. We'll get a modern suite put in if you choose this house, complete with shower.'

She looked at them regretfully. 'I agree. They're pretty and interesting, but not all that practical. That bath is so big it must take a huge amount of hot water, and I prefer showers, anyway.' She tried to turn on a tap and found it hard to move.

Des tried and managed to turn it on, but it gave out only a trickle of rusty water. He had even more trouble turning it off. 'Not good enough. The plumbing needs checking.'

'It might wear in with use.'

'I doubt it. Mr Greaves is well aware that this house and the fourth one aren't up to scratch, but we had no one coming to live here and two of the cottages in Top o' the Hill were perfectly functional, so he didn't think it worth having anything changed. Once I take over management of the trust, I may decide differently. We can't wait weeks to modernise the plumbing if someone comes to us in an emergency.'

'Does Rose have a lot of other descendants, then?'

'The more I look, the more I find. Some branches of the family seem to have had big families.'

'I'd love to find some cousins of my own age,' she said wistfully.

'I'll do my best to oblige. Now, let's check the attic before we go.'

From the back of the landing, narrower stairs led up to the roof space. This was lit by two dirty skylights and one light bulb on a long flex. This was swinging gently to and fro as a stray breeze crept in through some crevice or other. If she'd been of a nervous disposition, Gabrielle might have found that spooky, but she felt so at home in this house, so *welcome*, it didn't worry her.

There were dusty boxes in one corner, a jumble of furniture in another, and a large old-fashioned wardrobe on one side.

'One day when it's raining, I ought to come and make sure it's watertight.' Des walked round the big uneven space, studying the walls and ceiling. 'However, I didn't see any signs of stained plaster in the bedrooms, and I was looking, and there are no trails of leaks on the walls here, either.'

Gabrielle swung round to speak to him just as he stepped towards her and they bumped into one another.

He grabbed her to steady them both, then kept hold and pulled her closer for a kiss. 'In stage two of our relationship, regular kisses are obligatory,' he murmured as his lips brushed hers, then settled in for a proper kiss.

When he ended it, he studied her. 'Why are you looking so surprised?'

'That should be obvious! I wasn't expecting a kiss now. Anyway, you told me once we didn't have a relationship.'

'I lied. I didn't want to frighten you away. But after our night of mad passion, I think things might have changed just a teeny bit, don't you?'

She had to laugh at that. She loved the way his mouth twisted up slightly more at one side. He helped her see the amusing side of life in general, and their relationship in particular. 'You didn't frighten me away. And may I say that you're a very good kisser, Mr Monahan. Let's see if I can do as well.'

She pulled him back towards her and gave him another kiss, as gentle as his, and also, she hoped, as warmly arousing.

Then she stepped back, taking a deep breath to steady herself. 'Now isn't the time, tempting as this is. We have a house to choose and arrangements to make. I don't like being without a home.'

'I think we've found the house, don't you?'

'Yes. But we should still check out the fourth one, don't you think? What's it like?' She led the way downstairs to the kitchen, which she loved already, and waited near the window for his response, looking out on to the tangle of garden, itching to tidy it up.

'The fourth house is quite far out on the moors, used to be a farm, and it's seriously old. I'm not sure how old, because someone had started to modernise it, but perhaps eighteenth or even seventeenth century. I think this house is early twentieth century, probably Edwardian. I'll find out when I investigate the trust's papers.'

'Is the farm near any other houses or does it stand on its own?'

'There are no other houses in sight, not now, though there are one or two ruins across the old fields. The farmland up there was never very productive and has mostly gone back to moorland vegetation: scrub, boggy patches, tufty coarse grass and little streams. It's scruffy-looking scenery to southern eyes – comes as quite a shock at first – but as I learn more about the terrain, I'm beginning to appreciate it.'

She tried to picture the fourth house. 'I think I might feel a bit nervous if I had to live somewhere like that, absolutely on my own. Actually, I'm going to be nervous living anywhere on my own till I'm utterly certain Stu has forgotten me. I'm a real wimp where he's concerned. I could never stand up to him, however hard I tried. He was a good con artist, always had reasons for doing something his way.'

After a moment's hesitation, she confessed, 'Stu hurt me physically, you know. At the end. When I wouldn't reduce the price.'

'*What?* He beat you? Is that why you sold so cheaply?'

'Not exactly. Beating would have left marks. He proved that you can hurt someone physically without thumping them, though. He thought I gave in because of that, and I suppose I did in a way. I decided if he would do that to me, it wasn't worth waiting for more money. Since I wanted nothing further to do with him, it was the quickest way to cut the final ties.'

Des's face was flushed and his eyes were bright with anger. 'If I ever meet that sod, I'll make him regret hurting you.'

She was touched by this. 'Don't bother. He's not worth it. I know I'm free of him now. It's just . . . well . . . emotionally, I don't *feel* safe. I feel as if he might still pursue me. Isn't that stupid?'

'No. Not at all stupid. You know him quite well, so if you still feel nervous, then maybe you have reason. But you're not alone now.'

'Thank you.'

They stood smiling at one another for a few moments, then he said, 'First things first. Let's sort out a house for you, then make it safe. You've definitely chosen Brook House?'

'Is that its name?'

'Yes. Not very imaginative, is it?'

'No. But, then, it's a rather unpretentious house, don't you think? Straightforward. Cosy and homelike – not small, though not built to show off the owner's wealth. It's here to provide a home and withstand the weather.'

'I think you're right. That's settled, then.'

'Good.'

'There is one more thing.' He hesitated, but she was looking out of the window again. He hoped he was doing the right thing. He took a deep breath. This next step was so important . . .

Chapter Eleven

Stu waited till Radka had gone to work before he switched on his laptop. She'd told him first that she worked in a senior position in the accounts department of a large company, whose name was unknown outside the Czech Republic. Now, she said she was a partner, hinting that it was in something quite big.

She certainly lived in luxury, seemed to be able to take any time off she wanted, and she travelled regularly to other countries, which was how he'd met her. Was she telling the truth now? He shook his head. He didn't feel sure about anything she said.

First things first. He had to look into his ex's situation.

He let out a yell of triumph as he got into Gabi's online bank account easily, using her password. As he studied the amounts in the various sections of the account, he whistled softly at the totals. He hadn't expected her to be able to stash away so much of the sale money. She couldn't have had any debts at all to pay off.

The bitch must be living on the smell of an oily rag. Or else she'd found some guy to subsidise her.

That was easier for women than for men. Then it

occurred to him that he was in the same situation at the moment – a kept man. Radka let him stay in her flat in Prague, which saved him a good deal of money, but she only fed him when they went out to restaurants.

She was on to all the scams, had made an arrangement with a hotel to send regular bills to his company for his room. By the time the hotel took a cut, and then she did, Stu only got about half the amount. It helped, but it wasn't enough to do something worthwhile with.

He stared across the room at a locked door. She didn't let him into that room or even tell him what was in it, and she never opened it while he was around. He didn't feel it'd be wise to try to pick the old-fashioned lock, a skill he'd learnt as a youth, because he had no doubt there would be an electronic security system inside. She might even have a security camera recording what he did every day in the rest of the flat. Who knew with Radka?

He didn't take any money out of Gabi's account this time, not till he'd worked out somewhere safe to put it. If she checked the online log, she'd notice that someone else had been there, but she wasn't as tech-savvy as he was, for all she knew how to use the computer system at her work.

He'd wait until a certain friend of his was back in the UK and then get Carson to do the job of emptying her account for him. He'd make sure he was in Prague himself at the time and that he never went online that day, or at least not from his own computer.

It'd be worth paying a percentage of the account's contents to Carson to get that much money. Everyone took their cut when they did you a favour. It was how the world functioned.

Smiling, he logged off and got ready to leave for the UK the next day. When Radka got home, she'd just shrug about him leaving, in that annoying way she had.

If she hadn't been so eager in bed, he'd have been worrying about how she really felt about him. But she was eager. Very. She said he satisfied her as few other men had ever done.

Well, most of the time. It had only been once that he'd failed. How stupid of him to care about whether Gabi was injured or not. He couldn't afford to get soft. He still had to make that big chunk of permanent money he dreamt of.

When Radka came home, he danced attendance on her, as usual.

'I want you to put some bugs in the cars belonging to these people from your company and another group,' she announced, giving him a list of car numbers and locations. 'We find it useful to keep an eye on them. Just activate the bugs and slap them on the cars, out of sight, underneath the wheel rim. Then check that they're working. I'll download an app to your smart phone and show you how to use it.'

'Why the hell do you want to bug people's cars?'

'It is not of concern to you. Just do it. My friends and I live securely because we do favours for one another. You will join in by doing this. There are a couple of spare bugs. Throw them away after you've checked that the others are working properly.'

'But—'

'No buts. Just do it. Now, come to bed, you naughty boy. I need your body.'

She wasn't even going to tell him why he was planting the bugs, he thought, irritated by that. Still, it'd be easy enough to do.

He followed her into the bedroom. He wanted to stay annoyed with her, but she quickly made that impossible.

The following morning, Stu got out of the plane at Heathrow feeling stiff and grumpy. It might be a short flight, but the seats were cramped. He was too tall for economy class, but the damned company had started economising at the expense of their staff's comfort. Only the most senior executives now rated business class. As he wasn't flush with money, he'd decided not to pay the difference this time.

He asked to hire the cheapest car he could find, pleased when they couldn't supply one of that type and let him have the next size up for the same price. It was an omen, he was sure: a sign that he was entering another of those lucky patches in his life. But this time he'd not fritter away his money.

He decided to drive down to Wiltshire that afternoon to check up on Gabi. Before he made the snatch for her money, he needed to find out what she was doing with herself and feed that into the plan. He might be intending to organise something unlawful, but he'd be very careful how he did it. Oh, yes.

The journey to Worton seemed to take ages and he was feeling tired, thanks to Radka's demands the previous night. It'd be good to have a couple of rest days from her. She'd started ordering him around in bed, which was a big turn-off.

He stopped at a motorway service station and ordered a coffee to go because he hated sitting in such seedy places.

When he got to the village, he parked in a quiet spot just out of the centre. No one would recognise the car, but they might recognise him, so he pulled a hat over his betraying blonde hair and wound a scarf round his neck, even though it wasn't a cold day.

He'd bet Gabi was staying with her friend Tania, so he tried there first. When he peeped over the back wall of the big old house that had been subdivided into flats, he saw Gabi's car.

'Yesss!' He made a triumphant fist. *Spot on with your guessing, Stu*, he congratulated himself. His luck was definitely returning. Oh, yes.

He stayed where he was in the garden of the derelict house next to the flats, watching the windows carefully, especially Tania's on the ground floor. But there was no sign of life.

To make sure, he went and rang the doorbells of the four units, one by one, waiting each time for an answer, and ringing a second time before he moved on to the next bell. But there was no response from any of the flats.

Just to make certain Gabi was at work, he phoned the store and asked to speak to her, pretending to be a cousin from Australia.

'I'm afraid Ms Newman no longer works here,' the girl on the phone said.

Now, the bitch had surprised him. 'Oh dear. Do you know where Gabi's gone? I'm not going to be in England for long and I'd love to catch up with her.'

'Sorry, sir, we can't give out information like that.'

'But I'm going back to Australia next week.'

'Even if I knew where she was, I wouldn't be able to tell you,' she repeated. 'Perhaps her former neighbours know.'

Well, well. Had they given Gabi the sack or had she resigned? Either way, it didn't sound as if they knew where she was. Where could she have gone? Had she transferred to another job in the company or had something else cropped up? Whatever it was, her car was still in the village, so she'd be coming back at some point to collect it.

He got a clipboard out of his car and walked briskly round to the rear of the building, holding a pen, as if he had a reason to be there.

He tried the doors, but she'd locked the car. She was careful like that. And she'd taken her car key back from him. Stupid of him to let her do that without making a copy.

He grinned as an idea suddenly struck him. Good old Radka! She'd supplied him with exactly what he needed.

He bent down as if to tie his shoelace, activated the tiny electronic bug and slapped it firmly into place under the wheel arch.

Smiling, he went out of the back gate and returned to his car. He checked the app on his smart phone and set it to tell only him where his ex was, with a separate password to get the information.

Got you, you stupid bitch! he thought. *I'll know where you are at all times from now on.* Another thing going right for him. Once he found out where she was, it'd be fun planning how to upset her all over again.

He hated to think how much money she'd kept from the house. OK, she'd put more into it than him in the first place, but she was a nonentity, a plodder, who didn't *deserve* to be so comfortable.

Next thing was to go and see Mrs Starkey, their former neighbour. She had a soft spot for him. She'd probably know where Gabi had gone, and if he took the old lady some flowers and soft-soaped her, she'd soon tell him.

When he rapped on the door, it took a long time for her to answer, but he was used to this. She tottered along like an elderly crab – looked like one, too.

She smiled when she saw him. 'Naughty boy! You haven't been to see me in a long time.'

'I've been out of the country. Do you still make a good cup of tea?'

'Yes, of course. Come in, Stu dear.' She held the door wider and led the way to her conservatory at the rear. It was stiflingly hot, as usual, but he ignored that.

'I'll put the kettle on, shall I, Mrs Starkey?'

'I miss you and your blarney,' she said when he came back. 'I hear they're going to tear that house of yours down and put two others in its place. Did you know?'

'I haven't a clue what they're going to do with it. Gabi might know.'

'She's gone off with her new fellow. You let a good woman go there, Stu.'

That sort of explained why her car was at Tania's. He summoned up a convincing lie. 'She *is* a good woman, but, sadly, we weren't suited. I do need to contact her quite urgently, though, because something's cropped up. Have you any idea where they've gone? What's her new guy's name, by the way?'

The old woman shook her head. 'I've not got the faintest idea. When she found out that all her things had been stolen, she went down to the B and B for a night or two, then she went off with that man. He's not half as good-looking as you.'

'All her things had been stolen? What do you mean?' He hid his impatience as he listened to the tale. 'But her car's still at her friend's, so she must be coming back.'

'I expect so. If so, she might come to see me and I'll tell her you're looking for her.'

'Thanks. You're a honey.'

He sat and chatted for a tedious ten minutes longer, but got nothing more out of her, so took his leave.

'Any time you're in Worton, come and have a cup of tea with me,' she said at the door.

'I'll definitely do that.' He nerved himself to kiss her on the cheek. Ugh, he hated the feel of that papery old skin on his lips, but sometimes you had to do things that disgusted you.

He went round to the flats at the time Tania usually got home and waited for her in the car park. But she only gave him the frozen basilisk stare and refused to let him in to talk things over. She wouldn't even stay outside with him, either, and took advantage of another tenant's return home to go into the building with him.

Fat bitch! he thought as he drove off. She was cracking

on the weight. Who'd want to bed a sow like that?

After one more check that the bug on Gabi's car was working properly, he drove back to London and returned the hire car. When he went into his tiny serviced flat, he looked round in disgust. He was worth better than this claustrophobic hovel.

His only hope now for a better life – the life he was meant for – was Radka, even if working with her meant taking a few risks. But he might give Lady Luck a whirl one night after he got back – if it felt right, of course. After all, Prague had several casinos.

In the meantime, he had to go and make nice to his boss tomorrow. Damn Patrick! What did he want this time that couldn't have been said over the phone?

Des waited until Gabrielle had turned away from the window to ask his important question. 'What you said about Stu has made me wonder if you'd like me to move in with you? Will that make you feel safer?'

'Is that the only reason you'd move in?'

She was back in cautious mode, he could tell. Oh, she'd been badly hurt, his little love had. Was that just down to Stu, or had there been something go wrong before him? Once or twice she'd cut herself off from talking about her life prior to her marriage and changed the subject. He gave her a quick hug. 'No, of course it's not the only reason, Gabrielle. Surely you realise that? I've been trying not to rush you, that's all.'

'I think I'd rather be rushed.'

'Very well, then. I'd really like us to have a go at living

together. We get on well, in bed and out of it, and not just because we're both early risers.' That remark by the woman serving breakfast had quickly become a joke between them. 'I was going to get round quite soon to suggesting we live together, believe me.'

'You're a cautious man.'

'Takes one to know one. Then, of course, I realised that living with you would save me paying hotel bills, so I jumped in and asked you.'

She choked with laughter. 'You've done it again.'

'What?'

'Made me chuckle, defused the tension. You're very good for me, Des.'

'I hope so.' He put one arm round her shoulders and they stood for a few moments by the window, not needing to fill every second with words. He liked that about her. He liked so many things about Gabrielle.

When they pulled apart, she said, 'So that's settled. We'll move in together. Have we time for another look round this house? I need to check out what's needed to set up a home.'

'Sure. I don't think it's been lived in for a few years, but it ought to have all the basics, at least – even sheets and towels. Apparently, Mrs King bought the old place very cheaply, furniture and all. As they say in the house adverts, it's a fixer-upper.'

'If it were mine, I'd enjoy doing that. It has a nice, homey feel.'

'I'm sure the trust would pay for paint or for jobs to be done, if you want to make any small changes. It's to our advantage to keep the place in good order, after all.'

'I'd love to do a bit of refurbishing. It'll give me something to do till I can find a job.'

'Don't rush into hunting for work, Gabrielle. You look as if you desperately need some R and R. And you do get a stipend, remember.'

She grimaced. 'I have a mirror, so I know I'm not looking my best. I'm amazed you even noticed me. Actually, I feel convalescent – that's the best word to describe it. A lot of the strain has gone, now that the divorce is over and done with, but it took its toll. And then to be robbed . . .'

'Well, we'll do things at a more reasonable pace now. You'll need a new bathroom. I reckon, before we arrange for one to be fitted, we should find out if the present bathroom suite is worth something as an antique, as you thought. No use throwing away the trust's assets. I'd never have thought of it being valuable.'

'I may be wrong.'

He shook his head. 'I don't think you are. I watch those TV antiques programmes occasionally, and it sounds quite likely now you've pointed it out. I don't know why I didn't think of it myself. They sell the strangest items for ridiculous prices – things I'd call junk. Anyway, I know just the place to check about the bathroom suite.'

'Oh?'

'There's a wonderful antiques centre near Littleborough. I know the owners. You'll like Emily and Chad. We'll go there first of all, because changing the bathroom comes high on my list for making the home more comfortable. That and a new bed.'

He pretended to leer at her, making her chuckle again, but he could tell that all the teasing in the world couldn't quite dispel her sense of apprehension about Stu. He never ignored such signs, especially when the person seemed intelligent. Someone's life might depend on paying heed to details. No, that was fanciful. If Stu wanted anything, it'd be her money. He didn't seem like the sort of man who'd kill his ex, not when he already had a new woman.

But Stu hadn't hesitated to hurt her, had he? Well, the sod would have to walk through Des to do that again.

His stomach rumbled and he glanced at his watch. 'We should leave now, Gabrielle. We have an appointment with Henry and we need to stop for lunch on the way.'

'All right. We can't leave the hungry tiger unfed.'

He tried to put on a pitiful expression, but was laughing too much to maintain it for long.

As they left, she turned to look back at the house. 'Could we move in tomorrow, do you think?'

'I doubt it. There won't be any electricity switched on, and certainly no telephone. And what about the bathroom?'

He saw the disappointment on her face. 'Do you really want to camp out here? I don't mind moving in without a new bathroom, but I'd rather wait till we've made the place more secure and have electricity.'

'I suppose you're right. I know it's foolish but I've fallen in love with the house. How soon do you think we can get the electricity turned on?'

'I don't know. I'll do my best to hurry them up. But we'll also need to make the doors more secure. That big key may seem cute, but such locks are incredibly easy to pick.'

'Oh dear. What a pity! The big clunking sound made me feel safe.'

'I'm a very safety-conscious guy. We'll get good locks fitted *and* we'll continue to keep an eye out for your ex.'

Des frowned as he walked across the little bridge. He was still trying to work out why he too felt she hadn't seen the last of Stu Dixon. He wasn't usually prone to presentiments, but, then, it wasn't like him to fall in love so quickly, either.

Not that he was complaining about that. He hadn't dared say the three magic words to her yet, but they kept hovering on the tip of his tongue. *One day soon I'll do it,* he promised himself. *I'll tell her I love her, and if I'm really lucky, she'll say the words back to me.*

'Before we go, let me check whether there's mobile coverage out here.' He pulled out his phone and switched it on, nodding. 'Oh, good. Bit of luck, that. It's not the fastest but it's OK.'

'Another good thing about Brook House.'

'Yes. Come on now. I'm hungry.'

He ate a hearty meal but Gabrielle left half her food again. Judging by her clothes, she'd lost quite a bit of weight recently. And she wasn't the sort to feel it necessary to look like a stick insect. He didn't comment, trying instead to tease her into sharing some of his dessert. He was pleased about every extra mouthful he got her to eat.

He found himself humming as they drove to Mr Greaves'

rooms. It had been a while since he'd felt so happy.

What he'd been for a year or two – and had only just admitted to himself – was lonely.

The lawyer greeted them with a smile. 'You look more rested today, Ms Newman.'

'Do call me Gabrielle.'

'Thank you.' Mr Greaves inclined his head but didn't return the compliment. 'Please take a seat and we'll discuss the practicalities of your situation. Des? You'll stay?'

'Yes. For two reasons. One, because I'd like to accept formally the job you offered me managing the trust, and two, because Gabrielle and I are "together" as they call it nowadays, so what affects her, affects me.'

'Oh! I see.'

She felt Mr Greaves wasn't best pleased with this.

'Something wrong with that?' Des challenged.

'I'm happy that you've accepted the job, but is it wise to mix business and pleasure?'

'I don't think you get much choice about who you like and don't like,' Gabrielle put in.

Des nodded agreement. 'And, in this case, I think it's particularly useful that I'll be with her, because Gabrielle still worries that her ex will come after her, and I don't discount the possibility. I'll be able to keep an eye on her professionally as well as enjoying her company.'

The lawyer looked puzzled. 'Why would your ex-husband do that, Gabrielle? You're divorced now, and I think you said yesterday that you no longer have any financial links.'

'No, I don't. But I do have a considerable sum of money

from the sale of the house, enough for a generous deposit on another house. Stu can't even think of money without itching to spend it, or, more often, gamble it away. When he runs out of his own money, he goes after other people's.'

'Is he as bad as that?'

'Yes. He pinched money from my purse regularly till I realised what he was doing and kept a better eye on it.'

The lawyer shook his head and made a *tsk-tsk* sound. 'Shocking. Very well. Perhaps it is fortuitous that you and Des are together. And the house you've chosen?'

'Brook House.'

He nodded. 'My own favourite. It's a nice little place.'

'Needs some upgrading,' Des said. 'We can do a few of the decorating jobs while we're there, but the bathroom needs complete modernisation. There is money in the trust for renovations. I think Mrs King thought of everything.'

'She was very thorough – even made a list of what might need doing in each house, and that bathroom is on it.'

'Gabrielle thinks the old bathroom suite might have value as an antique, so we'll go and ask Chad about that tomorrow. We don't want to throw it away or take it out carelessly if it'll bring in money.'

'Certainly not.' Mr Greaves looked at Gabrielle. 'There is the question of money for you – a living allowance.'

'I think I should pay my share of the household bills,' Des put in quickly. 'We'll get Mrs H to OK my figures about that, shall we? I can't OK my own payments, after all.'

Mr Greaves' expression lightened a little. 'Good idea. We'll pay you the same stipend as we were paying Libby, my dear. That should cover your living costs nicely. Just one more thing. Do you have a car?'

'Yes, but I'll have to go back to Worton to fetch it. Des drove me here in his.'

Des intervened again. 'I can get a friend of mine to collect it, check it for bugs and then bring it up here.'

'Bugs?' The lawyer looked rather surprised. 'Is it . . . very old? If it's infested with insects, you should get rid of it.'

'Electronic bugging devices, designed to track Gabrielle.'

She was horrified. 'Do you think Stu will do that? Why would he? He's in Prague and he won't know where to find the car, even if he comes back.'

'Does he know who your best friend is and where she lives?'

'Oh. I see. Yes, of course he does, and anyone can get to the car during the day, because everyone in the building is usually out at work. I wasn't thinking straight or I'd have left it somewhere safer.'

'Don't get your knickers in a twist. My friend will check it out before he brings it here,' Des said.

She turned to him. 'I'm annoyed because I should have been more careful. I'm not a child, and I shouldn't need looking after.'

The two men exchanged glances and she realised how sharply she'd spoken. 'Sorry. It's just that I promised myself not to be dependent on other people once I was free of Stu.'

Mr Greaves surprised her by saying, 'We're all dependent on others, to some extent, my dear. I don't know what I'd do without Mrs H here and my wife at home. Now, let's go on to the other things.'

She frowned. 'What other things?'

'Mrs King's bequests. She's left a box for each person – well, for the first half-dozen relatives to take up her offer, anyway. The contents of the box are to be used or disposed of as you please. For Libby, she left the ornaments she had in her little house. They proved to be quite valuable. You get the contents of quite a large cardboard box.'

'What does it contain?'

He shrugged. 'I don't know what's in any of the boxes. Mrs King said they were not to be touched by anyone else. Mrs H will hand the box over to you as you go out. And if you'll let her have your bank account details, Gabrielle, she'll see that your stipend is paid into it every month.'

'How kind of Cousin Rose!'

'Yes. She was kind. Very kind indeed. Quite my favourite client.' He glanced at the clock on the mantelpiece. 'And now, I'm afraid, I must let you go. I'm expecting another client shortly. Des will show you round town and help you settle in, I'm sure, given the – er, circumstances.'

As they walked out, Mrs H looked up from her huge, comfortable desk. 'Ah, Ms Newman. Could you let me have the details of your bank account?'

'I'm changing my bank account, so I'll give you the details when that's sorted. It's high on my list of things to do tomorrow. My ex knows all the details of the old bank account, you see. Well, apart from the password. And I really must get a new computer.'

'Good idea to change your bank account. One can't be too careful with money. You'll pop back and let me know as soon as you have the details?'

'Yes, of course. Tomorrow.'

'And we'll collect the box at the same time,' Des added. 'All right to leave it here?'

'Yes, of course. I won't put it back in the cellar. I'll get the caretaker to help me shove it into our suite's store room.'

When they went outside, the sun was shining.

'I think that went well, don't you?' Gabrielle said to Des.

'Yes, it did. I'll put a new computer on the list of things you need. They're not expensive these days.'

She gave his hand a quick squeeze. 'I'm so lucky, to have found a home and you so quickly.'

He smiled. 'We're both lucky. Now, we've got the evening to ourselves. I know a good Chinese restaurant. Let's abandon practicalities and get ready for a meal and a couple of drinks. I'm famished.'

'You would be.' Greatly daring, she added, 'And when we go back to the hotel, I'll have my wicked way with you. If you're not too full up to move, that is.'

He nodded approvingly. 'Sounds like a reasonable plan. I like the way you think, Ms Newman. Very practical.'

She pretended to hit him. 'Is that all you can say?'

'No. But we'll wait till later on for some of the other things I want to tell you.'

The hungry way he was looking at her made her breath catch in her throat. He might be a quiet sort of man, but it was clear that still waters ran deep.

She hadn't expected to meet someone else so quickly.

Surely nothing would go wrong with a man like this? She found herself studying him sometimes, glad to see how fit he looked, how his skin had a healthy colour to it. She liked the steady gaze that met hers squarely, the way he didn't scan the room for more useful people to talk to, but gave her his full attention.

She felt Des wanted to be with her and didn't care too much about what was going on around them. That made her feel good.

Chapter Twelve

Stu strolled into the company's building, watching others rush to the lifts or stairs to get to their desks before the heads of each section came to work. It was rather like going to jail, he decided, coming back here. His footsteps faltered for a moment before he brushed the shadow away.

You had to earn a living, so he followed the herd and made his way to Patrick's office. He'd deliberately come in early, knowing his boss wouldn't be in yet, wanting to be there first. *Eager beaver, moi!* he thought and sniggered.

Then he saw that the PA bitch was already at her desk. Bronwyn by name, Brunhilde the Valkyrie by nature. She stared down her nose at him, so he smiled as if she were a dear friend. He always smiled but he'd never yet got her to smile back.

Patrick came in shortly afterwards, stopped at the sight of Stu, as if he'd forgotten Stu was coming in today, then sighed and said, 'You'd better come into my office, Dixon. Bronwyn, please join us.'

Stu shot a quick glance at her. Was it his imagination or was she looking extra smug this morning?

She took a seat to one side and Patrick gestured to a

chair. 'Sit down, Dixon. This won't take long.' He waited till Stu was settled to say, 'We've been reviewing our staffing levels and they're still too high.'

Stu held his breath. Surely this didn't mean . . . they couldn't!

'I'm afraid we're going to have to let you go, Dixon. Analysis has shown that we have too many people at your level.'

It was out before he could prevent it. 'But I've done well for the company in Prague, dammit! And before.'

'Yes, you have. And therefore we'll be giving you an extra month's salary in your severance package as a bonus, and a really good reference. You're not the only one going, but you're the only one with the extra bonus.'

Stu held in his anger.

The bitch was actually smiling at him now, from where Patrick couldn't see her.

'When do I finish?' he managed.

'Straight away.'

'But I've got a lot of my things still in Prague. You collect possessions when you're posted somewhere for a long time.'

'Hmm. Well, we'd better spring for another fare there and back. See to that, Bronwyn.' He looked back at Stu. 'Now, I'm afraid I'll have to send for Security and ask you to clear your locker and leave the building immediately thereafter. Nothing personal, just standard procedure. Please don't try to return. The reference and any other documentation necessary will be sent to your home address. Good luck.'

He had the gall to come round the desk and hold out his hand.

Stu shook it but couldn't summon up any snappy farewell remark and certainly not a smile.

Fuming, he waited in the outer office, turning his head away from the bitch's desk until Security sent up two men. What the hell did they think he was going to do, tear the place apart?

Grimly he checked and packed the things from his locker. His desk had been cleared when he went to Prague so that the office could be used by someone else, and the contents of that were in boxes. He took his time confirming that everything was there, after which the security men helped him carry the boxes out of the building and load them into a taxi.

They turned away without a word of farewell, and that was that.

Stu looked back at the tower block as he was driven away. Damned egg crate of a building. It looked as soulless as the people inside it.

He understood now why people planted bombs.

What the hell was he going to do? Jobs at his level weren't plentiful and this wasn't a boom time.

And he had debts still.

'Penny for them,' Des said next morning when Gabrielle sat staring into space instead of finishing her breakfast.

She pushed her plate with its half-eaten toast to one side. 'I was just wondering which bank I should move my account to. Or even whether I should move it. There are safeguards on people's accounts, after all, so am I wasting my time changing?'

'You should definitely move it, and the sooner the better. As for which bank, well, that's up to you. I agree: if it weren't for Stu, you wouldn't need to bother. But you said he'd stolen from you before, so better safe than sorry. After all, someone did steal your laptop.'

She could feel herself blushing. 'I forgot how much information is on it. Passwords and such. It's so hard to remember them all.'

He pushed her plate back in front of her. 'You should finish your breakfast. We've got a busy day ahead of us visiting banks and I don't want you fainting on me.'

'What? Oh, hadn't I finished? Just to reassure you, though, I'm not the fainting sort.' She began nibbling the piece of toast again without looking at it. 'I suppose you're right about changing my bank, but why the hurry? I don't think Stu is a *criminal*. He wouldn't steal money from a bank. He knows I'd call in the police.'

'He might think he could charm you into not prosecuting him for what he took.'

She considered this, head on one side. 'I suppose you could be right. He might think that. But he'd be wrong. Only, every time I admit to myself that he's not a good person, I feel more stupid than ever. I thought I'd fallen in love with him, so I married him, let him order me around, and it took me months to realise what he was really like.'

'Stop saying you're stupid. You're not. You're honest and decent, with a clear-thinking brain. It's hard for many people to admit they've made a mistake in their marriage. Some never do and put up with the situation all their lives. I married the wrong person, too, remember, so I know how easily it's done, how appearances can deceive, how life goals can change.'

'Your ex didn't steal everything you owned, on top of the settlement.'

'We don't have proof that Stu arranged the burglary.'

'No, but I'm sure he did. I still haven't figured out how he's disposed of my things. He's not very practical about details and that robbery just wasn't his usual style, except . . .' Her voice trailed away.

Des waited.

'Stu did have mood swings, ups and downs, and then he wasn't always rational.' 'Bipolar, do you mean?'

'Not that bad, no. But I looked it up once on the internet and you can have a milder version of it. There's even a name for it, but I can't remember what it is.'

'Did he admit he had that problem?'

'Definitely not. He'd have denied it with his dying breath. I didn't even mention it to him, because he'd have gone mad at me. He could be fun in the upbeat moods, but he was hard going when he felt aggrieved at the world. Sometimes he talked about getting his own back on people he believed had treated him badly. I thought it was just a lot of hot air because he never boasted of having done anything specific to anyone.'

'Do you think he has a grievance against you?'

'I can't think why he would have.' She stared out of the window again. 'What are we talking about Stu for? Let's go into town and the first bank we see will be the one I transfer my account to. I'll get it over and done with today.'

'You might look at the terms the banks are offering first.'

'I'm not being very practical, am I? Strange. I'm usually very careful with money. Now, well, it seems less important than getting my life together.'

'I think you're in recovery mode from a stressful time, and you aren't your usual self.'

'I don't feel I know what my usual self is any more.' She straightened up. 'Enough of this introspection. I'm going to focus on being more cheerful from now on. Which won't be hard with you around, Des.'

'What a lovely compliment! For that, I'll take you to the antiques centre after we've done the banking and you've signed up for electricity to be switched on. You'll love the centre.'

He was glad to see her brighten up still further at that prospect. He was particularly happy to see her coming out of her lethargy.

'We also have to call in at the lawyer's to give them my new bank account details. Oh, and what about the box we're supposed to collect?'

'I think it can sit there for another day or two, don't you? Till we move into our new home, in fact. Or are you desperate to open it?'

'I'll be interested to see what's inside it, but such a big box would be in the way in our hotel room, and I'm more interested in getting a home again, even if it's only for a few months.'

'OK. Before we set off, I'll just ring my friend Leon and ask him if he can pick up your car and send it to us.'

'Won't he want paying for doing that?'

'He owes me a favour. He'll probably use the car

instead of paying a fare for one of his employees to go somewhere. He sends people all over the place on jobs. We might have to wait a day or two to get the car, though. Do you mind that?'

She shook her head. 'Not as long as you're here to drive me around.'

'Good. I'll ring him while you're getting ready. I have something else to discuss with him, about a client, so you won't mind if I make this a private call?'

'No, of course not. In your job, you must have to keep information confidential most of the time.'

While she was getting ready, he walked outside and rang his friend from the hotel car park. Leon ran a little-known government security service which took care of minor 'clearing-up' jobs, as Leon described it. One of the things they did quite often was help people to disappear from dangerous situations and lives. Des had done a couple of minor jobs for Leon, and done them well, if he said so himself.

Rapidly, he outlined Gabrielle's situation and explained that he had a feeling something funny was going on with her ex. When he mentioned the name of the company Stu was dealing with in Prague, there was a quick intake of breath from the other end.

'Are you looking into their activities as well, Leon?'

'You know I can't discuss specifics. Let's just say you and I may have interests in common. For your ears only, we did hear there was a new player being groomed, but we weren't sure who it was. We'll check out this guy Stu, in case it's him. You don't happen to know who his new lady friend is, do you?'

'Just a minute. There's someone here who might.' Des looked across at the car and saw Gabrielle waiting for him, her face raised to the sun. He strode across to her. 'Did you ever hear the name of Stu's new lady friend?'

'Radka. But I don't know her surname, I'm afraid.'

'That'll help. Nearly finished my call. Sorry to keep you waiting.' He fumbled his car keys out of his pocket and gave them to her. 'You might as well wait in comfort.'

He walked back to the secluded corner of the car park and resumed his conversation with Leon. 'She thinks the woman is called Radka.'

'Ah.'

'You know of her?'

'We know it's one of several aliases for a rather clever woman. We call her the Black Widow, because she uses men and tosses them aside, just like that female spider who eats her mates. We're working with Interpol on this, but no one has pinned anything on Radka yet. We're not even sure what she looks like. We had one sighting, but the operative couldn't take a photo. Anyway, you know how women can change their appearance. No one ever saw a female of that description again. She must have found out she was being watched.'

Des waited, but Leon didn't volunteer any more information. 'So you can get the car to us?'

'Yes, of course. Mind if we use it for a delivery en route?'

'Feel free.' He shut down his mobile and stowed it in his pocket, then rejoined Gabrielle. 'Ready to go?'

'Are they bringing my car?'

'Yes. In a couple of days. No charge.'

'Wow. Do you cause miracles often?'

'It's not a miracle. I have a lot of acquaintances because I meet new people all the time in my work.'

She wasn't sure she liked the idea of that, because it was how Stu had operated. Contacts. No, Des wasn't at all like Stu and he called people like this Leon 'friends'. What was she thinking of to compare Des to Stu?

The banking changes took a full hour to put in place. Luckily, Gabrielle had her driving licence and passport handy. She was grateful to whatever good angel had made her sling them into her handbag rather than packing them in one of the boxes. She smiled. People teased her about how big her handbag was and how much stuff she could pull out of it, but it had worked brilliantly for her during these troubles.

After that, she and Des went down the street and he signed in the name of the trust for the electricity to be reconnected. They were promised that 'within three to five working days'.

As the woman at the counter turned away, Des whispered to Gabrielle, 'Cry pitifully.'

After one startled glance, she began to sob.

'This poor woman is homeless and she's not got the money for hotels,' he told the clerk.

'It's all right. I'll camp out there. The water's on, at least.' Gabrielle dragged out a tissue since she hadn't been able to produce tears on demand, and hid behind it.

'Isn't there any way you can help her?' Des pleaded. 'My trust has provided a home, but we can't switch on the electricity.'

'Oh dear. You poor thing. I'll see if we can fit in an emergency reconnect.' The woman picked up the phone, explaining, nodding and listening.

Gabrielle emerged from the tissue and made a play of wiping her eyes and blowing her nose. 'Sorry.'

The woman put down the phone. 'You're in luck. Pete doesn't mind getting in some extra overtime, but he can only fit you in early. Really early. Can you be there to let him in at seven o'clock tomorrow morning? On the dot.'

'I can be there at any time if it'll get the electricity switched on.' Gabrielle gave her eyes a final wipe, amazed that she had been convincing.

'It's very kind of you,' Des put in. 'We're grateful.'

'We do our best for our customers. But Pete will have to check that everything's working safely in the house. Our records show it's been a few years since the electricity was connected. Has the house stood empty all that time?'

'I'm afraid so,' Des said glibly. 'It belonged to an old lady and has been left as a trust for homeless young women.'

When they got outside, Gabrielle pretended to punch his arm. 'You sneaky devil!'

He smirked. 'Part of my job description, being sneaky. And you caught on quickly about why I wanted you to cry, so you're pretty sneaky yourself. You're not complaining, surely? Your fake sobs will get us the electricity far sooner.'

'It's a good thing we're early risers. You'd better ask the people at the hotel to leave us a simple breakfast outside our room.'

'And later we'll go out for a hearty lunch.'

'You think with your stomach, Des Monahan. You're lucky you don't put on weight.'

'I have excellent genes. All of them.'

He waggled his eyebrows like Groucho Marc pretending to be sexy, and made her laugh again.

'Come on. We'll go to the antiques centre now.'

He drove out of town, through Littleborough and up towards the moors, waving towards a pub on the left near the foot of the slope. 'We'll have a late lunch there afterwards. They serve food all day. If it wasn't for that chocolate bar you had in your handbag, I'd be fainting from hunger by now.'

'I'm going to nickname you Piglington.'

'Whatever you like as long as you stay with me.' He slowed down behind a heavy lorry and gestured up the slope towards the right. 'That's the centre.'

It wasn't a building so much as a collection of buildings and outhouses, a sprawling complex whose various architectural styles were united by house walls rendered and painted white, and dark slate roofs at different levels. A big sign at the entrance to the car park said CHADDERLEY ANTIQUES.

As they entered the centre, Gabrielle stopped for a moment to stare round the spacious room at the gleaming displays of items, some under glass, some lit up by spotlights, all of them immaculately clean.

It felt welcoming, as if she was supposed to come here. She blinked in surprise. What a strange thought!

A woman came towards them. 'Can I help you – Oh, Des, it's you! Were we supposed to know you were in the area?'

'No. I'd meant to warn you, but we've been so busy I didn't get round to it. I didn't think you'd mind us popping in. Gabrielle, this is Emily and—' He turned towards the sound of footsteps. 'And this is Chad. These two are the owners of this tumbledown old shack.'

Emily chuckled and moved to shake hands.

'Your showroom is gorgeous,' Gabrielle said. 'I've never seen antiques so beautifully displayed. This is quite an old building, isn't it?'

'One part of it dates to the seventeenth century, we think, but there are additions from every century. We still have some buildings at the back to renovate, but we haven't decided what to do with them yet.'

After shaking hands, Chad turned as footsteps echoed their way across the spacious sales area and a young man joined them.

The newcomer had Down Syndrome. Indeed, he seemed very confident, utterly at home here.

'This is Toby, who lives in one of our three special units. He helps out in the centre and he's a demon at finding treasures at flea markets.'

The young man beamed at Emily as she said that, then came to stand in front of Gabrielle. After studying her solemnly, he bobbed his head as if in approval. 'The Lady told me you were coming to see us, Gabrielle. She said be careful. A bad man is coming. Very bad. But you have good friends. They'll help you.'

'Toby senses things sometimes,' Chad said quietly. 'And it doesn't do to dismiss what he says, however cynical you are about psychic phenomena.' He looked at Gabrielle.

'If you ever need help, as he clearly thinks you will, don't hesitate to come to us.'

She nodded. 'I will. Thank you for telling me to be careful, Toby.'

The young man nodded, turned to Emily and said in quite a different tone of voice, 'Mrs Lawford has some new stock. It's pretty. Ashley is washing it.'

He turned and went away.

'Ashley's another of our special needs people,' Emily said. 'We have three of them. They're all at the higher end of ability and capable of living independently with a little help and supervision.'

But Chad was watching their visitors. 'Is something wrong, Gabrielle?'

'How did Toby know my name? He wasn't here when Des was introducing me.'

'He sometimes surprises us like that.' Emily hesitated, then said, 'We have a resident ghost, who seems to communicate with Toby more than anyone else. Don't worry if you don't believe in ghosts; it's not obligatory. But he's never wrong when he passes on messages from the Lady.'

'I'm not sure whether I believe in ghosts or not. One of my friends claims to see them. I never have. I don't know whether I'd be scared or fascinated if I did see one.'

Des surprised her. 'I believe in them and I've sensed them a few times. It's the Irish in me. My grandmother was fey. But this is an unusual place, and if there are ghosts anywhere, they'd be here, don't you think? But they'd be good ghosts, I'm sure. The centre has such a warm, feel-good atmosphere.'

Which gave her a lot to think about, because she had felt that warmth quite strongly. She let Des explain why they were here today.

'Sounds interesting. I'll come and look at your bathroom suite,' Chad said. 'If it's in as good a condition as you say, then it would be worth enough money to rescue it carefully.'

'How much approximately?' Des asked.

'Anything from a few hundred to two or three thousand pounds, depending on condition and rarity.'

'That much?'

'Yes. But it'd better be taken out carefully. I have a woman who does that sort of job for me. She's a good plumber, too, so she might put in the new bathroom for you while she's at it. I'll drop in at Brook House later this afternoon to check the suite, if that's OK with you – around six? Emily and I are going out for a meal this evening with some friends, and it's not too far out of our way to come to you first.'

Des looked at him thoughtfully. 'Your rapid response probably means you know someone who's looking for a genuine antique suite.'

'Guilty as charged. I'm doing a lot more work online and taking commissions via the internet since I've moved up to Lancashire. The suite would be for a fellow in Edinburgh, who's setting up a family museum on his estate.'

He glanced towards the window. 'I've just seen a car pull in and it looks like – yes, it's the Torbins, my next appointment. Why don't you take a look round the centre while you're here?'

'Then come back and have a coffee with me,' Emily added. 'You can bring me up to date on what you're doing up north again, Des. Did you decide to accept the job Mr Greaves offered?'

'Yes.'

'Good.' She looked at Gabrielle, clearly wondering what her role was.

'My friend here is another of Rose King's connections. She's going to stay in Brook House, and since you're bound to find out, O Gatherer of Gossip, she and I are together, so I'll be staying there with her.'

'Nice that you've found someone, Des.' She turned to Gabrielle. 'People who interact with the old Drover's Hope, which is what the old inn here used to be called, often seem to end up finding a life companion. I'm new enough to that state to wish everyone as happy as I am with Chad.'

Her smile was glorious and revealed so much love that Gabrielle felt drawn to her, as well as envious. 'I'd love to follow your example, Emily. I've had two failures at partnerships so far.'

Des looked at her sharply and she realised she'd given away her secret. Oh dear! She didn't want to talk about Edward, not to anyone. It upset her too much. She was just getting herself together.

But she couldn't just leave it at that, would have to explain to him.

Oblivious to this, Emily smiled at her. 'Don't mind our nosiness. We've grown fond of Des. We must introduce you to Libby when she gets back next week. She and Joss are taking a little holiday break in Brittany with Ned. She's another of Rose King's protegées.'

'I've heard about her and I'd love to meet her. I wish I'd known Cousin Rose.'

Des took Gabrielle to the area behind the showroom, a huge place two storeys high, with the ancient wooden rafters showing. It looked like a converted barn but no attempt had been made to modernise the interior, which was full of little stalls, only a few of which weren't occupied. The stalls weren't selling the usual junk and bric-a-brac, but genuinely old articles of various sorts, smaller stuff that didn't command the high prices Chad's items did.

'Can I leave you here for a minute or two?' Des asked. 'I want to check something out with Emily.'

'You could leave me for an hour or two with so much to look at.'

'I won't be long.'

Almost immediately, she found a stall selling Moorcroft pieces and stopped, entranced. There was one small bowl for only forty pounds, soft pink pansies on a dark blue background.

She'd always loved Moorcroft blue pieces and had promised to buy herself one someday. Perhaps that day had come. She smiled at the seller. 'May I pick it up? I'll be very careful.'

The man shrugged. 'If you drop it, you pay for it, but with that proviso, go for it. It's a popular pattern, that.'

She loved the bowl. It wasn't large. She'd never let

herself buy a large one. But this was affordable. She took a deep breath and said, 'I'll take it.'

When Des got back he stared at her. 'What's brought that blissful expression to your face?'

She explained and showed him the bowl, then let the seller wrap it carefully in bubble plastic.

'I've drooled over pieces like that for years, but I never even thought of buying one while I was with Stu, or even with Edward. Stu would have mocked it and taken all the pleasure out of owning it. Edward wasn't into antiques and, anyway, we were saving for a house, then paying off a heavy mortgage. We had to be very careful with our money.'

'I'm glad you've got your Moorcroft then, and if it helps, I like Moorcroft too, though clearly not as much as you do. Who was Edward?'

'I'll explain later.'

'Very well. Shall we go and find Emily now?'

'Yes.' She put the bowl into her shoulder bag, making sure it couldn't fall out.

'I'd better warn you,' he said quietly as they passed the little snack bar in the corridor between the two selling areas. 'Libby is Emily's daughter, who was stolen from her as a baby. It was a miracle that Leon helped her find her daughter, and both women are delighted to be in each other's lives. As Emily said, this place seems to foster loving relationships of all kinds.'

'And this Leon friend of yours seems to have his finger in a lot of pies.'

'He does. But he's one of the good guys.'

While they chatted to Emily, Gabrielle commented on how attractive the stalls in the selling area were and displayed her purchase, stroking the shining glaze with a loving fingertip. 'There are still a few empty stalls, I see.'

Emily grimaced. 'There shouldn't be any, but it's taking more time to organise it all than I'd expected. I think I'm going to have to find someone to take over part-time because Chad and I like to nip off at the drop of a hat to go hunting.' She saw Gabrielle's surprise and let out a gurgle of laughter. 'Hunting antiques, I mean, not animals.'

'What sort of person would you need to look after the antiques market?'

Emily looked at her thoughtfully. 'Are you looking for a job?'

'Yes. And I'd prefer part-time. I need to build a new life for myself and I'm not quite sure where I'm going yet.' She shot a quick glance at Des, who gave her hand a quick squeeze and nodded as if to encourage her.

'What were you doing before you came north?'

She grimaced as she explained. 'I just couldn't get excited about selling soap powder and things like that.'

'Who could? Perhaps you'd like to come and spend a day with me once you're settled into Brook House? We'll see if we get on all right, and also if you like dealing with sellers, who aren't always the most reasonable people on earth, I have to warn you.'

'You should meet aggrieved customers in supermarkets! Some of them were very difficult to satisfy, and often over items that cost less than a pound. I'd love to spend a day here.'

She beamed all the way out to the car.

'Well done for offering your services,' Des said. 'You were quick off the mark there.'

'I love antiques. And I'll feel better when I have a job.'

'I think you'd do well at Chadderley Antiques,' Des said. 'You understood the selling and displays in a way I didn't.'

'I really like Emily, too. I'd love to work with her.'

He waited expectantly and she could guess why. Her pleasure faded abruptly. 'We'll talk about . . . my past after we get back to Brook House, if you don't mind. Let's go and buy that late lunch now. And maybe we should get something to make tea and coffee with at the house as we're getting it ready to move into.'

'And some biscuits, in case we get hungry.'

'In case *you* get hungry.'

'You ought to eat more.'

'I don't often feel hungry.' She was relieved when he didn't press her to tell him about her secret now. But she felt at a greater distance from him than before.

She ought to have told him sooner. He'd been so open with her.

The trouble was, she hated telling anyone about Edward, because she always ended up in tears, and it wasn't just the tears. She felt destroyed by guilt all over again.

Chapter Thirteen

Stu took his possessions back to his tiny flat, scowled at them and decided to go for a walk. He didn't want to stay in this dump, staring at the ruin of his working life. He kicked one of the boxes out of the way as he moved towards the door.

Half an hour later, he realised suddenly that he hadn't planted the bugs as Radka had instructed. What would she say if he went back without doing it? That was a no-brainer. She didn't allow any leeway when she wanted something doing, even the minor tasks around her flat.

Anyway, it'd be a bad tactic to ask her help in finding a full-time job if he'd just demonstrated inefficiency in other areas.

Sighing, he got out his list and travelled from one part of London to another, using the Tube to save money. He went into one business car park after another, doing as he'd been ordered, finding the cars exactly where she'd said.

All the time, his thoughts kept wandering. Why did she want this doing? How the hell was he going to earn a living, even with Radka's help? He didn't speak any foreign languages fluently, only knew a few get-by words and phrases in French, German and Italian. Bilingualism was becoming increasingly useful in Europe and he'd met people who were fluent in several languages.

The trouble was, in the UK he'd muddied the waters in one or two places in his haste to trample his way to the top, and word about that sort of thing spread.

He didn't always think clearly when he was feeling high – couldn't understand why. At those times he always assumed things would go well. And they often did, for a while at least. But nothing lasted. That was one lesson he'd learnt the hard way.

He didn't know whether he was glad or sad to get on the plane going back.

In Prague that evening, Radka was waiting at the flat. She greeted him with 'You got the sack!' in an accusing tone.

No greeting, no commiserations, he thought angrily. 'I didn't. I was made redundant and that's not the same thing at all. I wasn't the only one made redundant, either. They're cutting back a lot on staff. Streamlining, they call it.'

'Why you? I thought the project here had gone well.'

'It had. They're giving me an extra month's pay as a bonus because of that. But I'm still going to have to look for another job. And I'm . . . a bit short of money. I had a few debts, had to pay something on account before I left England.'

'I know about your debts.' She sat staring at him, her expression giving away nothing of her feelings. 'I will give you a trial working for me.'

He relaxed a little. 'I'd like that. Doing what? Running your company's relations with the UK?'

She laughed. 'No. We have no relations with the UK and we're not going to. That was only a pretence to allow me to come to London. I'm talking about my own company now, not the one you were dealing with here.'

'You said you worked for someone else, then you said you were a director. What do you do exactly?'

She shrugged. 'I say what is necessary, and I do what is necessary as well. Now be quiet and listen. I do not give people top jobs when they first start working for me. Never. They must work their way up, doing whatever is necessary when I need it. Even if it is something menial, they must do it.'

She was talking to him differently, not bothering to sugarcoat what she was saying. He tried to keep an interested expression on his face, but he was starting to feel apprehensive about what she'd want him to do and whether she'd really help him to gain a higher position or just use him.

'You have stopped listening to me.'

He jerked to attention. 'Sorry. I'm a bit tired, Radka.'

'As your employer, it is not my concern whether you're tired or not, and it is your duty to listen to me when I am talking. Still, you have had an unpleasant shock, so I will make an allowance this time. We will go over again what I need. Tomorrow morning will do.'

Her voice changed tone. 'Now we will go to bed. I have missed your attentions. That, at least, you do very well.'

'Sounds good to me. It's easy to love a woman like you.'

She didn't smile back at him. Looking thoughtful, she picked up her handbag and led the way into the bedroom.

And there she continued to give the orders, acting far more arrogantly than before.

He didn't enjoy their lovemaking that night.

He didn't at all like the helpless feeling of having to do what she said.

Gabrielle didn't feel hungry, and, for all Des's urging, she left some of the food she'd ordered. He cleared his plate, then she realised he was studying her face, looking thoughtful.

'Is what you have to tell me so bad? Are you worried it'll frighten me away? If so, I have to tell you that I don't dislodge easily once I consider someone a friend.'

She shook her head. 'It's not that . . . well, not exactly. Let's go somewhere private.'

'I'll pay for our meal and meet you outside.' She walked up and down as she waited for him, dreading what was to come. No matter how many times she told herself she wasn't guilty, she couldn't believe it. She *was* guilty. Morally, if not actually.

Des didn't try to chat as he drove back to Brook House, for which she was deeply grateful. Her stomach was churning and she felt sick at the thought of reliving the worst months of her life.

As they walked towards the house, he put his arm around her shoulders and gave her a quick hug. 'I'm on your side, you know.'

'Mmm.'

Inside the house, she moved instinctively towards the kitchen, with its views along the valley. They called to her, those views did, made her feel part of a more peaceful world. She went to stand by the window and could feel him nearby, waiting for her to start.

But she suddenly remembered that the people from the antiques centre were coming to see the bathroom suite. 'We shouldn't start this till Chad and Emily have left. I'll be too upset to speak to them if we do.'

He frowned as if puzzled, then gave a slight shrug. 'Whatever you think best. Or I could put them off.'

She looked at her watch. 'They're coming in half an hour. We could go into the garden till then. It's not all that warm today but part of the back is fairly sheltered. I think I'll feel better outside.'

It seemed a very long half hour and she was relieved when they heard a car come up the lane and stop outside the house.

Chad and Emily were as charming as before. Chad said the bathroom suite was particularly valuable and in excellent condition, so they made arrangements to contact the plumber he used in these cases.

Emily reminded Gabrielle about coming to spend a day at the centre, so they arranged for it to take place while Des was away.

Normally, Gabrielle would have enjoyed their visit but today she was glad to see them go and could hardly force out a word of farewell.

As she closed the front door, she turned to Des. 'Let's get it over with now.' She sat down at the kitchen table opposite him. She couldn't face the kindness in his face, so stared down at her clasped hands.

He followed suit, calm and patient as always, reaching across to give her hand a quick squeeze. 'If this is so painful for you, you don't have to tell me. Truly. I trust you absolutely, Gabrielle.'

'No. I need to be honest with you. Something slips out occasionally and it's better that you know. If you . . . still want me, you'll need to understand why I get upset.'

'Very well.'

'I was married before Stu,' she began.

He went very still, didn't comment, except to give a small nod as if to encourage her to continue.

'We were happy together, Edward and I. Very happy. The only problem was I couldn't get pregnant.' She gathered the strength to say the next words aloud. 'Then he fell ill . . . and the doctors sent him for tests, so many tests, till one day they told us it was cancer.'

She could feel the waves of panic and grief rising, as they always did when she spoke of the few agonising weeks that had followed. Only a few weeks, but it had felt like a dark, sunless eternity as they lived through it.

'That must have been dreadful.'

'It was. When we discussed treatment with the oncologist, he was very kind. He promised to do everything he could to cure the cancer. But after we went home, we got online and found out just how low the survival rate for acute lymphoblastic leukaemia was.'

She tried to breathe steadily, to hold back the tide of grief.

'I didn't know when we married that Edward had had leukaemia as a child. That apparently increases the risk of developing ALL. That was why I hadn't become pregnant.

He had a low sperm count because of the treatment. I was angry about not having known. I needn't have had all those ghastly fertility tests. And I was furiously angry about him falling ill again.'

She took another deep breath. '*Angry!* How stupid was that? But I couldn't help it. Edward didn't deserve it. *I* didn't deserve it. How could it happen to us?'

She paused to gather her strength. 'I tried to hide the anger, be supportive. I tried so hard, Des, I really did. And I – I . . .' She began sobbing. She always wept when she had to tell anyone about this part, which was why she never spoke of it if she could help it.

'Take your time. Or don't tell me anything else if you don't want to.'

Des reached out to her again, but she couldn't bear anyone to touch her while she was telling the tale of her shame, and jerked her hand away.

'It turned out we'd discovered the cancer too late. The ALL had spread to the area around his brain and spinal cord. And . . . he had the Philadelphia chromosome, which meant there was very little hope of a cure. No hope at all, really, but they never say that to you.'

She dug her fingernails into the palms of her hands to hold back the tsunami of grief that threatened to overwhelm her. Even that small act brought back memories of how often she'd had to dig in her fingernails during those final weeks, to distract herself by the pain of it when dealing with Edward.

'That must have been hard for both of you.'

She nodded and forced out the final revelations. 'It was

hard to get through every single day. They arranged to start the chemo and said Edward had to take another drug as well because of the chromosome problem. But he felt so ill and was going downhill so rapidly that he decided to stop the treatment after a week. He said it was no use, and he didn't want his last weeks to be so desperately uncomfortable.'

Des nodded, but, to her relief, he didn't reach out for her again. Thank goodness.

'Edward gave in, Des – *just gave in*. I couldn't *bear* it. I shouted at him, begged him to try, begged him not to die.'

She was sobbing loudly, speaking jerkily, about to lose control of her emotions, but couldn't do anything to stop that. It had to be told. Des deserved that honesty.

'In the end, Edward took his own life – and it was my fault. He left a note, saying it would be easier for all concerned. But he meant easier for me, I know he did.'

'Didn't he have any family?'

'Yes. Parents. A brother. They were devastated. They too wanted him to continue the treatment. We all harangued him, Des. We didn't mean to add to his burden, but we did. Only, I was worse than the others because I loved him so much. I was so *selfish*!

'Dear heaven, you can't be blaming yourself about what he chose to do.'

'But I do.'

'How did he . . .' Des broke off.

'Edward got hold of some drugs. They told me afterwards it wasn't painful; he'd just have gone to sleep. He even went to a hotel, so that I wouldn't be the one to find him. That was the kind of man he was.'

There was silence, then she said, 'I had a breakdown, and it took a while for me to get on with my life. But if ever I have to talk about it, tell people, I fall to pieces. Even now, years later. So I don't tell anyone if I can help it.'

'I feel honoured that you'd tell me.'

'I was bound to slip up and say something. Anyway, I love you, so I won't lie to you.'

'May I hold you now?'

She nodded and let him pull her to her feet and put his arms round her. Then she gave in to her pain, knowing it was inevitable that she'd weep herself senseless. She always did.

He held her the whole time.

Des held her close as the sobs lessened, and even after they'd stopped. He had never seen anyone weep so painfully. Twilight deepened around them but he waited for her to make the first move.

How could she blame herself for what had happened? That didn't make sense.

He thought it'd been brave of Edward to cut short the time of suffering for his wife and family. He wondered if he would have been as brave.

Only when Gabrielle pulled away and let him guide her to the sofa in the nearby living room did he say quietly, 'I love you, Gabrielle. I've been wondering whether I dare say it for days. I love you dearly.'

'How can you, after what I just told you?'

'Because you're you. A fallible human being, like the rest of us. I don't think it'd be easy to live with a perfect human being. Anyway, what happened wasn't your fault. It wasn't anyone's fault. Bad things simply happen sometimes. What you've told me hasn't made any difference to how I feel about you.'

She studied his face as if trying to tell whether he meant it.

He stretched out one hand to caress her cheek, and when she didn't jerk back, he moved towards her. He didn't try to kiss her on the mouth, but touched his lips to her forehead, then to each damp cheek. 'I love you and I intend to go on loving you for as long as we both shall live. I can't guarantee not to fall ill, but I'll do my damnedest.'

'You don't . . . blame me?'

'Of course not. I'll repeat it a hundred times if that's what it takes to convince you.'

'I love you, too, Des. So very much.'

A few more tears rolled down her cheeks, but the faintest trace of a smile was there behind them now, as delicate and fragile as a rainbow peeping through the unfolding clouds.

He gave her a quick hug, then let her go. 'There now, we've both said the words I've been longing to use, the words that start to bind two people together: I love you.'

'You don't usually sound Irish, but you did just then.'

'When I'm very moved by something, it comes out – shades of my grandmother, who never even tried to get rid of her Irish accent, even though the Irish weren't liked by many people in the UK in the days when she and Granddad moved here.'

Her voice was almost a whisper. 'Will things really be all right between us?'

'It won't be my fault if they aren't. What you've told me makes no difference whatsoever to how much I love you. And I've never been a quarrelsome fellow.'

The room was dark now, except for the moon shining through the window, turning all the colours to black and white, like an old movie.

Des's voice was full of love. 'We need to go back to the hotel and get some sleep now. We have to be here again by seven o'clock in the morning.'

'It's hardly worth going back.'

'There's no food in the house. And you ate hardly anything of our late lunch. Let's buy something to eat at a supermarket, maybe a bottle of wine, too, and picnic in our hotel room.'

He led her to the door, and she moved at his guidance, as meekly as an exhausted child.

She didn't speak while they were driving back, but once, at some traffic lights, her hand rested for a moment on his thigh and she squeezed it slightly. He felt that was a good sign.

They stopped at a small all-night supermarket and she wore sunglasses to hide her swollen eyes.

He walked into the hotel between her and the reception desk.

In their room they unpacked the food and he ate some, teased her into eating too and gave her a glass of wine to relax her a little. He hoped he was doing the right thing. He'd have to find someone with the appropriate expertise – a psychologist maybe – and ask how best to help her shake off the unnecessary guilt.

In the meantime, he finished his food and turned to make a casual remark about a celebrity who had just appeared on the TV news. Only Gabrielle was asleep, her glass tilted to one side, so that the last of the wine had spilt into her lap.

He took away the glass, used a tissue to mop the damp patch, then picked her up and carried her across to the bed.

She muttered sleepily as he pulled off her shoes, but she didn't wake. When she turned over, she seemed to fall instantly asleep again. He cleared up their food before joining her in bed.

He loved her more because of what she'd told him, not less, because it showed how deeply she could love. She'd said she loved him, but he knew how fragile she was about love.

It wouldn't be his fault if they didn't stay together and settle down to build a happier life.

But would she allow herself to let go of the guilt?

In the morning Gabrielle woke with a start, to find Des already awake, lying on his side next to her, smiling. The memory of what had happened stabbed her sharply, making her gasp, and she searched his face, trying to see whether he was looking at her differently.

His voice was quiet, casting hardly a ripple of sound into the morning stillness. 'I still love you.'

'I find it hard to believe you can.'

'Why are you so hard on yourself?'

She closed her eyes, muttering, 'Let's not talk about it again. Ever.'

'Is that really what you want?'

'It's what works best.'

'We'll see how we go. I'm not promising anything, except to continue loving you.'

'I don't deserve you.'

'Of course you do, my darling Gabrielle. Now, let's see if they've left some breakfast outside.' He opened the door of their hotel room. 'Ah. They have. Shall we take it with us and eat it at Brook House?'

'Yes. I'd like that. Our first proper meal there.'

He put his hands on her shoulders and gazed into her eyes. 'We not only have a house to open up and bring to life, but we start living together properly from today.'

She rubbed her cheek against his hand, then became brisk as they got ready to leave.

He didn't say anything more about what she'd told him. There were times when silence spoke more loudly than words, and the merest touch was all it needed to affirm the existence of love between them – to offer comfort, too.

Chapter Fourteen

Stu found himself living a dual life and working very hard indeed. In the daytime, he did menial jobs, helping load and unload vehicles, clean them out, deliver goods – all sorts of filthy or tedious tasks he'd not done since he was a student.

He hated it, but told himself Radka was testing him. Inside, he felt angry that she'd even feel the need to do that, especially as she still required his services every night in bed. Just once she went away and left him in the flat, with instructions on where to report for the next two days.

The man he worked for hardly said a word, and then only in heavily accented English. But Stu suspected that the fellow understood English perfectly well, even though he didn't volunteer a word that wasn't connected to his work, because his eyes betrayed an understanding at times when Stu muttered to himself.

Radka hadn't said where she was going. He hadn't liked to ask. Once work was over, he spent most of the time she was away sleeping. She had exhausted him.

When she came back, she looked rather tired but seemed pleased about something.

* * *

She wasn't pleased in the morning. 'You talked about *that woman* in your sleep again! When are you going to forget her? Was she better in bed than me? Was she?' She punched him in the chest.

He fended her off. 'No, of course not. I haven't even been thinking about her.' This was a lie, because he had wondered several times how Gabi was coping without him, and as he struggled with his own washing, since he couldn't afford the price of having his clothes laundered, he remembered with regret how well she'd looked after him and their house.

'I don't know why I should talk about her in my sleep. For heaven's sake, Radka, no one can control what they say when they're asleep.'

She scowled at him, but let her fist drop. 'I do not like it.' She studied him for a few moments, then said, 'I shall require you to prove your devotion to me and to my company.'

'Oh? How?'

She frowned as if still thinking something through. 'I want you to run a little errand for me.'

'Just name it.'

'You will go back to England and find out what your ex is doing, then work out whether you can steal another houseful of furniture and goods from her.'

He gaped at her. 'What? But she won't have anything.'

'She is an intelligent woman and will have received insurance money. Of course she will have household goods – new ones, too. She will have found somewhere else to live. You will discover where.'

'But why—'

'To show me you don't care about her any more. And because I want it. But do not take risks. If it is not feasible, then steal the furniture from someone else. We can deal with her later.'

He gaped at her. 'Me? Arrange a burglary?'

'Yes, you.'

'But Gabi will be on her guard now.'

'Then you will have to be very clever.'

'If she still has nothing, how the hell do I find someone else to steal from?'

She shrugged. 'That's your problem.'

He wondered if she'd gone mad. She was jealous of Gabi – he'd realised that a while ago, just couldn't understand why. 'Look, darling, even if I found a house where people were away, I don't have a removal truck. And if I stole one – I'm not sure I'd know how to do that, by the way – the police would soon pick it up. They've got everything on computers these days, you know. They just call in your vehicle's number plate.'

'You have the sense to understand that, at least.'

'I'm *not* stupid.'

She studied him. 'No. But you are sometimes rash. I do not like rash behaviour. It can have bad consequences in my line of work.'

'Hell, Radka, I don't even know what your line of work is – not really. Isn't it about time you told me?'

'I tell you what you need to know. No more. Now, about this project. I will supply you with a removal truck and a very strong man and woman to load it and pretend to be the owners of the furniture. If anyone asks, they will say they are coming back to the Czech Republic because they couldn't settle in England. You will supply them with a houseful of possessions to move. Then you will come back to Prague by road with them.'

'Is there a point to this?'

'Oh, yes. There is always a point when I do something.'

'Such a lot of trouble to get back at Gabi. It's not worth it. I really don't care about her. I never did. Look how I treated her. Was that like a man who cared?'

'It's not just to get back at her. It is also to prove to me what you can do. There is perhaps one other thing you should know now.' She smiled. 'Last time we brought something else back in the removal truck – something very valuable, as you know. We shall be doing that again.'

His heart sank. 'Not . . . drugs?' He hadn't asked what it was last time, but even though she refused to tell him what exactly she wanted bringing back, he knew it must be drugs. That had to be what her business was. No wonder she had so much money.

She continued to smile at him. 'I don't know why you look at me like that. It was you who gave me the idea to do this.'

He couldn't deny that. He'd been desperate to find some way to make more money and she'd offered it, so he'd stolen Gabi's things. He felt a bit mean about that, and he had put a few of the things aside – family treasures that insurance money couldn't replace. They were in his flat in London. One day, he might find a way to give them back.

He shivered as Radka continued to smile at him. He hadn't intended to get involved in drug running. If he'd had any alternative whatsoever, he'd have left there and then, and run for his life. Well, he'd have left the following day while Radka was out. But even that thought sat like lead in his brain, because he knew he didn't dare risk it.

She'd find out where he'd gone. She'd send someone after him. She might even order him killed, because he knew about her now. Not much, but enough for her to want to keep him quiet.

Maybe if he did what she ordered about Gabi this time, Radka might let him off being directly involved in drugs afterwards.

It seemed the best he could hope for.

Hell, his luck had never been so poor!

The next day, Gabrielle and Des moved into Brook House. The landline wasn't connected, but would be the following morning.

As he was boiling the kettle for a coffee break, Des's mobile rang. He glanced at the caller ID. Leon – though of course it didn't say that name, but Auntie Mary.

'How are things?' the familiar voice asked.

'Mainly good. And you, Leon?'

'I'm all right, but I'm afraid a drunken driver sideswiped Gabrielle's car yesterday.' 'No one was hurt?'

'Thank goodness, no, but the idiot was driving a four-wheel drive and it did a lot of superficial damage. Naturally, we'll get the bodywork repaired and it'll be good as new, I promise. In the meantime, we'll pay for a hire car. I know you'll each need your own transport.'

'I'm afraid so. We're going to be dashing around all over the place setting up house here, plus I have a follow-up meeting with a client I can't neglect. I promised to be there when she meets her birth son for the first time. Her parents insisted on him being adopted and she doesn't want her husband and other children to know about him until she's sure it's all right between them. She won't even tell the birth son her address. I've been handling the correspondence, organising the meeting.'

'There are some sad tangles due to forced adoptions.'

'Yes. I've handled a few. I don't think Gabrielle will need a car until I leave, though.'

'Just go ahead and hire one as soon as you like. I'm embarrassed that we've damaged hers. My staff are all good drivers, but when a drunk skids on a narrow country road, there's not much avoidance action possible. You pay for the car, tell me how much and you'll be reimbursed by bank transfer.'

Des was used to the way Leon avoided any direct financial contact. 'Fine. Um – you don't think it was someone deliberately trying to hurt Gabrielle who rammed the car?'

'Definitely not. We checked. Young fellow. Known as a heavy drinker in that district, and not his first accident. He'd only just got his licence back, too, the idiot.'

Des put the phone down and saw Gabrielle waiting in the kitchen doorway, looking anxious. 'Bit of bad news, I'm afraid. Someone's crunched your car. My friend will pay for the repairs, but we'll need to hire a car for you in the meantime. He'll pay for that, too.'

'How did it happen?'

'Sideswiped by a drunk.' He saw Gabrielle's wary look, suspicion creeping across her face. 'They checked and are quite sure it wasn't your ex trying to get at you. And they're very thorough, so it will really have been an accident.'

'That's a relief. And you're still going away?'

'Just for a couple of days. I can't let the client down when I promised follow-up action.'

'Do I really need to bother hiring a car?'

'Definitely. You can't stay out here without a vehicle. And what if I'm delayed? I don't expect to be, but you never know, so we'll make sure you have wheels.'

She sighed. 'I suppose.'

'Will you be nervous on your own?'

'No.'

He couldn't hide his disbelief at that. She would never have made an actress.

'Well, perhaps I'll be a bit nervous,' she admitted after a slight hesitation. 'We could have a bolt fixed to the inside of the bedroom door before you go, if you don't mind.'

'I can do that. I'm quite a handy fellow when it comes to small jobs. But maybe you should stay at the hotel for those two or three nights.'

'Good heavens, no! I'm not *that* nervous. I'm probably being silly and will never see or hear from Stu again. But I will sleep better with a bolt on the bedroom door.'

'I'll put extra bolts on the front and back doors, as well as the bedroom. These old doors are pretty solid, but the locks are easy to pick. What'll you do with yourself while I'm away?'

'I'll go and see Emily. A part-time job would be good, don't you think?'

'Yes, I do. And even if you don't get a job, they're nice people. It's good to make friends.'

'I lost a lot of friends when I married Stu. He didn't know the meaning of the word, or care about anyone else. He only wanted to bother with "useful contacts". There's only Tania that I see regularly now. I must phone her and catch up.'

'Another good idea. Oh, and how about tomorrow we fetch that box of yours from the lawyer's? Aren't you eager to look inside?'

'We've been so busy, I've kept telling myself we'd get round to it tomorrow – but I kept forgetting.'

He knew she would be nervous while he was gone and would sleep badly, bolts or not. Pity he couldn't take her with him. He'd have to see if he could set up some nearby support system for her, someone she could turn to.

He wished Joss and Libby were back from their holiday. As an ex-policeman, Joss would have been ideal in the role of protector.

But Emily and Chad would help her if she turned to them. He added calling them to explain the situation to his mental list of to-dos.

The next day, Gabrielle and Des drove to the lawyer's office as soon as it was open and picked up the box. It was a good thing Henry's office was on the ground floor and they could use the caretaker's trolley to take the box out to the car. It wasn't heavy so much as big and awkward, and it took both of them to lift it into the car boot.

Gabrielle glanced at him. 'Shall we just take a peek?'

'Your box, your call – but I must admit I'm curious to see what's inside.'

She took out her penknife and slit the tape that held the box top in place.

'Every woman should have one,' Des teased.

'What?'

'A penknife.'

'Oh, that. I've had it since I was a child and I needed it sometimes at work. There are a lot of boxes behind the scenes in supermarkets.'

When she lifted the flaps of cardboard, she found photos and diaries in small, neatly labelled packages. 'How lovely! This is another thing I can do while you're away: start reading these.'

'Am I allowed to see them, too?'

'Of course you are.' She lifted up the edge of the top layer. 'Oh. There seem to be other things underneath. But it's the diaries I'm looking forward to reading.' She beamed down at the box as she pulled the flaps over it again. 'That's really whetted my appetite to see what's inside it.'

'We said we'd sort out a hire car for you today as well. I'll pay and Leon will reimburse me.'

The lawyer's receptionist had given them the name of a local car hire firm, which she said was cheaper than the big chains, so they tried there first.

'I'm all for supporting small businesses,' Gabrielle said as they pulled up outside.

'This one's not exactly small.'

'It's not part of a soulless chain, though.'

They found the woman who handled car hires very helpful and she had the sort of medium-sized vehicle they were looking for.

Just as they were about to start on the paperwork, Des's phone rang.

He stood up. 'When it rings with that tone, I need to answer it straight away. Can you finish filling in the forms, Gabrielle? I shouldn't be long.'

'Yes, of course.' She glanced through the window and saw him listening intently, nodding once or twice, then explaining something with much gesticulating. She picked up the pen and tried to concentrate on filling in the forms, but kept sneaking a quick peep outside.

'That's all the details filled in,' the saleswoman said a few moments later. 'We'll need to wait for Mr Monahan to come back before we sort out the finances. He said he was going to pay, if I remember correctly.'

Another glance showed Gabrielle that Des was frowning and still listening intently to whoever it was on the other end. 'It doesn't matter who pays. You can take it off my credit card.'

Even when she'd completed the transaction, she could see that Des was still listening and looking serious. Had something gone wrong for one of his clients? Or was it this Leon person? She turned back to the woman. 'If you give me the keys and other stuff, I'll go and get used to the car.'

'Sure. I'll come with you to point out any features you might not have noticed at first glance, and I'll show you how the CD player works.'

'No need. I don't listen to CDs when I'm driving and this is only for a few days anyway.' She didn't want to chat, just keep an eye on Des, so she got into the car, looked quickly at the controls and nodded. 'I've driven this model before. I'll be fine, thanks.'

'Well, I'll leave you to it, then. Give me a call if you want to extend the hire period.'

A couple of minutes later, Des folded up his phone and put it in his pocket.

Gabrielle waved to him and he walked across to join her.

'I've already paid for the car, to save time.'

He looked at her in dismay. 'Oh dear! I wish you hadn't, especially with what I've just found out. We don't want anyone following your money trail. Well, it's too late to do anything about it now, and you did say Stu wasn't good at the finer technicalities of using the internet. But if he gets help . . .' He shook his head, frowning. 'You can trace anyone these days if you have the skills.'

She focused on the main thing. 'What have you just found out?'

He glanced across at a man working on another car. 'We'll talk about that when we get back. Will you be all right driving this?'

'Yes, of course I will. I had to drive various cars at work.'

'Let's go straight home, then.'

She followed him, not even noticing that she was driving a strange car, because she was even more worried now. This phone call had something to do with her, she knew it, and perhaps to do with Stu, who still seemed to be casting a shadow over her life.

Was she imagining things? Or was he still threatening her – or, rather, threatening her finances?

When they got back, they lugged the big box inside and left it on the unused dining table.

Des picked up the kettle to fill it. 'Might as well have a coffee while we talk.'

'Let's just talk.'

He studied her face. 'Sorry. I didn't mean to worry you that much. What Leon told me probably won't affect you, but you need to be warned.'

She waited, biting back the urge to tell him to hurry up.

'It seems your ex has got himself involved with a group of people suspected of drug smuggling. Well, more than suspected. No one's been able to pin down the main players, so the authorities haven't pounced, but they're quite certain that's what's going on.'

'Stu's into drug smuggling?'

'Looks like it.'

'I find that hard to believe. He'd fiddle expenses, yes, tells lies at the drop of a hat – oh yes, he'd do that – but commit major crimes? No, not Stu.'

'You said he was a gambler. He may not have a choice if he's in debt to someone. They like to use people without a criminal record.'

Silence wrapped doubts round her certainty and it began to crumble.

'There was no sign of any involvement in drugs while

you were together? He wasn't a drug user, even casually?'

'None at all. I don't think his highs were drug-related. There were never any marks or signs. But he did gamble and lose sometimes . . . well, quite often actually. He borrowed a chunk of money off me once when we were first married, and refused to pay it back. He tried to make a joke of it, us being husband and wife, but I'd never gone for joint finances. In the end, he yelled that he didn't have the money and refused to talk about it again.'

'That was the only time?'

'It wasn't the only time he asked, but I refused to lend him any more money from then on. I worked too hard for it. Even with Edward, I'd kept my finances separate.'

'A lot of people do nowadays. Did Stu go away on trips?'

'Occasionally. But only for a day or two, usually to business conferences or meetings – ones you could check on the internet.' And she had checked them as her love for him faded. Oh, yes.

'I wish to hell I wasn't about to go away and leave you. Leon thinks something's brewing. Maybe I should cancel.'

'No, don't. I still can't imagine Stu doing that sort of thing, but even if he's involved, why should it concern me?'

'He might seek shelter with you if anything goes wrong, or try to get money out of you. He doesn't know about me.'

'He doesn't know where I live now.'

'You've laid a trail with that credit card. You still kept the same credit card and number, didn't you?'

'I told you, it was too much of a hassle to change that.

Anyway, Stu wouldn't know how to hack into anything.'

'But he knows a lot of people, and some of them might have those skills. And he *is* living with this Radka female, who is a person of great interest to Interpol, and to my friend Leon, as well.'

'I still can't get my head around Stu being involved in that sort of thing.'

'Leon doesn't usually make mistakes. Look, before I go away, I'm going to get you to memorise his emergency phone number. You're to call him if you have any doubt whatsoever about your safety, or if Stu shows up here and tries to bully you, or if you think you might have useful information. Promise me you won't let the fact that you used to be married to Stu stop you turning him in.'

She stiffened. 'Of course I won't. I despise drug dealers. They sell death and misery, as far as I'm concerned.' She repeated the phone number after him.

'An electronic voice will tell you that they'll ring back, and you put the phone down. It only takes a minute for someone to call, usually.'

'OK.'

'Can you remember all the places you've used your credit card since we left the south?'

'At the supermarket. At the antiques centre. For the car hire. That's all.'

'Damn! I'd forgotten about the antiques centre. I'll tell Leon.' Des beckoned her over to listen as he made the call. A mechanical voice told him to put the phone down. He waited and two minutes later his mobile chimed. He explained what had happened, nodded and disconnected.

'Don't get involved in this stuff, whatever you do, Gabrielle. Run away and hide in a hotel, if necessary. It's big league and nasty. Let the authorities deal with it.'

He came across to hold her and kiss her gently.

This simple action made her feel loved as Stu never had done. So she said it aloud: 'I love you, Des.'

'And I love you. Please . . . be very careful while I'm away.'

Radka brought two people to the flat to meet Stu. She paused to let them study one another, seeming amused by the situation.

The man was huge, at least six foot three tall and very muscular. He had the high cheekbones you often saw in Slavic countries and long, straight hair, greying. There was a suspicious expression on his face and he was studying Stu as if he didn't trust him. Beside him stood a stocky middle-aged woman, equally suspicious.

Radka made the introductions. 'Josef and Nada. For our purposes, they are man and wife. They speak good English, so you will have no trouble understanding them. They will wait in London and meet you when you phone them to say where the house you've chosen is. Don't take too long to find out what we need to know and work out how to take the furniture.'

She was watching him like a cat watches a mouse, Stu thought, and every time she mentioned Gabi, her face twisted with anger. He was surprised at how jealous she was. There must be some way to exploit that. But not now. Now, he was at her mercy, deep in debt, and had to keep her happy.

He hoped his half-smile was steady. He thought it was, since it was an expression he'd practised carefully in the mirror years ago.

Radka continued her instructions. 'On the way back, you will pose as their cousin. I have suitable clothes for you to wear on this trip, clothes made here, not in London. You will leave all your English clothes behind.'

'Right. Yes. Clever thinking.'

She uttered one short phrase in Czech and the two others left. The package they'd brought sat on the table, wrapped in newspaper.

'Well, aren't you going to look at your new clothes, Stu?'

He opened the package, grimacing at the cheap trousers and jacket inside. The shirt was worn, faded. The underwear looked second-hand, which made him cringe. What would he look like in such rubbish?

'Is this really necessary?'

'Yes. Customs officers are trained to notice such details. Here is a Czech passport. Use it when you come back. Use your British passport to go into and out of the UK.'

He took the passport reluctantly. What would customs officials think if they found this on him with another name on it?

'This mobile is programmed to call Josef and me. You will use it for nothing else. You will use your own mobile for all other purposes. Is that clear?'

He nodded and, when she didn't offer, he had to ask. 'I'll need some money for expenses.'

'You always need money. You won some at the casino the other night. Use that. Invest in my business.'

'I'd like to, I really would, Radka, but I had the money paid into my bank account and then I got online and paid some more instalments off my debts.'

Her voice rose dangerously. 'You owe money here, even?'

'No, no. Debts from my time in England. I had a run of bad luck just before I left.'

'Gamblers always do. I will make sure you stop gambling from now on.'

He ignored that remark. 'I still need to pay a bit off the old debts every now and then, to show good faith. Otherwise, I'll be in trouble with people who are very . . . violent in their persuasion methods and who wouldn't hesitate to wipe me out.'

He couldn't hold back a shudder. He was in over his head and didn't know how to get out of this hole.

She muttered something that sounded like a curse. 'How much? And do not try to fool me. Exactly how much do you owe in England? Do not leave anything out because this is the only time I will help you.'

When he finished telling her, she slapped him across the face, yelling and shrieking. He didn't dare hit her back and ended up cowering in a corner of the sofa while she continued to shout and kick or punch any part of him she could reach.

He might not understand the words she was saying, but he did understand the utter fury behind them.

Eventually, she stopped and poured herself a drink of wine, slumping in a chair by the window.

He got up cautiously and straightened his clothes.

'Get a whisky and then sit down again,' she ordered.

He did as he was told, making it a generous slug of whisky.

'Now, understand this, Stu. I will see that your debts are paid. This time only. And you will *not* gamble again – not if you value your personal valuables.'

She patted her crotch suggestively, and he couldn't help wincing at the implied threat to his manhood.

'Thank you, Radka. I'm very grateful.'

'I will give you enough money for this journey and you will keep an account of every penny of mine that you spend. Every – single – penny.'

'Of course.'

'And one day, you will repay all of it to me.'

'How?'

'I will provide the means for you to earn money, do not worry.' She gave him a nasty smile. 'Until it is all paid back, you are my tame monkey.'

He swallowed back an angry retort. He didn't dare do anything to upset her. He rubbed his cheek gingerly. She could be . . . terrifying. The longer he was with her, the more he could sense his confidence slipping and his fear of her increasing. She didn't love him as Gabi had. Radka loved only herself and kept him near her because he could satisfy her sexual needs.

But surely if he got away, she'd let him be? He'd leave a promise to pay her back, and he would – he definitely would. His luck was bound to turn.

She wouldn't go as far as murder. Not after all they'd done together.

Would she?

He remembered her chill determination and it occurred to him for the first time that dealing in drugs could lead to killing. He felt sick at the thought.

Dealing with Gabi would be easy in comparison – and rather fun. He'd take her money from the bank while he was at it, but not to give to Radka. No, he'd put it safely away in a bank account of his own, something for a rainy day. Well, he'd tuck most of it away.

He might have a little flutter with Lady Luck now and then, but only when he was away from Radka.

Chapter Fifteen

A few days later, Gabrielle watched Des pack his things for an early departure. He didn't need her help, but they chatted as he packed. She was going to miss him more than she wanted to admit, for the pleasure of his company and for other reasons. She felt safe and cherished with him.

As if he knew what she was thinking, he said suddenly, 'I don't feel good about leaving you on your own. This is an isolated house. Are you sure you won't change your mind and go to the hotel?'

'We've been over that, Des, and the answer is still no. You've fitted bolts on the bedroom door and it's a very solid one. I'll be fine here.'

'Leon has promised to keep an eye on Stu Dixon if he comes back to England. Suspects don't often get away from Leon and his unit.'

'So you keep saying.' She could see he was still worrying about her and went to stand in front of him, a hand on his shoulder. 'Des, I'm an adult. I'm responsible for myself. And you're only going to be away for a day or two.'

'Very well.' He continued packing.

His last words as he left the following morning were, 'Don't forget, I can be back within three hours and—'

She stopped him continuing by kissing him on the mouth.

'Pity I have to leave,' he murmured, keeping his arms round her and returning the favour.

'A great pity,' she agreed as she came up for air.

It felt strange to be in the house on her own. Gabrielle strolled round the garden for a while but it began to spit with rain. The rain grew heavier, so she went back inside. She got out the diaries, looking forward to getting to know more about Cousin Rose.

The pages were filled with beautiful handwriting, not copperplate but close. They showed a warm, caring woman pouring out her heart. Rose had been unable to have children of her own. Eventually, she'd managed to adopt a little girl, the child of a distant cousin who'd become pregnant as a schoolgirl and rejected the child in favour of continuing her education.

Rose had written only intermittently from then onwards, mainly at crisis points in her life. She had clearly loved being a mother.

As the pages continued, Gabrielle found that Rose had never told her daughter that she was adopted, because the birth mother had moved to Australia and deliberately lost touch with her family. She worried in the diary that this would seem too much of a rejection for the child.

In a cruel twist of fate, Rose's daughter had also been unable to conceive and had adopted a little girl they called Libby, a child who had appeared one day without warning.

They'd been on a list for ages, they'd told everyone, but notice of the child had come through suddenly.

Libby had grown up near her grandmother, and the two had been close till she was twelve. But then her mother had married for a second time and moved away from the area. Her stepfather had cut off all connection with his wife's past, saying the old woman was interfering in his marriage, which had upset Rose dreadfully. He was a control freak, she decided.

From then onwards, she'd had to pay a private investigator to get news of the child *she* never stopped regarding as her granddaughter. Des had come into the picture when the first PI retired.

What a sad tale!

The phone rang and Gabrielle hurried to answer it. 'Tania! How are you? Did you have a good holiday?'

They settled down for a long conversation. Gabrielle told her about the antiques centre, and Tania had actually heard of Chadderley Antiques, because her boss dealt with them. What a small world it was sometimes. Tania's main topic of conversation was her latest guy. She ended the call suddenly when she realised she was going to be late for a date with him if she didn't hurry.

Gabrielle smiled as she put the phone down. She hoped this new guy would continue to make Tania happy.

After that, she realised it was one o'clock, so she went to get a belated lunch, sitting down with a book to read as she ate, as she'd done when living alone. Only as she was clearing up did she realise she'd forgotten to ask Tania not to give anyone her phone number.

'Damn!' She picked up the phone and pressed 'redial' but a couple of clicks took her to Tania's landline answering service, where she left a message to ask her friend not to pass on her phone number, or any other information about her. Then she went back to her favourite TV programme.

She didn't stay up late that evening. She was going to the antiques centre the next morning to spend time with Emily, and she wanted to be bright-eyed and alert, just in case there was a chance of a job.

Without Des, the house was too quiet. She'd quite enjoyed the first few hours on her own, but as she lay in bed, she began to feel anxious. She didn't know what all the night noises were and jerked to attention a few times, heart pounding. But nothing happened, so she tried to focus on something more positive.

She was looking forward to visiting the antiques centre, rather fancied working in this area. The antiques shows on TV had been among her favourites, and she and Tania had watched them together quite often.

If she got this job, she'd give it all she had. She yawned, and the next thing she knew, it was morning.

Des arrived in Shropshire to find his client very much on edge and worried sick that her birth son wouldn't turn up, or that he'd be too like his father, who'd run away when told she was pregnant.

After calming Marla down, Des went ahead of her to check out the venue and the hotel, because she wouldn't even consider going there till he'd done that. He found nothing untoward, and though the son hadn't arrived, he booked a room for himself.

It was probably a lot of fuss about nothing, but Marla was in such a fragile state that Des couldn't deny her the support she needed.

If he had to go back to Lancashire, he'd find someone else to stay with her. He'd already alerted a friend in the industry, who lived nearby. Tom had agreed to step into the breach if necessary.

Des couldn't stop worrying about Gabrielle. It wasn't like him to imagine things going wrong. Why was he being so fanciful this time?

He didn't consider himself quite as foolish when he got a call from Leon to say that Stu Dixon was on his way to England.

'Has he found himself another job?'

'Not that we can discover. He's still living with the Black Widow.'

'What's he coming to England for, then?'

'I don't know, but it was someone at a subsidiary of her company who booked the flight, so it seems highly likely he's here on her business.'

'Damn. And I'm away from Gabrielle.'

'We have an operative in Yorkshire on another job. I'll warn him to be ready to go to her aid if her ex shows any sign of heading north.'

'Thanks.'

'The net is closing in on the group Dixon's entangled with. Unfortunately, these things take time.'

'Yes, I know.'

'Interpol is working closely with us on this. They've asked us to tail Dixon when he gets to England. We won't lose him. Don't worry. We'll see that your friend is all right.'

'She's more than a friend.'

'Yes. I guessed that from the way you speak of her. Good luck to you with that. Finding a life partner can be a damned sight harder than any other job in life. I've given up on it.'

It was unusual for Leon to confide anything about his personal life. Clearly, he had had his disappointments, too.

Des didn't phone Gabrielle with the news that Stu was in the country. She wouldn't need to know unless he headed north, in which case Des would get her out of that isolated house quick smart, whatever she said.

Once again he agonised over whether to return to her straight away, but Marla was so vulnerable and afraid. He'd compromise by phoning Gabrielle and enjoying a long conversation with her tonight.

He'd only be away for three nights, after all. And Leon was keeping an eye on Stu.

England looked grey and cold as Stu got off the plane. There was a delay in customs, and then his bag was late coming out. As soon as he picked it up, they took him aside to search it and pat him down. That annoyed the hell out of him. He was a British citizen, yet they were treating him like a foreigner.

Was this random or . . . It couldn't be because they knew about Radka and the drugs, could it? Surely not. His heart started to beat faster, but he kept a pleasant expression on his face, commenting ruefully about being delayed but doing all they asked of him with calm cooperation.

It was a relief when he noticed a nearby female officer questioning an older woman in a similar way. Did they think someone like that old granny might be bringing in illegal substances? How stupid could you get!

It must be a random set of searches, then. Didn't they have anything better to do?

On the other hand, he hoped desperately that they stayed stupid.

When at last they let him go, with apologies for the delay, he could have murdered a drink of whisky, but decided to wait till later. He just wanted to get the hell out of here. And he had some very good whisky in his flat.

He left the airport as quickly as he could, shivering as a cold, damp wind tugged at his unfamiliar, cheap-looking clothes and ruffled his hair. He wished Radka had given him a warmer coat, but there was one in his flat. Nearly summer and yet it felt more like winter. He took the Tube into London and went straight home.

He stopped in disappointment just inside the door. The tiny flat felt shabby and alien to him after the luxury and spacious elegance of Radka's apartment. Whatever she was doing was certainly paying well. He scowled round the small, stuffy room, living and kitchen combined. He sometimes told people airily that he had a service flat, which was perfect for someone who travelled a great deal. But, actually, it was all he'd been able to afford when he'd won a chunk of money once.

He intended to keep this place. It was a sign that Lady Luck did smile on you sometimes.

The mortgage was the first account he'd made a payment on from the casino winnings in Prague. He'd fallen behind, should have paid the whole mortgage off when he got his settlement from the divorce, but he'd been certain he was on a winning streak and hadn't done it.

He had to control himself better financially, would do that from now on. He hated being dependent on Radka.

He opened the cheap suitcase she had given him, then stopped and looked round again. The flat felt slightly wrong, as if . . . It was as if someone else had been in here.

He started to look around carefully, worried, though he didn't know what exactly he was worried about. He had nothing illegal here and everything seemed to be in its usual place. And yet . . .

There was a knock on the door and he flung it open, not wanting to be disturbed.

The caretaker stood there. 'Begging your pardon, Mr Dixon, but I thought I should tell you that we had to have the water people in to check all the flats. There was a leak in one of the other flats and it caused a right old mess, so we had everything in the building gone through. They tried not to disturb your things, but you might notice and worry.'

'I did notice. Thanks for letting me know.' He slipped a small tip into the old man's always-ready hand and closed the door in relief. Someone *had* been here, but not the police or one of Radka's minions. He was seeing dragons round every corner.

Pull yourself together, Dixon!

He unpacked and grimaced at the stale sheets and used towels, then faced the annoying necessity of doing some washing. This meant a couple of trips down to the machines in the communal laundry area.

When he got back, he dusted, then went to fetch his washing from the dryer and put his underwear away, feeling virtuous.

A glance at his watch told him his friend Carson might be around, so he left to chase him up. He wanted Gabi's money transferred from her bank account as quickly as possible. He didn't even try to get into the account himself. He knew his own limitations, wanted to leave no trace.

He found Carson in a seedy little all-night bar and offered him fifteen per cent of the total amount.

Carson laughed. 'Fifty per cent or nothing doing, Stu.'

'Look, I really need that money.'

'So do I. And I'll be the one running all the risks.'

'Thirty per cent, then.'

'Forty. And that's my final word.'

'Oh, very well.' But wait till Carson wanted a favour from him next time. Just wait!

'You might as well stay here, Stu. It's a small job and won't take me long.'

Half an hour later Carson came back to the bar. 'No such account. She's moved her money to another bank.'

'Damn! Can't you trace her?'

'I can. But not today. I want to do that from another computer. Meet me here tomorrow night, same time.' He grinned. 'Don't worry. If she's made any financial transactions, I'll find her.'

'Good.'

Could have been worse, Stu decided, drinking the

last of his whisky. This gave him a day's grace, and even Radka couldn't blame him for what someone else would and would not do.

He turned to see if Carson wanted another drink, but he'd already finished his wine and left. One minute he was there, the next he wasn't. Stu had always envied him that ability to slip through life almost unnoticed.

He stared down at his glass. Should he order another? A woman a few tables away was giving him the eye. No, better not. If Radka found he'd been near anyone else, she'd throw a fit. Who'd have thought she'd be the jealous type?

Besides, this bar was distinctly shabby. Not his sort of place at all. And the woman wasn't exactly young.

He walked out and stood on the pavement, wondering whether to go to the casino and watch the play. Watching cost nothing.

No, better not. He might be tempted to have a flutter, and his luck hadn't been good lately. He wasn't doing any more gambling until it felt right and only when he was away from Radka.

Anyway, he was tired. He went home to bed.

His last thought before he fell asleep was: see, he could kick the gambling habit if he had to.

Gabrielle drove to the antiques centre, looking forward to her day with Emily.

The young woman on reception showed Gabrielle into Emily's office.

Over a cup of coffee, the two women talked about Gabrielle's work experience, then took a leisurely walk round the complex, with Emily explaining various details of how things were organised.

She also pointed out the secured exhibits, too valuable even to trust to the surveillance cameras. 'Chad has a knack of finding rather special pieces. He won't hide them away, says people should be able to see beautiful things, but I must admit I worry sometimes about thieves breaking in.'

'I'd have thought he'd be better selling such items in London, if you don't mind me saying so.'

'He had a big gallery in London, but he was looking to take things easier – not exactly retire, but not work as hard.' Emily gave a wry smile. 'I suppose he has slowed down a little, but he's still very busy. He and I like to make a virtue out of a necessity, so when he has to travel to check out a new piece, I want to go with him, if I can. My friend sometimes helps out but she's in Australia visiting her son and his family.'

'Sounds as if you're making a great lifestyle for yourselves.'

Emily's smile was glowing. 'Yes. Chad and I only found one another a couple of years ago, so we're not wasting a minute.' She cocked her head on one side. 'Tell me to mind my own business, but how long have you known Des?'

'Only a few weeks.'

'It doesn't take long to fall in love, does it?'

Gabrielle could feel her cheeks heating up. 'Is it that obvious?'

'For both of you, yes. Something in the way you look at one another, or the way your eyes soften with fondness. I like to see people in love.'

'Did Des tell you about my possible problem?'

'He did mention that he was a bit worried about your safety.'

'Yes. It's my ex. I don't know why, but I can't stop worrying about him. We split the property and he got more than his fair share, so he ought to have headed for the hills with it. But he's a gambler and often runs out of money. He knows I have some left from the house sale and I'm afraid he'll come after it.'

She flushed. 'He fooled me into marrying him, but the so-called love didn't last long. I didn't leave a forwarding address and changed my bank account, but you know what things are like these days. If someone wants to find you, they only have to go online.'

Emily patted her arm gently. 'Rose King's houses come in useful for women in crisis, which is what she hoped. She gave shelter to my birth daughter, you know, before Libby and I found one another. I gather you're a distant blood relative, while Libby was a sort of adopted granddaughter to Rose – no less loved for that.'

'Yes. I only just found out from her diaries. Small world, isn't it?'

'Yes. Let's go to the snack bar and grab a coffee. They make much better coffee than I do.'

When they were sitting down, Emily said with a smile. 'I think you'd fit in well here, so I'm happy to give you a try-out. But I wonder if you could come in straight away and dive in at the deep end, so to speak. You see, Chad and I want to inspect a collection of old silver in Ireland. Quite rare and by a valued maker. They'll only hold it for three days.'

Gabrielle beamed at her. 'That's wonderful! I'd love to work here, if you think I won't make a mess of things. I'm hardly trained.'

'But you seem to love antiques.'

'I do.'

The young man Gabrielle had seen before came into the café with a young woman and they ordered a cappuccino each.

They stopped to say hello to Emily.

'Do you remember Gabrielle?'

Toby nodded, then frowned at her. 'Yes. I remember you. Be careful, Gabrielle. Be careful of the bad people.'

Ashley tugged at his sleeve. 'Come and sit down. They want to talk.'

He followed her meekly.

'She looks after him like a little mother,' Emily murmured.

'Why did Toby warn me about bad people?'

'I don't know. But he's usually right when he talks in that tone. In some ways he's an idiot savant. He can pick out a valuable antique from a pile of junk, you know. It's quite amazing to watch him do it. And he can sense things.'

Gabrielle was glad about the job, but what Toby had said worried her.

She hoped Des would ring tonight. She wanted to tell him she had a job.

Most of all, she wanted him back. She couldn't get Toby's words out of her mind.

Chapter Sixteen

While he was waiting to see Carson again the following evening, Stu got busy on Radka's business. He phoned Tania first to see if she knew where Gabi was.

Her voice was curt when she found out who it was. 'Even if I did, I wouldn't tell you.' She slammed down the phone.

Which meant she probably did have some idea – and knowing how scatty Tania was, she'd have written it down somewhere.

He decided to get his car out of the basement and drive down to Worton. It needed a spin if the battery wasn't to run down.

He'd see if he could get into Tania's flat and have a good poke round. Serve the bitch right if he trashed it! He wouldn't, of course. He wasn't a vandal. He just wanted to find his ex, so that he could get hold of her furniture to placate Radka. Though how the hell a man was supposed to control what he said in his sleep, Stu couldn't work out.

Surely if he proved himself, she'd find him a better job and forget about Gabi?

As he drove through the village, he sighed. He should

have stayed in Worton and put up with a more pedestrian lifestyle. When he looked at his marriage in retrospect, he decided that Gabi had a lot of good qualities. Even Radka's sex appeal had worn thin now, and he admitted to himself that he wished he need never see her again.

There was no one in at any of the flats, so he felt along the top of the lintel of the rear door, which opened into a small courtyard. He smiled when he found the key. The silly bitch had even boasted about where she kept her spare key one evening when she'd had too much to drink. How stupid was that?

He opened the door and strolled inside, but his smile faded as a search of the small flat failed to disclose any sign of an address book. He did find a crumpled pile of twenty pound notes stuffed in her knicker drawer, so he took a couple out for himself, on principle.

When he noticed a light blinking on an old-fashioned answer phone, out of curiosity he played back the single recorded message.

'Bingo!' He played it again, just in case he'd missed anything.

Gabi's voice echoed around the room, sounding tinny and blurred, but it was definitely her. 'Tania, I forgot to tell you not to give anyone my new mobile number, especially Stu. I don't want him to find out where I am.' She chuckled. 'He'll never think of me finding a job in an antiques centre in Littleborough, let alone such a famous one.'

'You always did give away too much information,' Stu muttered as he erased the message.

He called in to see Gabi's old neighbour again, in case she had any more details, but Mrs Starkey hadn't heard from his ex, so that was a wasted half hour. It would be his last visit to the old hag, he hoped. What a yawn!

He drove back to his London flat and grabbed something to eat. Tinned corned beef on bread that had been in the freezer wasn't exactly gourmet dining, but the sandwiches filled the gap.

Sipping a second cup of coffee, he got online and soon found where this Littleborough place was. He had a bit of luck, finding an article in the local newspaper that mentioned the latest show in a well-known antiques centre, which had opened up there the previous year from London.

The name Chadderley Antiques meant nothing to Stu, but if the place had been in London before and rated such an effusive article, there was a fair bet this was the place where Gabi was working.

He had such a strong feeling that he was on the right track that he called Josef and told him to drive up to Littleborough the following day with Nada and wait for further instructions.

It wasn't late, but Stu wasn't driving up to Lancashire tonight. Not only was it raining, but he was tired. Besides, he had to meet Carson again. He had to get some money behind him, in case things went pear-shaped with Radka, and the only person he knew with money was Gabi.

After a moment or two's thought, he also phoned Radka to report progress. To his relief, she didn't linger to chat, just said 'Good' and hung up.

He wondered who she was sleeping with tonight. Perhaps if the fellow was able to satisfy her, she'd consider releasing Stu.

And perhaps not. He owed her money. Very fond of money, was Radka.

Stu watched a TV programme till it was time for his meeting.

The bar was dimly lit, as usual, and Stu didn't see Carson till he slid into the next seat.

'Well, did you find her new account?'

'Of course.'

'How much?'

'What you said, Stu. Sixty per cent of her money is now in a new bank account, which I opened in your name yesterday.' He handed over a piece of paper. 'Here are the details. Learn them by heart and burn this.'

'Thanks. Can I buy you a drink?'

But Carson had gone. Strange, that. He usually stayed for a drink.

Stu stuffed the piece of paper in his pocket and sipped his drink. For a moment he thought a guy standing by the bar was staring at him, but then a young woman walked across to join the guy. As she gave him a hug, they turned away from him, and he realised he was getting jumpy.

He looked at the empty glass regretfully as he set it down. Not the time for a booze-up, and, anyway, it wasn't the same drinking on your own. Besides, he had a long drive the next day, not to mention important business to attend to, so he'd better go home and get some rest.

As he passed the bar, the young woman swung round without looking and bumped into him, spilling some of her wine over him.

'Oh, sorry. I wasn't looking what I was doing. We're celebrating our anniversary, you see. Can we buy you a drink to apologise?'

Who cared about a ratty old jacket like this one? Stu dredged up a smile. 'No need. You didn't spill much. Enjoy your celebrations.'

The young woman cuddled up to her partner and watched Dixon leave. 'I planted the bug on him. We'll be able to track where he goes.'

'Clever girl. Drink up and we'll go home. This is not my idea of a fun place.'

Des was woken by Leon's ring tone. He came instantly awake as he picked up his phone from the bedside table. 'Yes?'

'Dixon has been down to Worton and broken into Gabrielle's friend's flat. Do you know this Tania woman?'

'I've heard Gabrielle mention her, that's all.'

'Any idea what he might be after? Did Gabrielle leave anything there?'

'She had nothing to leave. The thieves took everything.'

'Maybe he was searching for information.'

'Perhaps he was after Gabrielle's address. Tania knows where we are. That settles it: I'm going back to Lancashire straight away.'

'Yes, I was thinking maybe you should. We'll send our operative over from Yorkshire to keep an eye on Brook House as well.'

'No need. I'll be there.'

'Better safe than sorry. Two of the Black Widow's most adaptable and ruthless workers have also arrived in England, pretending to be husband and wife, driving a truck. Our operative is armed.'

'Maybe I should be, too. Something's clearly brewing.'

'I reckon. And our Interpol liaison thinks so too.'

'Oh, hell. And Gabrielle is right in the middle of it all.'

'Yeah. Not only that, but there's another matter of interest for you to add to the mix. Someone has emptied Gabrielle's bank account. We can't pin this to Dixon – yet – because the money was skilfully moved overseas and simply vanished. But the coincidence of this happening the day after Dixon's return to England strongly suggests a connection.'

'You'd think so.'

'She'll get her money back from the bank, because they let themselves be hacked.'

'That's not the point. Her ex is still hounding her.'

'It was very cleverly done. We haven't been able to trace the money to anything but an internet café and a service provider in the Middle East. Is Dixon that good with computers?'

'I doubt it. From what Gabrielle has said, he's too impatient.'

'Then that's someone else who needs removing from the action afterwards. I don't need to tell you to keep out of sight in Lancashire, Des. We want to catch them, not chase them away. Do not mess this up by joining Gabrielle unless her life is actually threatened, because if they see you, they'll back off.'

'But—'

'I mean it: stay nearby and keep watch or I'll have you removed. We're too close to breaking this gang to risk anything.'

'I'll be very close by, then, and if there's any doubt about her safety, I'm going in, whatever you say.'

'As long as no one sees you while you're keeping watch. Need a different car?'

'No. I'll change mine for my friend's when he takes over this job for me. We've done that before.'

Des didn't like the idea of staying away from Gabrielle, but he could see the sense of not giving the criminals even the faintest hint that they might be in the sights of the law. Damn! He should have listened to his instincts and handed over the final stage of Marla's meeting with her son to his friend.

He'd stay in the shadows – reluctantly – unless Gabrielle was in real danger. But he wasn't letting anything happen to her. If he had to, he'd go in and rescue her. She was too important to him to take risks. This was one time where he'd take his gun.

While Nada drove the truck up to Lancashire, Josef stole a car and headed north. When he was about halfway there, he turned off the motorway and dumped the car in the first small town he came to, planning to steal another from a shopping centre.

He watched a young woman park a car and head into the centre with her friend, chatting away. He didn't have to follow them far before he found an opportunity to lift the keys out of her handbag. He made sure what he was doing was hidden from the surveillance cameras by passers-by – well, as much as it was possible to hide what you were doing these days.

He smiled. The car's owner would get a shock when she came out to get her car. He wished he could stay to watch.

By the time the police were informed, he'd have dumped her car and stolen another further along the trail. He needed his own transport to keep an eye on that English fool.

He smiled. He always enjoyed this part of a job. The fool was in for a big shock.

He changed cars again in South Yorkshire, then doubled back across the Pennines towards Littleborough.

When his phone rang, it was Stu.

Josef sighed and prepared to listen to the fool. No, this guy was more than a fool; he was strange – there was something wrong about him. No one in the group could understand why an intelligent woman like Radka would employ him in the first place. There were other men who could satisfy her in bed, surely? She didn't usually keep any of them with her this long.

'Josef? I think I've found which antiques centre she's working at. It's called Chadderley Antiques and it's on the road into Littleborough from Yorkshire. I'll go and check that she's there, then I'll follow her and phone you again.'

'Right.'

'Is that all you can say?'

'What else is to say?' He always pretended his English was worse than it was with people he didn't trust.

Besides, you heard useful things muttered sometimes.

He pulled to one side and studied the map on his mobile phone, then phoned Nada and told her what was happening. When he set off again, he continued on the same road until he saw a big sign saying CHADDERLEY ANTIQUES. He laughed aloud. Fate was definitely on his side on this trip. Or, as the fool would say, 'Lady Luck'.

Stu was heading for trouble if he didn't watch out. Josef had seen how Radka had lost patience with him, and if the fool didn't toe the line on this job, he'd be in more trouble than he realised. Or didn't he realise exactly what Radka would do to keep the money coming in? Didn't he know how important she was?

Josef turned into the antiques centre, got out the photo of this Gabi woman that Radka had supplied him with and studied it again. Even if she'd changed her hair colour and style, he'd recognise her.

He went inside, strolling past exhibits that shrieked valuable. Might be a good place to raid one day.

A quick study of the room changed his mind. The place was well guarded, and then you had to get the stuff out to the coast or to an airfield. No. There were easier targets. The owner of this place knew what he was doing.

Josef strolled on, following a sign that said MARKET HALL towards the back of the building. He found himself in what looked like an old barn, the sort that had belonged to monasteries in the past, or to very rich people. Lots of stalls. Nice selection of goods.

A young man with a big moon face stopped dead near him, then hurried out of the hall. What had caused that?

Josef wondered whether to leave, because he didn't want to attract anyone's notice, but a small bronze figurine caught his eye and he lingered to study it.

Two minutes later, the young man was back with a woman. Josef tensed.

She stopped to ask, 'Can I help you, sir?'

'Just looking.' Josef was amazed to realise it was *her* – the one Stu was looking for. More good luck.

'He's a bad man,' the young fellow said. 'Tell him to go away, Gabrielle. Tell him to go away.' He kept his distance, tugging at her arm.

Josef had already realised that the guy was a natural, born with less of a brain than the rest of the world. Why was he saying that Josef was bad, though? They'd never met before, and he couldn't possibly know why Josef was here. Or that this woman was the target of the whole trip.

'Toby, that's not polite.'

'He hurts people. He's bad. Tell him to go away.'

Josef didn't want to cause a scene, so he shrugged and said in his best English, 'I was only looking around to fill an hour. If I'm upsetting your poor friend, I'll leave. Are you in charge here? It's a lovely place.'

'I just work here.' She walked to the door with him, the young fellow trailing them, a few paces behind.

Was she making sure he left? Or only being polite? Josef couldn't tell, but kept a smile on his face as he went across the car park to his car.

She stayed at the door, so he had to drive away.

He could have done without the annoyance. He'd have to ditch this car quickly now, in case she recognised it following her. Damn the idiot! People of his sort should be locked away, not let loose in the community.

He parked further down the hill, waiting to see if Stu turned up at the antiques centre.

He smiled as he saw Stu drive past shortly afterwards. The fool was using his own car for the trip. How easy he'd be for the police to trace.

Stu found the centre, but he didn't go inside. He parked as far away from the door as he could, around a corner in a sort of overflow car park. He opened the bonnet and pretended to be fiddling with the car, which gave him a clear line of sight to the entrance.

As the day began to fade, people started leaving, so he crouched down, hoping no one would come to this part of the car park. They didn't. They got into their cars and drove away.

By the time Gabi came out, the car park was empty. She hurried across to a car Stu didn't recognise. What had happened to her other one? Had she wasted money on a newer one, when she hardly drove anywhere?

He waited till she'd left the car park, then followed her, knowing she'd never seen this car, so wouldn't realise it was him. She went down the hill, but didn't go into the town. Turning on to a side road, she cut across country to a minor road that ran along a shallow valley.

He could afford to fall back here, because he could see a long way ahead. At one point he stopped to cram a hat on his head and stuff some papers in the corner of the dashboard, hoping it'd make the car look a bit different.

Gabi turned left and went slowly up a hill, along a road signposted NO THROUGH ROAD. If it was a cul-de-sac, there was no need to follow her yet. Stu drove past the turning and parked by the side of the road at a small rise. He got out and stood on the higher ground to watch where she went, using the small but powerful binoculars Radka had given him.

The top of Gabi's car was visible all the way up the slope and she didn't stop until she came to what looked like the last house. He watched her get out and walk along a path to the front door, which she unlocked. Aha! This must be her new home.

'Gotcha!' he muttered and went back to lock his car. There was no one around, so he strolled up the lane, taking care to do nothing that would draw attention to himself. If anyone asked, he'd claim to be stretching his legs in the middle of a long drive.

He needed to find out whether this house was worth stealing from. He shook his head. Stupid of Radka to insist he hit on Gabi again. But women could do stupid things when they got jealous, even though it surprised him that a savvy woman like Radka could have such a weakness.

The lane turned into a path with a sign indicating a hikers' trail that led up on to the moors. Bit of good luck, that. The residents would be used to people walking up their lane.

The hiking path skirted the garden, which was surrounded by a drystone wall. He stopped when he found he could see into the rear of the house, which was brightly lit with no curtains drawn.

He got out the binoculars again and studied the interior. Yes! Plenty of furniture to fill the truck. Looked like some of it was antique stuff, too. Might be worth a bit. Trust Gabi to set up a place worth robbing. She cared a lot about her house and would have had the insurance money to buy furniture. Where had she got the antiques from, though? The centre where she was working?

Or was this a rented house? He smiled. He hoped it was: then she'd be in trouble for letting someone else's furniture be stolen.

Lady Luck was definitely moving his way again.

He suddenly remembered that he had to let Josef and Nada know where she lived, so he crouched behind the drystone wall and rang them.

'Where are you now?' he asked.

'I am parked in Littleborough, as you told me,' Nada said. 'If I am not needed yet, I'll get some food before I come to you.'

'Yeah. You do that. But don't be long.'

Josef answered just as quickly and Stu gave him the same information. 'Where are you?'

'A few miles away from Littleborough. I need to steal another car and then I shall join you.'

'Well, be careful you don't get caught. I won't be doing anything till after it gets fully dark. Got to give people down the lane from Gabi time to get to sleep.'

Stu broke the connection and went back to his car, where he settled down for a boring wait. Gabi couldn't get out of here without passing him. No need to draw attention to himself by staying too close to the house – not until it was time to act.

* * *

Des arrived in Littleborough mid afternoon, later than he'd planned because his friend's car had had a flat on the motorway. He had cursed as he changed the tyre, his heart heavy with anxiety for the woman he loved. What the hell did Stu want with her?

He parked just off the main road, in a farm access track that wasn't used very often. He reconnoitred the area near their house. No cars parked in the lane, no sign of anyone walking on the moors.

He liaised with Leon's operative by phone and they agreed to find observation points slightly uphill from the house, one to each side.

The other guy was hidden behind a wall, and Des made sure he found a good place to hide and observe, too, behind some raised ground with a few shrubs on it. The grass he had to lie on was damp and it was chilly, but all he cared about was keeping Gabrielle safe.

He waited, but could see no sign of anyone at the house, so he slipped down the hill into the house. His phone vibrated, but he ignored it. His had to get his gun. He didn't like using the damned thing, but these were serious criminals.

It was clear that no one else had been inside the house since Gabrielle left for work this morning. Her mug had been rinsed out and left on the draining board. He touched it briefly, as if it would bring her closer, then shook his head at himself. He'd got it bad for that woman.

He wished he hadn't agreed to do things this way, wished he'd stayed with her in the first place.

Moving outside again, he went up the hill. He still

felt worried and couldn't figure out why. Her ex was a thief, not a hit man. But the two with Stu added another dimension to the situation – a more dangerous one.

His phone crackled to life again and this time he answered it.

'You weren't supposed to go inside,' Leon said.

'So shoot me. I was unarmed, needed to get my gun, given what you've told me about these people with Dixon. And I wanted to make sure that that no one else had been there since she left, that there were no unpleasant surprises waiting for her.'

'And the place was clear?'

'Yes. She won't be back from work until about six o'clock, by the way.'

'All right. But don't go into the house again.'

'Not unless I have to.'

He continued to half sit, half lie on the damp, windy hillside, wishing he had his thermal underwear.

At last a car turned up the lane. He got out his binoculars. Gabrielle was home. She looked happy as she got out of her car. Clearly she'd enjoyed her day.

Something caught his eye and he watched another car pull into the side of the main road just past the turn-off into the lane. A man got out – a man whose face he recognised from photos the minute he brought it into focus: Stu Dixon. He must have followed her home.

Des shook his head in bafflement. What the hell was going on here? Why was the fellow pursuing his ex? Was he obsessive about her? He didn't sound to be the sort to care about anyone but himself.

He was about to communicate the identity of this new arrival to Leon's team when he saw another car drive past and stop further down the main road. There wasn't a lay-by there, only the rough, gravelly verge, so there was no reason for anyone to stop. The car didn't appear to have broken down.

A tall, powerful-looking man got out and stretched, then crouched by the car, using binoculars to observe Stu. He looked like a Slav of some sort, Des decided, with straight dark hair, high cheekbones and almond-shaped eyes.

No operative of Leon's would be so obvious about following someone. So who was this? One of Radka's people? Must be. Why the hell was he following Stu, though? They were supposed to be working together.

Anxiety made Des's pulse speed up and his whole body tense for action, but nothing happened for a few minutes.

Dixon continued to watch the house, and the other guy watched Dixon.

Gabrielle didn't come out again.

When Dixon got back into his car, the other guy hastily did the same, as if afraid of being spotted.

Puzzled about what was going on, Des kept his binoculars focused on the driver he didn't know and saw him speaking on a mobile phone. When Des flicked back to Stu, he was on his phone, too.

Which seemed to suggest they were talking to one another, and therefore working together. Only, if so, why was the big guy hiding from Stu?

Curiouser and curiouser! Des was beginning to feel like Alice in Wonderland, only this wasn't Wonderland – it was Crazyland.

Dixon couldn't be stupid enough to try to steal Gabrielle's houseful of possessions again, surely? Or nasty enough? Not to mention arrogant enough to think he could get away with it.

Perhaps he was an undetected lunatic. Des would make sure he was a very sorry lunatic if he hurt Gabrielle in any way.

It must have been Dixon who'd had her bank account emptied – must have been. But if he had stolen her money, that made it even more stupid for him to follow her to Lancashire.

Baffled, Des called Leon to report what was happening and give him the numbers of the two cars, then he continued to watch the players in this drama.

Leon got back to say the other guy's car had been reported stolen a short time ago, but Dixon's vehicle had belonged to him for five years.

Which solved nothing. Hadn't Gabrielle mentioned her ex driving a luxury car? Yes, Des remembered that distinctly. Well, this car was quite old and definitely not a luxury vehicle. So where had Dixon kept it hidden?

None of this information made it any clearer what was going on. Des thumped the soft ground with his clenched fist in frustration.

He could only watch and wait.

Happy to be home, Gabrielle changed out of her working clothes and put on jeans, a T-shirt and a cardigan, because it was a cool evening. She smiled wryly. This was now her only cardigan, and she possessed two pairs of jeans and three tops, as well as a few basic business clothes. She needed to buy some more clothes now that she was settled for a while and had money coming in.

She hummed as she began to cook a simple stir-fry for tea. She had so enjoyed her day at the antiques centre. Friendly people to work with and fascinating objects everywhere.

It had been strange, though, the way Toby had taken a dislike to the tall man with the slight accent. She couldn't place his nationality.

Remembering the incident, it occurred to her abruptly that the guy might be from one of the Slavic countries. He had those high cheekbones.

It hit her then. Stu was in the Czech Republic.

A shiver ran down her spine and her light-hearted mood evaporated abruptly. Was the man connected to Stu? Toby had been so certain he was 'bad'.

She left what remained of her meal to go cold and went round the ground floor, making sure the doors were locked, the old-fashioned sash windows screwed down tightly, and all the curtains drawn. Getting her mobile phone out of her handbag, she tucked it into her cardigan pocket for easier access. She could dial the police or contact Leon with one click. But the police would take ages to get out here and so would anyone Leon sent.

Should she ring Des and ask him to come back straight away? No, it'd take him several hours. He'd be here tomorrow anyway. She just had to get through the night.

She could nip down and ask the neighbours for shelter. Only she didn't know any of them and they'd probably think her crazy. Still, at a pinch she might be able to slip out at the back and run down the hill.

She cut such thoughts short. No need to get paranoid about this. She had no proof that Stu was going to come after her.

She passed an uneasy evening, unable to settle to reading her novel, not wanting to switch the television on in case it masked the sound of anyone approaching. She went to peer out of windows in the darkened rooms a few times after she'd heard noises she couldn't figure out.

She wished the house had double glazing, because that made it harder to break the window glass. If the house was hers, she'd have it put in. It must get very cold out here on the edge of the moors in winter.

When she went to bed, she took with her the phone, a heavy walking stick from the hall stand for self-defence and a chair to wedge behind the door. OK, there was a bolt on the door, but she'd feel better with a chair jammed under its handle as well. No one need know how timid she'd been, not even Des. She didn't want him to think she was a coward.

She didn't switch on the bedroom light at first, but went to look out of the window, trying to work out whether she could escape that way. If she had a rope, she might manage it. It wasn't a sheer wall: it had windows with wide stone sills and there were solid lintels above the windows on the ground floor, but only Spider-Man could have got up there without a ladder.

She was tired after her busy day. She'd soon get to sleep.

Only she couldn't, just couldn't. There were so many noises in the night that she hadn't noticed before.

And she was more afraid than she'd been last night. As if trouble were coming nearer.

Could you sense such things?

Chapter Seventeen

Stu sat in his car, tapping his fingers impatiently on the steering wheel. He toyed with the idea of capturing Gabi and telling her he'd been behind the theft of her furniture and money – and was about to steal her things again. He'd love to see her face when she found that out.

No, that was only a fantasy. She'd be able to tell the police who her attacker was if he did that. He'd have to send Josef and Nada in first to grab her quickly, before she could phone for help. Then they could tie her up, blindfold her and get on with stealing the furniture. He was quite sure Josef could handle that.

He wasn't sure how they'd put the drugs into the furniture, but no doubt they had experience. He shivered. What if they got caught getting it through customs?

No, Radka's people were too experienced. It'd be all right.

As daylight faded, Stu waited for the others to join him. He was starting to feel in control of his life again, now that he was away from Radka.

When Josef joined him at last, Nada was with him, but there was no sign of the removal truck.

He got out of the car to join them. 'Where's the truck?'

'Change of plan,' Nada said. 'Radka's decided she wants the woman taking out and never mind the furniture.'

Stu was so shocked by this casual announcement that he couldn't form a single word, just stood there with his mouth open. Never, even in his wildest nightmares, would he have thought he'd get tangled up in murder.

'No,' he managed at last. 'She has no reason to kill Gabi.'

'If she thinks she has a reason, that's what she'll do. She's a very jealous woman, so you must have made her think you cared for your ex.'

'Well, I don't. Not at all. But I won't allow you to murder her. That's going too far.'

Nada smiled and took out a small handgun. 'If you cause any trouble, you'll go too. Today you must show you're loyal to Radka. This is your real test, and if you fail it, we'll take you out.'

Stu froze, staring from the gun to Nada's face, then to Josef's. No sign of emotion, no sign of caring on either of those faces.

'Well?' Nada prompted.

He shuddered, still finding it hard to speak.

'He's weak,' Josef said. 'He should be taken out anyway.'

Stu rushed into speech. 'No. No, I'm not weak. I was just . . . surprised. I wasn't prepared for that.'

They exchanged glances, then continued to study him.

'You will kill her, then, as Radka wishes?' Josef asked.

'*Me kill her?*'

'You know how to fire a gun. You told Radka you'd been a member of a gun club for a while.'

'Yes, but—'

Nada raised her weapon and pointed it at him, smiling.

He rushed into speech. 'I'll do it! I'll kill her, if that's what it takes!'

Nada smiled grimly. 'What do you think, Josef?'

'I don't think he can do such a thing. He is weak.'

Stu interrupted them. 'You don't have to worry about me doing it. If it's my life or hers, then of course she'll have to go.'

'Very well. We will give you the gun when we get into the house. Radka wants your ex to know that you're the one killing her.'

Nada took over again. 'Afterwards, we leave quickly. You can leave your car here. You won't be coming back to England.'

'How are we going to manage it?' Stu asked, his voice sounding thin and strained to his own ears.

'I will climb into her bedroom and capture the woman. You will wait downstairs with Nada. I will bring this Gabi downstairs. Then you will kill her.'

'Let's go, then.' Stu didn't let himself be sick. Somehow he controlled the nausea. This was a nightmare, the worst he'd ever had. Surely he'd wake up and find it was all a product of his imagination?

But he knew it wasn't.

He knew he'd have to do it.

Through his night glasses, Des watched the two strangers talking to Stu. He saw the horror on Stu's face and the way he argued, then saw the woman threaten him. After some earnest talking, Stu nodded, then all three climbed into his car and drove slowly up the hill, not switching on the lights. That didn't bode well.

He listened carefully. There was no sound from inside the house. The faint light was still on in the bedroom, though. Couldn't she sleep? Could she too sense that trouble was brewing?

The hell with it! he decided suddenly. He was too far away up here to help her. He didn't care what anyone told him: he was going closer. He'd be careful – of course he would – but he was moving in on them.

He was relieved that he'd retrieved his gun and that Leon's operative was armed. He'd no doubt Radka's people would be carrying weapons.

When he kicked a stone, it gave him an idea, and he bent to pick it up and slipped it in his pocket. It might be useful to have something to toss to one side, to draw attention away from himself.

He stopped running and began to move quietly as the car stopped outside the house. Had Gabrielle noticed them? She might have heard the car, but they were on the other side of the building from her, so she'd not be able to see who it was.

He was sure she'd have locked herself in the bedroom, which would delay the intruders a little, at least.

He was beginning to feel sick with anxiety about her safety. He couldn't just run forward and tackle three people – two of them experienced thugs by the sound of things. He had to wait till he saw an opening.

* * *

Gabrielle heard a car coming up the lane. It didn't stop at the other houses, but came right up to hers. And it didn't sound like Des's car, not at all.

She slipped out of bed and went to stand by the window, opening it to listen, her heart thumping in her chest. No one knocked on the front door.

She rang the police and told them she had intruders and was scared. They said someone would be with her in half an hour.

She told them she could be raped or dead by then.

It made no difference.

Feeling shaky, she rang Leon's number. Waiting for someone to call back was agony, because she could hear the intruders moving about but couldn't see what they were doing.

Whatever they threatened, she wasn't coming out of her bedroom. They'd have to break down the door to get to her.

How long would it take for help to arrive?

Her phone buzzed faintly and she answered at once, telling Leon what was going on.

'Stay on the line and talk us through it. We have an operative nearby and Des is out there too. Have you any idea how many people there are?'

'No idea whatsoever. I'm at the other side of the house.'

She nearly jumped out of her skin as someone hammered on the front door. Pressing against the bedroom door, she tried to listen to and analyze every sound.

They must feel very confident, to make so much noise. But why wouldn't they be? The nearest house was a couple of hundred metres away and the rising wind would mask most of the sounds they made.

Dear heaven, what was going on?

There was the sound of a window smashing downstairs, then she heard the front door open. She saw by the line of brightness underneath her door that they'd switched on the lights downstairs.

'Keep talking to us, Gabrielle,' Leon urged.

But before she could say anything, there was a gunshot and the bedroom window smashed into pieces that were flung across the bedroom.

'They've shot out my bedroom window!' she yelled.

She picked up the walking stick as a dark figure smashed the shards of glass away from the bottom of the window frame and clambered into the room.

'He's climbed into the bedroom!' She began screaming for help.

She lashed out with the walking stick, but the intruder laughed and grabbed it, yanking it out of her hand, nearly twisting her shoulder out of its socket as he did so.

Then he grabbed her, holding her easily as he covered her mouth with one hand.

She'd dropped the phone, didn't know whether Leon could hear enough to know what was going on.

'Shut up, or I'll kill you now,' her captor said.

Nada smiled at Stu as the screaming upstairs stopped abruptly. 'He's got her. He's a good climber, Josef. He's good at many things, can kill a person in a blink of an eye with his bare hands.'

Stu hoped his terror wasn't showing.

There were a couple of bumps upstairs, then a door opened and heavy footsteps came down the stairs.

Josef came in, carrying Gabi, who had a gag in her mouth and a thin cord binding her hands together. He threw her to the floor and she lay there, staring round.

From across the room, Stu could see the pulse beating rapidly at her temple. He wanted to vomit, but he didn't dare. He wanted to turn and flee, but then they'd kill him too.

So he stood there, waiting, waiting for their next orders, unable to bear the thought of what they wanted him to do, but determined to do what he had to in order not to be killed himself.

It's self-defence, he told himself.

Nada moved a chair forward and dragged Gabi on to it by her hair.

Gabi somehow managed to wriggle off the chair before they could bind her to it. Nada kicked her hard in the ribs, causing her to whimper with pain. Again, she picked Gabi up and this time held her in place while Josef tied her to the chair.

Then they turned the chair around to face Stu, who'd been standing as far back as he could.

He saw the shock on Gabi's face. He didn't know what to do.

Josef moved across the room to stand beside him. He smiled as he came to a halt and handed over the gun, jerking his head towards the bound woman. 'Don't kill her yet. Radka will want a photo of it.'

'What if I miss?'

He laughed. 'It isn't hard to kill at such close quarters. The gun's ready to go. Just point it and fire. Fire as many times as necessary.'

Stu took the gun, making sure it was pointed down. He held it tightly but not too tightly, as he'd been taught.

Josef watched him carefully. 'You seem to know how to hold it, at least. Have you ever killed anyone before?'

Stu shook his head.

'Then this will be your first. But not your last, if you stay with Radka.'

The horror on Gabi's face, the pleading look she was giving him, made Stu feel even worse, if that was possible. He shook his head slightly, trying to let her know that he couldn't do anything to help her.

Best to concentrate on the gun. Only he couldn't get the image of Gabi out of his mind as he waited: Gabi in bed with him, Gabi making love with him, Gabi cooking meals for him.

He watched numbly as Nada got out a mobile phone to take the photo.

He was beyond thinking, beyond anything but holding the gun steady.

Des heard Gabrielle screaming but didn't make the mistake of rushing blindly to her aid. He moved round the side of the house, since he could see Dixon and a woman standing in the kitchen.

Where was Gabrielle?

The front door was open. As he approached it, he had to duck back because a big man came down the stairs holding Gabrielle in his arms. She was bound and gagged. The man walked through to the rear of the house and Des slipped inside, following him.

It didn't seem to occur to the man that anyone else would be around, but he did kick the kitchen door shut with one foot.

Damn!

Des moved back and crept through the house the other way, going into the unused sitting room and from it into the dining room, which led to the kitchen.

What he saw there made him freeze in shock. Gabrielle was tied to a kitchen chair and Stu was holding a semi-automatic, holding it as if he knew how to fire it.

'Aim for the forehead,' Josef instructed.

Where the hell was Leon's operative?

Des pulled out his gun and a stone as well. Could he distract them for long enough to save Gabrielle?

Stu raised the gun and aimed it carefully at Gabi, as he'd been taught.

She was moaning behind the gag, trying to speak, and he was glad he couldn't make out the words; if she said anything intelligible, he might not be able to do this.

'Come on!' Josef snapped. 'Don't take all day about it. We have a long way to go tonight.'

Then Stu saw a tear track down Gabi's cheek and he had to gulp down more vomit. He knew then that he couldn't do it. He just couldn't. Only if he didn't, they'd kill him.

Suddenly, there was a clatter to one side of the kitchen and Nada spun round, gun at the ready,

A man appeared in the doorway and Nada blocked his way to Gabi. 'Do it now!' she yelled, adding something in her own language.

As the newcomer threw himself to one side, out of the line of fire, Stu realised he had one chance to avoid killing Gabi. He turned the gun on Josef and fired.

His hand was shaking so much he missed, but he fired again as the big man launched himself across the room, roaring in anger.

Josef fell to his knees, blood pouring from his chest, a look of astonishment on his face.

The woman was crouching, trying to get a clear shot at the newcomer.

When she saw Josef fall, she aimed her gun at Stu instead.

Another shot rang out from the back door and the woman fell to the ground. She scrabbled for the gun with her uninjured hand.

Since Dixon was standing, shivering like a leaf and sobbing, Des rushed round the big table and kicked the gun away from her. She lay very still as he raised his own weapon.

'Lie face down!' he yelled.

She glared at him, but did so, looking more like a heap of dark-coloured clothing than a person.

Des moved across to Dixon and snatched the gun from his hands, because it was wavering about wildly now and he was afraid someone would be shot by accident.

Leon's man was framed in the back doorway. 'There were only three,' he said. He walked across to look at Josef. 'This one's dead. Good shot.'

'He did it.' Des indicated Dixon as he moved to pull the gag from Gabrielle's mouth. He used the kitchen scissors to cut the cord that bound her to the chair and secured her wrists. Then he pulled her into his arms, shaking with reaction now, leaving it to Leon's man to secure the scene.

Gabrielle clung to him like a leech, not saying a word, shaking violently.

As he held her close, Des checked to make sure that there was no further danger.

Leon's man had handcuffed the woman. 'You all right here?' he asked.

'You don't think I'm frightened of him?' He gestured to Dixon, who had collapsed into a chair and was weeping hysterically.

'I'll take Gabrielle into the other room, give her time to recover.'

The man nodded, his eyes not leaving Dixon as he pulled out his mobile phone. 'I'll tell them what's happened.'

'I hope nothing ever scares me as much as that did,' Des said as he helped Gabrielle to walk out, hoping it'd help her if he talked to her gently. 'When I saw what they were intending, I died a thousand deaths.'

He sat down on the sofa, pulling her on to his knee and into his arms. 'You'll be all right now, my darling.'

He could feel her nodding against his chest, but she hadn't yet said a word.

'Would you like a brandy?'

'No.'

'Anything?'

'You, Des. Just . . . hold me.'

There was the sound of a car outside. He was up immediately, pushing her quickly aside and going to stare out of the window. But the blue flashing light was a giveaway. 'The police,' he said unnecessarily.

Leon's man came into the room, looking at the shaking woman. 'I'll let the police in and explain what's been happening.'

Des gathered Gabrielle to him again. 'You don't need to speak to them till you're ready.'

'I'm starting to feel human again. I thought . . . I thought I was going to die.' She looked at him. 'Stu saved my life. I can't believe that.'

'Surprised me, too.'

'What will happen to him now?'

'He'll assist the police till he goes on trial, only it'll be Leon and Interpol he's helping, and if I'm any judge, he'll sing loudly.'

'Why did that Radka want me killed?'

'Who knows? Perhaps she was jealous of you.'

'Jealous of me? Impossible. She's utterly gorgeous.'

'She could be jealous because you're normal and she must know she isn't. Getting Dixon to kill you might also have been a way of testing how useful he'd be to her in a crisis. Who knows what really drives such twisted people?'

A police officer came to stand in the doorway. 'Are you all right, Ms Newman? Anything I can get you?'

'Give us a little time to pull ourselves together,' Des said. 'It was a close call.'

'So your colleague said.' The policeman whistled softly. 'You're lucky to be alive, lady.'

'I know.' Gabrielle looked towards the window. A moon was riding low in the sky. 'I'd like to go outside and breathe some fresh air. Would that be all right?'

'We'd like to get you seen by a doctor as soon as possible,' the officer said.

'I'm not hurt.'

'Maybe not physically, but it'll probably affect you mentally.'

'I'll keep an eye on her,' Des said. 'I'd like some fresh air, too.'

'It's spoilt the house for me,' she said as they went to sit on the stone bench at the side of the garden. 'I don't want to stay here any more.'

'Neither do I. We can go to a hotel tomorrow, or to one of the other houses. Whichever you prefer.'

'A hotel, one full of n-normal people and simple problems like what time they serve breakfast.' She shivered.

'Then that's what we'll do, my love.'

She was shivering partly with cold now, he thought.

'If you'll let me go for a few minutes, I'll pack some clothes for you and—' he began.

'No. I'll pack my own bag.'

'Are you sure you can manage?'

'Yes. I may have nightmares, though, and you have to promise to hold me if I do.'

'Any time. You're a brave woman, Gabrielle.'

She shook her head. 'I was helpless.'

'I mean now. No hysterics and you're even starting to function properly again.'

'I'm alive. That is . . . an amazingly sweet thought. It'll help me get through whatever's coming.'

As they packed, she said quietly, 'At least Stu didn't kill me as he'd been ordered.'

'He was playing way out of his league, but he led us to the Black Widow. She'd have killed him sooner or later, but now he'll help put her inside for the rest of her life. An Interpol team has been waiting to pounce on her.'

'She must be evil.'

'Some people are. Stu will be locked away for a good long time, but he'll probably get a lesser sentence because he turned on them and saved your life.'

'Yes. I suppose so. I hope I never have to see him again.'

'You may have to give evidence, but you'll not be near him. Oh, Gabrielle!' Des suddenly pulled her close. 'I love you. I love you so much.'

She smiled up at him. 'Good. Because I love you, too.'

But she shivered and stopped a couple of times for no reason as she was packing.

They both let out a long sigh of relief as they left the house.

Epilogue

A month later

All the lights were on in the small house in the centre of Top o' th' Hill, where Des and Gabrielle were now living. Even the three-storey house had been too far away from people for her to live comfortably there.

'You're all right about going to the party tonight?' he asked. 'There will be a lot of people.'

She nodded. 'Of course I'm all right. Stop treating me as if I'll melt in the rain.'

'You're still having nightmares.'

'And you've been there each time to hold me till I recover.' She gave him a quick hug then turned back to the mirror to finish pinning up her hair.

'My counsellor says I'm doing well, and working at the antiques centre gives me something positive to look forward to. Actually, it's Toby who helps me most. He comes to greet me every day when I arrive, and tells me the bad man won't ever hurt me again. He's going to show me the secret room next week.'

'Chad and Emily are great with those young people, aren't they? In fact, they're a lovely couple. I'm glad we're going to their party.'

'Yes. And Emily's daughter might not be related to me by blood, but Libby and I have decided to consider each other cousins.' Gabrielle stepped back from the mirror. 'There. How do I look?' She twirled round in front of him.

'You look wonderful.'

'You make me feel wonderful.'

Chadderley Antiques was lit up brightly, like a giant jewel nestled against the darkness of the moors that surrounded it.

There were security guards on duty outside, checking each car that pulled up.

'Can't be too careful with such valuable antiques,' Des commented. He let a burly young man park his car, showed their invitation and offered Gabrielle his arm.

They walked slowly up the steps to the entrance and stopped inside to say hello to their hosts, then moved on towards the café and corridor area where the guests were assembling.

Toby immediately rushed towards them. 'I found a ring for you. I found a ring.' He held it out. 'You need a ring to get married. I'm going to marry Ashley.'

He thrust a tatty box into Des's hand. The ring inside it looked grubby but was quite pretty. Some piece of costume jewellery that had caught the young fellow's eye, Des thought. He wanted to buy a much more splendid ring for his wife-to-be.

Chad came past just then and stopped to look at what Des was holding. 'Where did you get that?'

'Toby just gave it to me.'

'I found it at the market,' Toby said. 'You need a ring to get married.'

'May I?' Chad took the ring from the box, studied it and pulled out a small magnifying glass. 'It's gold.'

Gabrielle and Des looked at him in surprise.

He continued to examine it. 'And if I'm not mistaken, that's a rather good-quality diamond.' He turned to Toby. 'How much did you pay?'

'Five pounds.'

'You're very clever. This is a good ring.'

Toby beamed at him. 'It's pretty. You need a ring to get married.'

'How did you know we were going to get married, Toby?' Gabrielle asked.

'The Lady told me. I'm going to marry Ashley. So I need a ring, too. I have to find a ring for Ashley.'

As he spoke, the young woman came up to him. 'Is it a good ring?' Ashley asked Chad. 'Toby's been so excited about it.'

'It's a very good ring.'

'He wouldn't even let me wash it.'

'I'll do that for you. It needs some specialist cleaning.'

Des looked at him. 'Will that take long?'

'No, only a few minutes. It looks worse than it is. Why?'

'I'd like to announce our engagement tonight.'

Gabrielle tugged at his arm. 'You know I don't want any fuss.'

'But I do, my darling. I want to tell the whole world that we're going to get married.'

Ashley clapped in excitement, Toby beamed and Chad held out his hand for the ring.

'I'd better clean it straight away, then. I have an electronic gadget that'll do most of the work.'

Emily smiled at them. 'We've been waiting for you to tell us.'

'Is it that obvious?' Gabrielle asked ruefully.

'The love between you shines brightly. Don't even try to hide it.'

Later that evening, after Chad had made a gracious speech to his friends and favourite customers, he held up his hand to stop them moving away. 'There's one more thing. We have an engagement announcement tonight. Des and Gabrielle, will you please step forward.'

Blushing furiously, Gabrielle let Des take her hand and lead her into the spotlight.

Chad beckoned to Toby. 'Here. You found the ring. It's clean now. You can give it to Des.'

Beaming, the young man took it, studied it for a moment, then handed it to Des. 'It's pretty.'

'Very pretty. Thank you so much for finding it.'

Des turned to Gabrielle and raised her hand to his lips. 'We're getting married as soon as it can be arranged.'

'Not a fancy wedding.'

'No. That's not our style. But we will invite all our friends.'

'Yes. I'd like that.'

As he slipped the ring on her finger, she could have sworn a light shone in one corner. As the light faded, the troubles and bad memories seemed to slide gently to one side and she forgot everything but the man she loved and the life they would build together.

Hope shone brightly in her – no, not hope, *certainty* that they would be happy.

ANNA JACOBS is the author of over eighty novels and is addicted to storytelling. She grew up in Lancashire, emigrated to Australia in the 1970s and writes stories set in both countries. She loves to return to England regularly to visit her family and soak up the history. She has two grown-up daughters and a grandson, and lives with her husband in a spacious waterfront home. Often as she writes, dolphins frolic outside the window of her study. Inside, the house is crammed with thousands of books.

annajacobs.com